PILGRIM OF FATE
Volume 2

ISBN 978-1-941254-13-4
Omnia Mea Publishing
1. Kingdom of Biares–fiction. 2. Magical world of Dino–fiction. 3. Mount Athos and monastery Lanhidar–fiction. 4. The Balkan Wars–fiction. 5. Imaginary Advisors–fiction.

Librarey of Congress Control Number: 2022922576
Cataloging in Publication Program

To my ancestors and their eloquent descendants.

In memory of my mother Lilly,
My sisters Dragica and Dusica,
My brothers Aleksandar, Mihailo, Slobodan
My father Luka

THE PROLOG OF THIS LOG

Where I was born no one spoke the same language. Growing up in such a foreign environment gave me lots of headaches and confusion. My mom, a delicate and supposedly noblewoman, required much attention but because she spoke her own language, she could not communicate with my father, who was a foreign attaché in his own country.

Imagine now the seven kids our parents managed to manufacture in the sixteen years of their honeymoon. Imagine the kids' communications skills equivalent to the geese in our backyard, unable to understand each other or their parents.

Oh, please, don't get to any rapid conclusions. We had a nanny who understood our gibberish languages, and during these insane years, she raised us to become respectable children of our proud parents.

My father loved music, a mystic language I could never learn to speak. But he insisted that every one of us must learn how to play an instrument. He hired a young music teacher, and the lessons started every Saturday at 10 am and ended at 4 pm. No lunch. He often quoted Alexander the Great, "the way to a man's heart is through his stomach." Unfortunately, our stomachs learned the music faster than our hearts. The sounds of food processing organs played in tune with all four voices, while our instruments were on another screechy track, off-key, and undeniably unbearable.

Shortly after, our geese flew away, our dog howled every night, and our neighbors moved out of town. The popularity of our disharmonious band of instruments created no interest in a public concert. As soon as we lined up at the central square to demonstrate our musical talents, the main street became deserted.

My father didn't give up. He took us to the regional youth competition where twenty musical groups performed admirably until our turn came. We were booed in every way possible and in the end, their booing rhymed and became a popular tune.

We returned home and my father donated the instruments to the local college.

"Children, you don't have to play music anymore," he said to us with a sigh of relief.

Our music teacher and my seventeen-year-old sister, Neva, eloped to America. He had a rich uncle on some wide street in New York who had a job lined up for both. She washed the dishes and he swept the floors. My mom cried a lot, and my father cursed in some foreign language unbeknownst to us.

My hometown was small. So small it wasn't even printed in the official atlas of the Balkans. The town folks didn't mind this because they didn't care much for foreigners. These furners spoke another language and for my folks, who couldn't understand each other, it caused additional discomfort.

They turned to God. Every night, exactly at midnight, they sent their prayers to the heavens. Finally, God granted their wish. The only time our town folks could speak and understand each other was during the festival of saints. As I said before, prior to this holy period, they communicated with each other in their own Esperanto. The priest, who, before every Sunday's sermon depended a lot on energy drink named Slivovitz, organized the first rotary club in Biares. What was its mission? To outdrink every rotary club in our kingdom. Thank God our kingdom was small. Those were the happy times. But when the saints came marching in, most of our loony town folks marched out and never returned.

Based on the testimony of extra-terrestrials I encountered in my life, God didn't create the planet Earth. It was the Sun God who couldn't swallow an asteroid coated with a bitter taste of humanity and spat it out into the Universe. Tricky humans manipulated their way back into its orbit, and whenever the whiff of their stench passed nearby, the Sun would burst in anger sending a dire warning–nothing is eternal. From all this wisdom, from terrestrial and extraterrestrial knowledge accumulated in my pea-brain, I gathered the courage to create this book of joyful tales from the Balkans that I named Pilgrim of Fate.

Please read a few excerpts to bring you into my world, and if you get enchanted by my imaginary scenes and advisors, in the end, you will hear a beautiful Balkan tune, "Get out of my way on this clear day."

ONE

June 8th, 1913

Images of landscape rushed by our fast-moving train. In each one, I saw Galia, my newlywed wife from Chestnut of Maradonia. I missed her so much. I was a married man returning home, but my military duties as a captain of the Royal Guard allowed only three days for the stop in my hometown. The short time to share the happy news with my family made me sad. Reflections in the window revealed sadness on my unshaven face. Tunnels appeared and gobbled the light. For a second or two, this vision danced between daylight and darkness. Was it an imitation of my life? From an early age, I realized that life was not what happened to you, it was how you were prepared to face it. Was I ready? Had anxiety hijacked my soul? I gathered myself and walked out of the cabin.

"Next stop, Novo," the train conductor yelled through the open doors at the passengers in the next car. "There will be a fifteen-minute stop."

"Could we find something to eat at this station?" Someone asked.

"Yes, there is a restaurant and a wine shop." He paused and then added, "We also have a restaurant and a bar on our train, three cars ahead."

"Is the meal included with our ticket?"

"No, sir. Only if you are first-class passengers."

"Who do you think we are? The rich Brits?" another man commented.

I turned left and walked toward the restaurant on our train. The luxury of velvet, carved wood, and gold-plated moldings greeted me as did a gold-plated sign Wagon-Restaurant. On cushioned armchairs, needlepoint tapestries depicted scenes of nature. French porcelain on tables struck me as if I were in a palace on wheels. The waiter seated me at a table for two and brought a chilled bottle of wine. He poured some in my glass and waited.

"Good. It's what I need. Could you get me some stationery and a pen? I'd like to write a letter."

"Right away, sir."

I admired the elegant interior. Why would nations go to war when people could travel in this comfort? They would discover the beauty of the land, learn about different cultures, and share common knowledge. I spotted three other guests at the far end of the dining car. They talked or perhaps argued. Knives and forks in their raised hands gave the impression that battle was about to begin.

I smiled and gulped the chilled wine. The tingling of mild spirits spread through my tired body and calmed me. I drank another glass and leaned back. The relaxing atmosphere within the restaurant filled my soul with high hopes. I mused and brought Galia back into my daydreams.

The waiter interrupted. "Excuse me, sir, I brought the stationery and an ink pen."

"Thank you."

"Would you like something to eat, sir?"

"Yes, I like a good beefsteak. Would it be on the menu?"

"Certainly, sir. It is the Orient Express, you know."

"Very well, then. I'll have a steak with baked rolls dipped in butter and lots of tomato salad."

"How would you like your steak done, sir?"

"Flame-licked and juicy red."

From the window's reflection, I caught his glance of wonderment. He rushed back to place the order and pointed me out to the cook. The cook smiled and disappeared into his hot cubicle.

I placed the paper in front of me and gazed through the window. I dipped the fountain pen into the inkwell, and let my thoughts guide it over the light brown paper.

June 10, 1913

Darling Galia, my sweet wife,

I'm not a poet, nor a romantic scribbler to write endless pages about love. I know one thing for certain, I love you. Perhaps I didn't say enough of those poetic words but I hope you will accept me as I am. The mentality of a Balkan man may not be parallel to that of a Frenchman or an Italian. It is cultivated within the stringent boundaries of our traditions, nurtured with firm beliefs in marital laws, and practiced from the pagan times of our people. If I weren't a soldier, I would've stayed with you. But I am happy going home to tell my family that I'm married to the loveliest woman of Maradonia. I hope you can envision the joy on the faces of my mother and father when I bring the news about us. The struggle within me restrains the excitement of seeing my family soon. I cannot wait for my first leave to return to you. The moment the train pulled out of Chestnut, my heart wanted to burst. I ran to the last train car to get another glimpse of you. Far from my view, Chestnut changed into a fairyland. Magic mountains closed the passage, and only a dream of you passed over as a winter cloud. The words that I write now on this paper are a mix of nostalgia, yearning, and thoughts of you. With you, I had no other desires. Without you, I am facing a storm of uncertainty. Now that I am going to be a father, my worries about you and your well-being are growing uncontrollably. All other obligations to my family and our tradition will no longer be my primary concerns. It's my right to make decisions in my life, and I will always follow what my heart tells me.

I'm rekindling memories of our time together. I thought of the moment when we first let our feelings pour out, when our hearts trembled and our lips joined in a passionate celebration of love. I'm recalling your soft words, your gentle caresses, and your endless shedding of tears. From an unpredictable journey into the world, I have entered the age of maturity with you by my side. I have no fear and no doubts we will be together again very soon.

Your last words stormed through my head like a violent fire burning everything in its path. How could I leave you behind, alone, with our baby? The increasing distance tightened a rope around my neck. It choked my dreams, it silenced my screams, and for a moment, it took away the hopes of tomorrow.

By the law of the Almighty, in the church of our Christian faith, we became one. Our love has changed our future and now we are three. At the thought of the separation between us, I shudder, but I swear I will be back.

May the Lord keep you safe my darling wife, and may our time apart end quickly. I shall hold you in my heart until the day when I shall hold you in my arms.

Your Dino

The locomotive whistle ripped through the canyon, and the train slowed down.

"We're entering Novo," the waiter said and placed the platter of food on the table.

"Could I mail this letter from here?" I asked.

"If you have the letter ready, I'll drop it off with the station master."

"I'll have it done in a couple of minutes."

"No rush, sir. We have plenty of time." The waiter poured the remaining wine into my glass and walked away with the empty bottle. A minute later he brought another.

I smiled. "It's a long way to my hometown."

"We have many bottles in our cooler." He uncorked the bottle and filled my glass without a spilled drop. I handed him the letter and turned to my bloody steak.

The Orient Express stopped in the Novo station and a stream of passengers from the second-class cars rushed out. I opened the window. Two locomotives sat idling at the end of their tracks. A few lampposts illuminated the platform between the two trains. Steam engines released the pressure with a great noise.

The two spectacular Orient Express lines waited, one going north and the other south. Their massive locomotives and long passenger cars displayed large letters on both sides. Orient Express, the pride of the nations, traveled in its full splendor, visible from the hills above and from the valleys below.

The uniformed stationmaster held a lamp on his left arm and a whistle in his right hand. He stood firm, unmoved by the river of people from the two trains. Patient and calm, he represented a class of dedicated employees, regardless of their race or religion. He could've been another transplant, as my grandpa used to call Uncle Jonathan's masons from Maradonia.

I sat back and continued my delicious meal.

A loud knock on my cabin door alerted me. The voice outside announced, "Next stop, Nais."

"Nais? Didn't this train stop at Koles?"

"Yes, sir. It did a half-hour ago."

"Then why didn't you wake me up?"

"I tried, sir. You were sound asleep."

I glanced through the window. It was still dark. "What time is it?"

"Five o'clock, sir. We'll arrive at the station in ten minutes." The conductor walked away and continued knocking on other doors.

"Oh, my head." I writhed in pain from the headache and the stiffness of my body. I stood and reached for my bag. Sudden loss of balance threw me back on my bed. Was I drunk? That wine tasted so good. Where did the pain come from?

It reminded me of the time when at the age of seven I fell asleep next to the barrel of young Shirra[1]. My grandpa found me and asked if I had a headache. The first sip of wine tasted like a grape juice, but it carried the punch of a heavyweight. I guess all headaches of drunk people are the same.

Everything around me on the moving train swayed, and then it finally stopped.

I staggered through the car and onto the platform. Soberness returned, and I realized I missed getting off at my hometown station.

"Is there any train going to Koles today?" I inquired at the ticket counter.

"Not until tomorrow, sir. But, the Royal Daily will be departing in two hours from the Fort Lookout Station."

"Is that old mule still in service?"

"Oh, sure. Now with an expanded track, it connects the north and the south of Biares. It has become our main tourist attraction. Although it's sometimes unpredictable, it's still free for the people of Biares."

"There was never any certainty about the Royal Daily. Why should it be different now?"

"Well, sir, times have changed. Ever since the traffic increased, our people resented sharing their national pride. Some regular passengers boycotted the rides and complained to their representatives. A few who proclaimed themselves as patriots decided to rectify this injustice. Recently in some southern town, I believe I have saved the newspaper... wait, here it is. The Weekly Journal printed an article about the raid. The local patriots from the town of Koles stopped the train and kicked out the passengers along with the train engineers. Armed with jugs of brandy they occupied the train. They brought in a brass band and danced on top of the roof until everyone passed out.

"The following morning the town's constabulary came with horse wagons and carried away the inebriated bunch of boycotters. The two passenger cars had to be steam washed and cleaned from vomit and alcohol before returning to their scheduled service. This could only happen in the south, where our beloved kingdom is occupied with morons."

---

1   Shirra, first wine squeezed by a press

"I'm one of them," I said, "I'm from Koles."

He apologized and gave me the ticket. A horse-drawn buggy took me to Fort Lookout Station, and I stepped in front of a small brick cubicle with no attendant in sight. I sat on a stool and waited.

I reminisced about the rides on the Old Mule. My dreams took me through my years of silence. Scenes from the past brought back faces of train engineers, dark from the soot of burning wood and lignite. I recalled their smiling faces with white teeth and sparkling eyes every time they arrived in Koles. They had a repertoire of folk songs that echoed across the fields and lured the residents to the station. We called them the singing devils and on Sundays after church, they performed for us kids. The entire town turned up for their show. Accompanied by our local musicians, the singing devils went on for hours.

When Royals stopped in Koles the show would go on for days. The Old King Tarpe, the Queen Mother, and their escort enjoyed the show. There was never a schedule to meet or places to go. King Tarpe didn't believe in time-measuring devices. For him, time was a luxury humans could do without.

So, on any given day, events would take place on a whim. It's hard to explain how our minds worked at that time because my hometown folks never used clocks. Nature played a significant role in its solar and star alignments.

The Royal Daily arrived, as expected, four hours after the scheduled time.

I took a seat in an empty car and traveled through time in my dreams.

At 3 p.m., I stepped off the train in Koles and walked through the station. I passed by a small crowd of people. Their eyes checked me over and trailed on to another passenger. A small mirror on the wall reflected my unshaven face with a dark beard and mustaches. A flashback pictured a boy leaving his beloved hometown. Now the mirror, staring at a grown man, was the only witness of time who could recognize and welcome that boy.

It was a warm, mild kind of afternoon with a lingering fragrance of wild roses. Balconies on adobe homes, hidden behind neatly arranged pots of red, white, and blue begonias, resembled hanging gardens. Main street shops exhibited festive decorations usually displayed on Christmas, Easter, and King Tarpe's birthday. The street cobblestones glistened as if washed for a special occasion. Children promenaded between the Koles train station and the main square. Adults danced to music performed by a Gypsy band. Some gathered in the square and listened to the cacophony of speeches. Some sat on sidewalk benches in front of the pubs drinking homemade beer and brandy.

They all seemed to be occupied with an upcoming event. An air of expectation whirled through Koles. The self-appointed heralds yelled back and forth the news about the coming celebrity. "He didn't arrive," they announced and rushed back.

"Danton said he saw him pass this morning on the Orient Express heading for the capital."

"But Danton is blind. How could he see anyone?"

"He could sniff him. He can out-sniff any dog in the county."

I didn't wonder about the logic in conversations between my hometown people. It was all quite normal. But I did ponder about the visitor they were expecting. The square was full of people marching up and down with the local brass band. The hand-painted banners and decorations hung around the Monument to the Victors. At the other end, a large banner displayed, "Welcome Home, Dino, Our National Hero."

I almost lost my balance from the shock.

"What's happening?" I asked one bystander.

"Our hometown hero, General Dino Babic, is coming home from the front. He is very famous now. He captured the entire Jamal Pasha division and is awarded the Royal Medal of Honor for bravery."

"National hero? The whole division?" I commented.

"Yes, sir." He pulled a crumpled newspaper out of his pocket and pointed to an article. "See here, Dino Babic's triumphant victories, in full description. The Papagayo Daily never lies," he added with pride.

"The Papagayo never tells the truth either," I retorted.

"Why, you!" He stared at me with an obvious outrage. "Look here! You have no right to question this newspaper. Who do you think you are?"

"I am just another soldier coming home from the front. How did this general get to be a hero?"

This must've toppled his patience. He yelled at me and called me names I would not want to repeat.

His heated argument attracted the attention of a local crowd, and three gendarmes stepped forward and surrounded me. One of them addressed me.

"The entire county of Koles is celebrating the return of our national hero, Dino Babic. All Biares newspapers are printing a series of his heroic escapades. The delegation from the National Assembly is coming tomorrow to present him with the Black George Medal of Honor for his heroic deeds. Well, Soldier, if I were you, I'd leave the comments at home."

I sized up the situation and replied, "You are right, sergeant, I should keep it to myself. Sorry folks, I had no intention to dispute his heroics. I shall leave you in peace."

"That's a good soldier. All right, folks, make way and let this man pass."

In all my trials, I had never confronted a challenge like this one before. It was not easy to judge myself against public opinion, especially if most of it was based on Papagayo's reporting. After all, I was back in my hometown where everything was possible and everything was outstanding.

I found no one at my parents' house. The aroma of freshly baked apple pie frosted with vanilla sugar tickled my senses, and I spotted Mom's delicacy covered with a linen cloth on the kitchen table. She always baked something sweet for her boys. I couldn't wait to dig into it, and I cut a large chunk of the pie.

At the moment I opened my mouth to eat, three gendarmes stormed into the house and grabbed me. The sergeant followed shouting, "Now you've done it, soldier. How dare you break into the house of our hero?"

"But I didn't break-in. This is the house of my parents…" I started.

"Don't tell me that you are…"

"That I am, sergeant."

"Oh, my Lord. It is you. Let him loose, men."

"Who is he, sergeant?" one of gendarmes asked.

"Never mind. Get outside and disperse the crowd. Tell them it was a false alarm." He sent all three out and closed the door behind them.

"You don't remember me, do you, Dino?"

I peered into his eyes, looked over his face and his body, but I couldn't recall his image from the past. I shook my head.

"I'm Mitar, your relative. You and your brother, Petro, used to visit us on our farm when you were little boys. I used to take you fishing on the lake in our old boat."

Memories flashed, and I played back happy scenes of my childhood.

"Those were the happiest times of my life." I jumped in delight and hugged him. "I was about seven when you took Petro and me to the lake. That boat was a leaky tub, and I had nightmares it would sink and we'd drown. You kept us afloat by patching the holes with cow manure or something. I'm so glad to see you."

"I was fifteen then, and the three of us had a grand time."

"We sure did. It was the highlight of our summer vacation. And you? When did you join the constabulary? I thought you'd stay on the farm."

"After my grandma and grandpa passed away, my father didn't want to be a farmer, so he sold the farm and moved to town. I went to the constabulary academy and became a local gendarme. At first, I served in the northern province. Then I got promoted and moved back to Koles. I've been at it for five years now, and I like it. There is no crime here. Only drunks and idiots."

I smiled and patted him on the back. "Our kind of people, eh." Then I asked, "Where are my parents? Where is everyone?"

He lifted his eyebrows, paused for a second, and said, "They are at the parents of your future bride."

"Mitar, I just arrived, don't kid with me. It was enough to hear that Papagayo promoted me to the general who single-handedly conquered Jamal Pasha's army. What are you talking about? What future bride?"

"The whole town is waiting for you. Everyone wants to be a part of the celebration of your heroic deeds and the announced engagement between you and Isidora Maric."

"Are you mad? What engagement? Who the hell is Isidora?" I screamed at him.

"You know the family Maric from the village of Resava? Little Isidora grew up to be a beauty, and what a catch she is. Your father made a great bargain. She will bring twelve hectares of prime land and ten of their best milk cows. You'll be a rich man, Dino."

I stood there in shock caught between two impossible conditions. I needed to talk to someone; someone who would weigh in to help me resolve this problem. Who could that be? My father would not understand. The priest, maybe? But he was always drunk.

"I wish my Uncle Jonathan were around. He would help me." I spoke more to myself.

"He is here," Mitar spoke. "Back from India, he sits on the Gornik Rock every day and stares to the east. They say he is a Buddhist, whatever that

9

means. A skeleton that meditates. That's who he is now."

"I need to talk to him."

"Him? He's a goner. He doesn't talk to anyone."

"He'll talk to me," I said. "Mitar, please don't tell anyone I've arrived until I talk to my uncle. Now if you'd excuse me, I'm starving."

"I'm sorry, Dino. We'll be out of your way."

"I can offer you a piece of Mom's apple pie. I know how much you liked it when we were kids."

"Ah, yes. It was delicious. But it must be some other time. The town has gone crazy, and it'll get crazier when they find out you are here."

"You're the only one who recognized me. I passed a lot of townsfolk who stared at me, scratched their butts to remember, and talked themselves out of the idea that I was standing in front of them. They are waiting for the general, aren't they?"

He smiled. "We'll let the city fathers bail out of this mess by themselves," he said, and walked out.

While I gobbled the pie, Mitar yelled at the gendarmes and the nosy neighbors on the street. One of them said, "I could swear I saw an intruder inside."

"You are too drunk to see anything," another responded.

A half-hour later, dressed in civilian clothes, I rushed to Gornik. About a hundred meters above its base, a solid rock stuck out of the granite mountain wall. It overlooked Koles and served many needs for the area's inhabitants. Young lovers exchanged first kisses and vows, our bumbling idiots held an annual drinking party beneath the rock, and poets came to create new verses. Also, at this nature's wonder, uncle Jonathan discovered the formula for his famous perfume.

I found my uncle sitting crossed-legged on the bare ground. Wrapped in a worn-out kasaya[2] robe, his limbs exhibited the skin and bones of a near skeleton. On his bald head, a few strands of white hair fluttered in the wind. His facial skin, stretched by protruding bones, had a yellowish appearance. He stared to the east through the gray irises of his sunken eyes, as if seeing only the light of a prophet.

This sight of a man I once admired for his strength and wisdom shook me deeply. For a few silent minutes, I stood in front of him, waiting for

---

2   Buddhist monk daily robe

admission into his circle of vision.

"Uncle Jonathan, do you know who I am?" I asked.

No response came. I fought to keep my tearful eyes open. Through my clouded vision, he hovered and swayed. He turned to me. He confronted me with his eyes, deep in his skull. A toothless smile and a lifeless nod greeted me.

"Uncle, it is I, Dino." I rushed to grab his attention.

He nodded.

"I'm back from the war and have found myself in undesirable circumstances. I don't understand what's happening around me. I returned home to find peace and share the joyous news with my family. Instead, I discovered that I returned to the same mad town I left four years ago. The newspapers made me a hero and promoted me to general, and I heard my father is marrying me to some girl from the Resava."

My uncle sat calmly and listened.

"I cannot do that. I cannot marry this girl. Do you know why?" I raised my voice.

His nod shocked me. He motioned for me to sit down.

"How? Nobody knows about it, except for Prince George and Ms. LaGrange."

Uncle Jonathan nodded again and signed that he learned I was married on the day of our wedding.

"But, how? Tell me, how do you know?"

"From Buddha."

"Buddha? I don't know any Buddha."

"Buddha the Great Brahman is the master of our universe. He knows everything." He continued to sign in the language of my childhood. I stared at the slow motion of his hands. I questioned his sanity. Had he gone mad? Why was he talking to me this way?

"Uncle, why don't you speak to me? Please, I need your advice. I don't know what to do."

He opened his bony arms and hugged me. A slight tremor passed through my body, and then a flow of calmness inundated my soul.

He continued to talk in sign language. "My beloved nephew. I came back to see you again. The storm hovering over your fate urged me to return from the Far East, but only if I pledged that I would never utter words from my mouth. I gave my solemn oath to our abbot that I would not reveal the secrets of the Holy Light of Buddha. Ironically, you and I have switched. You are an orator now, and I'm a mute."

For a second or two, his incredulous discretion sounded convincing, however silly it was. He continued to pour out facts and I listened.

"Your father has become a slave to his ambitions. He is obsessed with the vineyard. All he dreams and talks about is the production of the best wines in the Balkans. He wants to expand the property and plant a variety of foreign grapevines. He works from sunup to sundown. My poor sister follows him, works alongside him the long hours, and if it wasn't for Petro's wife, Mira, she'd be cleaning, washing, and cooking all in the same day." He took a deep breath, held his frog-like pose, and released it in a sustained stream of puffs. He drifted into another state of meditation.

"What shall I do, Uncle?" My call of desperation seemed to have awakened him.

"You have broken a thousand year-old-tradition. In the history of our country, no one has ever tried what you have done. You have only one choice, my boy. Go back to your parents' house, write a note to explain everything, and then ask for forgiveness. Pack up and leave under the cloak of darkness, and don't let anyone recognize you. Pick up the Orient Express at dawn and return to your command post in the capital. The damage is already done and cannot be repaired."

"You mean without seeing my parents? My little sister, Anitsa, my brother, Petro, my sister-in-law, and my little nephew? I could never do that."

"Then you'll face the consequences. The humiliation and the embarrassment of you and your family will be trumpeted mercilessly. The disintegration of your fame and your heroic deeds will follow."

"I don't care about my fame and promotions, and I don't care about the fake titles and the heroics I never achieved. I care about my character and pride. I'm the one who will live with that, not those town idiots and drunkards. It's time that we face our destinies and decide about our futures alone as it was written in the first Constitution of Biares, by our Tsar Shandu six hundred years ago. No, sir! I will face them all and tell them it is my decision. It is how I want to lead my life, and not by the rules of our antiquated tradition." Exhausted by my sudden storm of protests, I heaved and gasped for air.

Uncle Jonathan nodded and went back to his meditation. I stayed with him for a short while and left without saying goodbye. I sneaked back into the house unnoticed. My restless mind and body searched for an oases of serenity within my tormented soul. I was tired, and I drifted into sleep on grandpa's ottoman behind the brick oven.

TWO

Turbulent dreams woke me up a few times. In the pitch darkness, I searched for images of my father. What would he say when I tell him? Would I be able to stand up to him? I envisioned his unforgiving face and our stormy confrontation. I found myself back in the mute years. A frightened, insecure little boy who awaited punishment under an umbrella of fear. Why? My father never raised his hand to any of us kids.

I must tell him. There was no other way. But how? The truth. Tell him the truth, you idiot. The walls around me were closing. The laws of tradition squeezed my remaining breath. Panic surged, and I gasped for air. I wandered again in the darkness. Consciousness stormed in. What had I done? How would my father take it? What would this horrible news do to him? I envisioned myself as an outcast. The prodigal son of the Babic family! No more a hero. No more our favorite son. In and out of sleep, I prayed for an answer. It seemed that the stairway to heaven closed on me.

With dawn, came the familiar footsteps. Rekindling of fire in the stove and a soft clatter of dishes took place. The twilight sneaked into the dark spaces and switched to daylight.

Mom's figure loomed over the plate settings. Through two decades of my life, she never changed. Lovely, vivacious, big-hearted Balkan motherhood always shined like a star. This time her tired, anemic face showed signs of aging. How old was she? Our parents never shared their age with us. Kids never bothered to know. Parents were old, and grandparents were too old. They often said, "Wait until you get old." The five-year-old, Bobby, replied, "Who cares?" He was the smartest kid around.

Sunrays lit up our kitchen. I stood up and stretched my arms. A gleam of joy flickered in Mom's eyes. I walked over and hugged her. She sobbed and trembled. Her whispers were almost silent. "My Dino, you've come home, you're home."

I pulled away and looked at her. She now cried tears of happiness.

15

"I missed you so much. It was too long," she mumbled between her sobs.

My sister-in-law came down the stairs and almost flew to embrace me with the baby in her left arm. Tears ran down her face while she kept kissing my cheeks and talking with great delight. My nephew kept sucking his breakfast undisturbed, big brown eyes staring at me. He was the baby replica of my brother, Petro, whose picture took place as the first son in our family album. But, by George, my nephew inherited our father's larynx. As soon as Mira pulled her breast away from his mouth, the deafening scream echoed throughout the house.

The deep voice of my father trumpeted his sentiments from the bedroom on the lower floor. "Is that my bugler? Is that my pride, my Yablan? Grandpa is coming. I'll be there, my boy. I hear you. Keep singing to your grandpa."

The room was full of sounds.

Mira talked to Mom, my father blabbered to his grandson, and my sister Anitsa came down the stairway. She screamed and jumped into my embrace, "Dino, my Dino!" She held me tight and spilled an avalanche of kisses all over my head.

The house came alive. My father walked in–broad smile, broad shoulders.

"Welcome home, son." His bear hug enveloped my entire being, body, and soul.

It had been so long since our last hug. Would he forgive me?

"Did you sleep well? Did Yablan wake you up? He is our morning troubadour. Every day I can hardly wait to hear his call at dawn."

"Yablan, hey? I wondered what name you'd chosen for him."

"That's what Petro and Mira wanted. They asked the godfather to name him Yablan, and he agreed. It's Mira's father's name, and he couldn't be happier when we christened the baby after him. He went to the capital and bought him an imported baby stroller with four wheels and cushion springs.

"Every Sunday, he'd take baby Yablan for a ride through the main street on the cobblestone road. He said going over the chuckholes, the baby never bounced but sat as if he was riding on a pillow. His grandpa bragged to some townsfolk about the stroller. He said he'd seen it in the capital where our noble citizens take their babies for a ride. But I..., to be honest with you, I'd like to have my grandson raised as you boys were. Let him feel the bumps and chuckholes on the flat-board stroller. He needs to toughen up. When he falls on his butt, he won't expect the pillow."

"Father, don't fret. Soon he'll be just like you," I said.

His eyes glistened in the morning light. Happiness spilled over his face, but a twitch of a nervous expression showed anxiety. The clatter of dishes interrupted his thoughts. He called out, "Well, Mother, is the breakfast ready?"

I couldn't take my eyes from my nephew. He was back on his mamma's breast. He pulled and sucked, his cheeks plump and pinkish, his eyes still staring at me as if saying, "Hey, don't bother me. I'm busy."

I thought of Galia and our future baby, our happiness of becoming parents. The anguish swelled within me. I sighed, and at that instant, my mother glanced at me. The stream of her worries drifted my way.

Mira placed the baby in the crib and sat at the table. We ate in an atmosphere of anticipation. My father wolfed down his breakfast. The greedy sounds of his gourmet appetite accompanied each bite. Savoring her breakfast, my mother searched around the table, ready to jump and serve the needs of her men. I resented her role and often questioned why Balkan women were so subservient to men. In the thousand years of male domination, a permanent barrier stood between men and women. Would I be a chauvinist pig with Galia?

From time to time, my father looked at me and smiled with a sense of jubilation. His eyes shone with excitement, and every time it stabbed my heart deeper. I lost my appetite and fumbled with the pieces of meat on my plate.

"Mother, I'm going out in the backyard. I need some fresh air," I said and got up.

She wanted to say something, but looked at my father and nodded.

"I'll come with you." Mira stood up.

I glanced at my nephew. He was already napping and kicking. The gurgle of his stomach gasses fell in tune with his happy babbles. What a joy he was.

"That's my boy. Fire one for Grandpa. Fire!" He yelled the command and his barrel of laughs thundered across the room. "When you wake up, I'm taking you and Dino to the vineyard," he added. "There'll be a great harvest this year. You and I will have plenty of work to do."

"Take it easy, Papa," I said.

"Oh, son, your father is growing old, and he can't cope with that," mother said. "He would like to be forever young, but his age is taking its toll."

Father turned to mother and said, "I'm not like your brother who sits on top of Gornik and stares to the east. He was foolish before, but now he has lost his mind completely."

"I visited with him yesterday, Papa. We talked."

He considered my words, narrowed his eyebrows, and slapped his hands in disbelief.

"He doesn't talk!"

"He talked to me," I insisted.

"How?"

"With the sign language. Remember?"

"What could he talk about with you? It must be all nonsense."

"On the contrary, Uncle Jonathan's mind is very sharp. He has acquired a lot of wisdom, and we could all learn from him."

"Like what?" My father snapped back irritated.

"Like telling the truth." I vented the agony of frustration.

"The truth? I have nothing to hide."

I raised my voice. "But I have God's truth to share with you all. The revelation that will shatter your dreams, Papa."

His eyelids narrowed, his lips tightened, and his hands turned into hammer-like fists. Every muscle of his body stiffened and bulged out.

I took a slow, deep breath and continued in a softer voice, "May the Lord forgive me for what I'm about to tell you."

Mira and Anitsa stood embraced, eyes riveted on me without blinking. My mother quivered in her chair. Anticipation fluttered in her eyes. My father took a defending stance, known to any of the Balkan men, ready to fight the invading forces. My time to tell the truth presented itself with a bang.

"I'm married!"

The crushing blow and immense surprise took place in dead silence.

"I married a woman in Maradonia one month ago. Her name is Galia Makarova. The wedding took place in Chestnut, and my best man was Prince George." My merciless words added to the pain on my father's face.

"But the tradition… Have you forgotten our tradition?"

"No, Father. I didn't. Our tradition is a thousand-year-old custom. We are in the twentieth century, and changes are taking place in the Balkans."

"Never!" he screamed. The painful cry in his voice echoed. The baby woke up and joined in with his howl. The women sobbed.

"You have disgraced me. You have disgraced the family, our name, and the town of Koles. The tradition, son, is the last and the most precious dignity our people have. For five hundred years under the Ottomans, our tradition stood alongside our people. It defied the invader's attempts to convert us to the Muslim religion. We fought against their laws, their customs, their traditions, and survived. Without tradition, our beloved country would not exist."

"But, Papa. General Savich gave me his blessing, and so did Prince George…"

"Don't call me Papa!" he thundered, angrier than before, his face red, his nostrils trembling, his eyes full of flame. "You're no longer my son."

"No!" my mother cried out. Pain blemished her pretty face. The fright in her eyes hung on the edge of panic. She twisted and rolled her hands in her lap.

Scolded and crushed, I lost my courage. His hatred was powerful. He turned and walked away. This was the last blow. I grabbed my bag and started for the door. My mom ran over and held me. Mira and Anitsa joined.

"You cannot go. He doesn't mean what he said. Please, son. This is your home. You were born here." The crying and panic in their eyes stopped me for a second.

I separated and said, "I must go, Mother. I have done enough damage, but I cannot reverse it, nor will I back out of my marriage. I love Galia. She is a wonderful woman. She is pregnant, and we will have our baby." The shock of the news left them speechless. I walked out distraught and defeated.

At the train station, a couple of posters of my heroic deeds faced me. I could only read that I was the black sheep of my family. The streets were empty. The peaceful ambiance suited me well. My town's drunks were recovering from yesterday's expectation of the 'general.' I boarded the morning Royal Daily North. The sad faces of disappointed tourists greeted me. They traveled to Koles to meet the general. I stood up and yelled. "Hey, I'm the general."

They smiled sarcastically, waved their arms in disgust, and commented, "Koles is full of pretenders. Everyone wants to be a hero. You better shut up or we'll throw you off the train."

"Son, don't make a mockery of our hero. He's fighting for our freedom," an old man reprimanded me. There was no lack of absurdity with my people.

THREE

The train entered the capital at 6 p.m. I checked in and reported to the command post of the Royal Cavalry Regiment. A clerk on duty registered my arrival and handed me an envelope. He addressed me as Lieutenant Colonel Dino Babic. I shrugged with a lack of interest.

"Sir, you've been promoted."

"Promoted? I was a general in my home town, yesterday."

I left him gawking after me. His face expression was that of my home-town people.

In the envelope I found a message from General Savich; the recommendation for my promotion to lieutenant colonel and the approval from the Supreme Command Quarters. At the bottom was a letter from Galia.

I tore open the envelope with trembling fingers and read with burning eyes the blurring sentences that spoke the longing words of love.

My beloved Dino,

Your letter arrived a day after your departure. Every word is a soothing cure for my loneliness. I read it often and I crave for you more. Days without you are unbearable, gloomy, and sorrowful. My longing for you begins in the morning and flows into the next day. It will not stop until you return. I dream of the days when we will be together.

My hopes are that you will find your family well and receive blessings for our marriage. In my dreams, they would accept me as they have done with your sister-in-law, Mira. I have no other hopes but to be your loving wife and their daughter-in-law. I don't ask for you to be a Frenchman. I love you, as you are, a kind and a gentle Balkan man, raised by the principles of our tradition.

Every day is becoming longer and lonelier. Come back to me, my love.

Your wife, Galia

I read it again and brought the letter to my heart. Perhaps she could feel me. But if she could…? I didn't want her to know. No, I wouldn't let her suffer. I pulled the letter away from my chest.

Most of the night I spent thinking about the meaning of the conflict and the consequences of the brutal moment of truth between my father and me. Who was right? Convinced it was the only choice, both of us stood behind our positions. My father with tradition, and I with progress. The painful and impulsive separation caused incurable wounds. By midnight, it penetrated and shook my confidence, then turned into despair.

The smiling face of my late grandpa appeared. Words floated in the twilight of dawn, "Good wisdom is part of our life; stubbornness is the base of our existence."

Grandpa, I hope you still play chess in heaven. Thank you. I'll write a letter to my father. I'll ask for forgiveness.

My adjutant, Lieutenant Rastko, knocked on the door and woke me up at 6 a.m.

"What's going on?" I inquired.

"An urgent message from the Ministry of War. Duke Simon Svetolik is ordering your presence at 9 a.m. I have arranged your car for 8 a.m. You'll have enough time to get ready. Your uniform is ironed and your boots are polished. The clean undergarments and your dress shirt are in the chiffonier."

"I'm starving. Would you order something for breakfast with a hot cup of tea?"

"Yes, sir, Colonel, breakfast will be waiting for you in the dining room."

I rushed to take a bath in steaming hot water in a small, unheated bathroom. Dipped to my waist, I rubbed my body and enjoyed the warmth. A minute later, I rose up and pulled the chain attached to the shower kettle above the tub. The shock from the ice-cold water resulted into a loud scream from me. Lieutenant Rastko rushed in.

"Is everything alright, Colonel?"

I stood naked, shivering, and pointed at the robe hanging on the nearby wall hook. "Hand me that robe, lieutenant. Who is the moron that attended my bathroom? Why was the shower kettle not filled with hot water?"

"I'm sorry, sir. This morning's orderly was a young recruit, Slavko, a farm boy who substituted for Corporal Deni. He didn't follow the right instructions. I will reprimand him."

"Strip him down and put him under the shower with cold water. No. Better yet, fill the kettle with ice-cold water and let him have it. He'll remember it next time."

"Yes, sir."

"Drop the order, dismiss the reprimand of the recruit. He wouldn't know about water for bathing. The only time farmers would use hot water is to remove pigskin hair and chicken feathers. Would you join me for breakfast, Lieutenant?"

"Thank you, sir, I'd be honored."

At precisely 8 a.m., the chauffeur arrived in front of the regiment's headquarters building. I grabbed my attaché case and walked out, Lieutenant Rastko behind me.

"Sir, don't forget to take notes at this meeting. Duke Svetolik is very particular about urgent matters in the Ministry of War. Every detail may be crucial in the decisions made this morning."

"Thank you, Lieutenant. I'm prepared. After the ice-cold shower, my senses sharpened."

"Good luck, sir. Crown Prince Kasander will also attend the meeting."

The presence of Crown Prince Kasander surprised me. For a moment, I questioned my role. As a regiment commander of two artillery battalions, I was a small link. My grandpa used to say, "Take it as it comes. Don't question the reason, follow the orders." But that only applied to him when my grandma chased him around the house with a broom.

Inside the office of the minister of war, tension greeted me. At the head of the table sat Crown Prince Kasander. On the right, Duke Svetolik, and on the left, Mr. Tanak Dud, Prime Minister of Biares. Chiefs of staff and other government officials occupied the rest of the chairs. Officers of various ranks filled the seats along four walls. A white cloud of tobacco smoke reached the cupola ceiling and lingered. Beneath it, a heavier layer settled above the assembly heads and looked like a rain cloud. The old bearded men in their shiny uniforms puffed their tobacco pipes in unison. God watched over me because I sat near an open door leading to the side offices and kitchen. The funneling effect drew out most of the smoke from officers and civilians around me.

Duke Svetolik stood up. He greeted his Royal Highness, Crown Prince Kasander, and the Prime Minister of Biares. He spoke in a quiet, distressed voice.

"Gentlemen, we have received a report from our elite scouts that the Kingdom of Thrace is about to attack our country."

An angry jolt of surprise echoed in the background. Duke Svetolik raised and lowered both hands and calmed the crowd.

"Our allies, Greece and Dachia, will join us in defense of our borders. Colonel Babic is here to point out the specifics of our enemy's strategy in this surprise attack." He turned around and motioned to his staff member, "Is Colonel Babic here?"

"Yes, sir, General."

"Colonel Babic, please approach," the captain called out my name from the other end of the table.

An uncomfortable silence took place. I realized it was not me who they were calling. They wanted my brother Petro, the decorated top scout of the Biares intelligence service. The captain repeated his call and then walked briskly over to me. He whispered, "Get up and follow me." His eyes shot flaming arrows with such anger that I jumped and rushed after him.

"Welcome, Colonel Babic. I must say your report is an excellent work of undercover intelligence. I'm proud of you, son. I congratulate you and your scouts on this extraordinary act of bravery." He applauded, Crown Prince Kasander stood up and joined in and the entire assembly thundered with applause.

I waited and took a deep breath before I spoke.

"Your Highness, Your Grace, please forgive me, but an error has been made. My name is Dino Babic, lieutenant colonel of the Second Regiment of the Artillery Battalion. My brother Petro is the one that you need here. He is the Colonel of the Biares Intelligence Service. My sincere apologies for the confusion this has caused. I have no knowledge of the undercover work my brother carried out."

"Son," Duke Svetolik addressed me in a shaken voice, "you have nothing to apologize for. You and your brother are the shining stars of our proud nation. We will remedy this mishap and send an immediate dispatch to bring Colonel Petro here. Go to your quarters and order the silent preparedness of your regiment. We may be at war any day. God be with you, Lieutenant Colonel."

I saluted and walked out gasping for breath. I wondered how much air was left in my lungs. Already filled to the brim with smoke from these small chimneys, I doubted it left any bronchial tubes empty.

Once outside, a long stream of exhaust poured out in two or three coughs. I inhaled the clean, fresh air of early summer. I kept my mouth open, walking back to my quarters. People stared. Soldiers saluted, and swallows flew over my head. What a beautiful day it was. Why would anyone want war?

The artillery regiment rolled out of the garrison on Sunday morning. The heavy guns, pulled by a team of horses, rumbled across the cobblestone streets. A cloud of dust swallowed the column on the country's dirt roads. We were assigned our future position southeast, between the Kupa Mountain and Bara Canyon. The map showed our destination point as being about three kilometers from the Thracian border, and about a hundred and twenty kilometers from our Capital. Major General Bogdanov, behind the thick growth of hair on his face, growled, "You have two days to get there."

In mid-morning the sudden storm from the North brought torrential rains. The wheels of the heavy artillery wagons sank into mud holes. In a battle with nature, men and horses used shear force. Time stalled. Anger and panic evolved. Low-rank officers screamed commands. The soldiers flogged the animals and looked up in desperation.

"God is not with us today," Simon the bugler declared. "We'll never make it in two days."

"Hey you, prophet! Get your ass in there and push," the second battery sergeant ordered the young bugler.

"Yes, Sergeant. What shall I do with my bugle?"

"Why, you …!"

Before I could hear the reply, the bugle flew to the side of the muddy road. The kicked body of the bugler splattered mud in all directions. He jumped up and grabbed the rear wheel spokes with mighty force. The horses squealed in pain. The whips flayed their hides. Blood spewed out of their nostrils. Shining bulging eyes reflected fear. The sergeants shouted in unison, and the echo landed on the far horizon. The soldiers dug in again and pushed.

Hura…! The wheels budged, and the heavy gun cart moved forward. The column crawled out of the mud. The two horses collapsed and died, open-mouthed, glassy-eyed.

When night came the heavens opened. Buckets of rain poured down. The road disappeared, the night came, and we stopped. Flames flickered from the small fires along the road. Shadows of men and animals fluttered in a blurry view. Deep darkness swallowed the shapes and figures. Rain came in torrents and soaked everyone in cold wetness while the night became a cradle of misery. Men shivered, prayed, and cursed.

Sergeant Stepan addressed me. "Sir, we must move. If we stay here overnight, half of the animals will die and half of our men will get sick."

I agreed. "Order the regiment to proceed. Use an extreme course of action. As soon as we reach the Roman highway, we will make camp."

The regiment moved. Men, animals, and guns meandered along the path through the night. A line of lanterns flickered and bounced off the wall of darkness. The rain kept bringing more misery. The regiment moved on.

At the break of dawn, we reached the cobblestone highway. The bugler trumpeted the stop. The column formed a straight line, and tents popped up along the road. A deep sigh of relief echoed across the valley. The clouds lifted, and the rain passed over the mountains.

Thank you, Lord. I ordered a short rest and a hearty breakfast before we moved on.

Sergeant Stepan walked into my tent and saluted. His tired eyes were half-closed. Signs of worry showed on his robust, weathered cheeks and forehead.

"We have only twenty-four hours to get to our destination," I said.

"Colonel Babic, sir, we need more time here. Some of the canon carriages need repairs, and most heavy guns require cleaning. We need fresh animals to replace the tow horses and oxen. We won't be able to move on until nightfall."

I raised my arm and stopped him. All of his arguments made sense. Men needed rest. The guns must be ready. As for the animals, yes, we need fresh horses.

"All officers will relinquish their horses. You will take my horse and hitch him to the front carriage. Order the cleaning and repairs immediately. The artillery crew will receive a short rest. All others will attend chores for readiness. We will move at noon. We must be there by tomorrow night."

"Yes, sir, Colonel," he saluted and walked out. A bright and sunny day greeted us in the morning. The wonderful warmth flourished over the area. Wheat fields in the distance shimmered in golden colors. In the nearby forests, birds sang a chorus of nature.

I overheard two officers in the next tent. "It's a shame that we must fight our allies. Now that we are free from the Ottomans, can't we live in peace and harmony as neighbors and brothers?"

"Yovan, you are too young to understand the history of the Balkans. Our people have always fought against invaders in defense of our beloved country. And it will never stop. This is our fate. Some call it God's will, but God has forgotten the people of the Balkans. We are doomed."

"I don't believe that," the young man argued. "God is always with us because we are his chosen people."

The bitter truth about the Balkan peoples was their unwavering belief. In all three religions, Catholic, Jewish, and Muslim, they were the chosen people. So were the Semites, Phoenicians, Canaanites, Ammonites, Edomites, and Philistines, all God's chosen people. With our unfounded convictions and beliefs, I wondered if God cared for any of us.

FOUR

We ran into our border patrol at the entrance to the gorge. They led us through a narrow passage over the gravel road. The heavy cannon carriages crushed the stone and made deep tracks. The patrol captain greeted us on the hilltop and pointed toward the Thracian border.

"We are about three kilometers from our neighbors. Their camp is on the other side of Storm Creek. We haven't detected any troupe maneuvers," he told me.

The 1st battalion took the left flank and the 2nd battalion took the center. I ordered minimal movement, low campfires, and lamps off.

A long night fell upon us. Orders from general headquarters provided no details about our next move. The courier from the capital caught up with us at dawn with a verbal message, "Wait for further instructions." We waited.

Heavens above revealed the beauty of our Milky Way Galaxy. The rising sun peeked over the edge of the earth. Golden rays from the east stripped off the vestments of the night.

I stepped out of my tent, lit my pipe, and blew a long puff of smoke. My thoughts drifted southwest in search of Galia. I considered the reasons for the upcoming confrontation. Fear within and a vision of a gloomy future lingered. I walked to the edge of the gorge and stared at the depth of darkness below. I thought about the claim that we are the children of God. For no human could pass through the gorge in the middle of the night without His torch.

Comforting thoughts of happiness and peace entered my heart. I sat under the tree and pulled out my notepad and pencil.

June 28, 1913
My adorable wife, my sweet Galia,
Days have passed since your last letter arrived and I beg you to forgive me for not responding sooner. Sudden changes are taking place that I have

29

no control over. The new course of my military career is taking me further away from you. In contrast, the visit to my family in Koles was an unhappy event that evolved into a series of obstacles to our original plans and our dreams. I am in despair writing to you about this unfortunate outcome, but my marriage announcement resulted in an irreparable clash with my father. He rejected my firm decision and renounced me.

It was a very painful separation from my mom, my little sister Anitsa, and Petro's wife Mira. I could not accept my father's demands for an annulment of our holy marriage. Angry and disappointed with his narrow-minded dogmas, and his thousand-year-old tradition of choosing a wife for me, I stood my ground. I told him to his face that I could only be married to you.

On my way to the new quarters in the capital, after a few hours of cooling my overheated mind, I regretted the confrontation with my father. I wish I had brought you with me. I know he would have instantly fallen in love with you and accepted our marriage, but our tempers flared up prematurely and the big divide happened. I left unforgiving, and he stayed behind the walls of our tradition.

Under normal conditions, I would've walked back and asked for his forgiveness, understanding, and acceptance of our marriage. Unfortunately, our fate is in the hands of warmongers leading our small country into another confrontation.

My career as a soldier was suddenly and unexpectedly catapulted, and the army promoted me to lieutenant colonel, commanding officer of the artillery regiment.

I am still puzzled about this extravagant advancement. But I believe Miss LaGrange and Prince George had mainly contributed to it with their embelished reports about my heroic deeds in the war against Ottomans.

The real hero is my brother, Petro. He is risking his life behind enemy lines collecting data and information about the Thracian military maneuvers. His scouting skills and courage in the war for liberation have had a remarkable impact on the outcome of clashes between the small armies of Little Antante and the mighty armies of the Ottoman Empire.

On this glorious morning, in the shadow of an old maple tree, I am envisioning your presence. My senses are mesmerized by an enormous longing for you. My dreams float between our yesterdays and tomorrows, while my heart trembles in the court of fear. I cannot explain how people of the same

Slavic origin could love and hate each other at the same time. However, here we are on the brink of another senseless dispute between our two countries.

My hope for tomorrow is to be with you.

With all my love, I pray for you and our baby. Let the Lord guard you and keep you well.

With all my love, Dino

The courier from Third Army Headquarters arrived the next day. "We are anticipating an enemy attack. Our orders are to position the artillery batteries and wait for the Third Army to join us."

From the Thracian border, the soft sounds of homemade pigskin pipes trailed our way. The melody entered our fighting souls and invited peace into our hearts.

The bugle awoke the soldiers. The loud commands set off a furious race to get ready, animals, guns, and supplies. It took only two hours to get our heavy guns ready and aiming at a target across the border.

My horse pranced. Sergeant Mika held him tight while I tried to get into the saddle. The horse jumped and knocked the sergeant down, and took off in the opposite direction.

I asked the sergeant, "What spooked him? He is usually very calm."

"Some horses have a sense of impending danger," he replied. "I'll go and fetch him. Before you ride, sir, he needs to be rubbed down. It will only take a few minutes."

"Very well, Sergeant. Go ahead."

The sergeant saluted, mounted his horse, and galloped away.

Captain Golich chose a few of our finest horsemen for a quick survey of enemy territory. A few minutes later, four cavalrymen rode off.

I worried about my inexperience in the case of an enemy attack. A lack of theoretical knowledge and artillery training could put the regiment in grave danger. Our commanding officer, Colonel Pavich, remained in the capital for some last-minute directives. I expected him to join us before the Third Army's arrival. I don't think the regiment officers had any confidence in me. Why would they? In feverish prayers, I hoped for the colonel's timely arrival.

My thoughts no longer justified the reasons for this war. Instead, I wondered why I was part of it. I couldn't find any explanations. I miss my imaginary advisors very much. Their arguments, their endless oratory, and their silliness were now things of the past. After all, they were from the beginning of time, and they had the answers to everything. Most were worthless, but they gave their opinion, like it or not.

At 2 p.m. gunshots echoed across the hills. Minutes later, two of our cavalrymen rode over the hilltop in a furious race for their lives. The gunfire continued. Our soldiers returned fire even though both sides were out of range. Only two scouts came across and slowed down before reaching our battery lines. A cold sweat ran down my back.

The cavalrymen approached. The horses slowed their paces. Captain Golich addressed the men. "What happened? Where are the other two?"

One of the men slid off his horse and dropped to his knees. He vomited violently. The other man looked over our heads and spoke in a deep voice. "The Thracians were waiting for us. Their border patrol shot at us before we got to the crossing point. They killed two other men. We couldn't see them. I had enough time to turn around and run. My horse got hit. Would you …?" He collapsed, face down in the grass. One long death rattle and he was dead. The Second Balkan War had started.

Colonel Pavich arrived in the afternoon. He ordered an immediate crossing into the enemy territory. Our regiment didn't encounter any resistance at the border. The scouts reported no signs of the Thracian army. Before dusk, we arrived at the outskirts of a small town. Two major roads intersected. One led southwest and the other north.

We positioned the four artillery batteries at an elevation overlooking the town and waited. There was no movement of any kind. I sent out two scouts and walked over to Colonel Pavich's tent to report. He stayed busy studying the map and motioned for me to approach.

"This town is a very strategic point for the Thracians. Their troops could cross into Biares southwest or northwest from here. But they must use the road through Jarmolo. The map doesn't show any other roads. There must be some units defending the town. What do you think, Lieutenant Babic?"

I disregarded his condescending address of my rank and replied, "We need to get the report from the scouts. They will give us a better picture, Colonel."

"If they don't show up in an hour, I will order an artillery attack on the town." He slammed his hand against the table. "We must occupy the crossroads and this town is in our way."

I said nothing. His anger frustrated me but I kept calm. He lit his pipe and smoked and puffed. His eyes flashed like lightning. Was this a sign of madness with all commanding officers at war? Darkness obscured the view. The full moon crept out and lit up the vast skies. Our battery units, and gunners stood at the ready. Time ticked away.

The two scouts returned and reported the pullout of an infantry division. One infantry battalion and about fifty militiamen was defending the town. There were four men in the town square tied to fence posts for execution. They could be local Biares citizens captured across the border or some of our scouts.

"Lieutenant Colonel Babic, send the advance unit to their observation points. Use the field telephone linemen to establish a link between us, and order the first battery to fire warning shots. If the Thracians don't pull out, order the second battery to aim at the town," Colonel Pavich ordered.

"But, Colonel, the four hostages may be in danger. What if they are our scouts?" The thought of my brother being tied to a pole hit me like a thunderbolt. I almost screamed in pain but held strong and said, "Sir, may I suggest that I go down and negotiate a peaceful solution? If I don't return within two hours, you may order an attack."

The colonel studied my resolve, then turned to the side and said, "All right, but remember, you have only two hours. Godspeed, son."

I picked two cavalrymen, and the three of us galloped up the hill. The town from the top appeared like an enchanted place surrounded by the morning fog. We trotted downhill cautiously and dismounted at the town's marker. The weathered sign was illegible. We tied the horses to a post and left our guns behind. I pulled out a white flag, unwrapped it, and walked toward the town square, the two soldiers behind me.

About fifty meters ahead, the line of Thracian soldiers and militiamen waited, guns pointed and ready to shoot. I waved the flag and hollered, "We've come to talk. We have no guns."

An officer with a long beard stepped forward and yelled. "Proceed, but keep your arms up."

I ordered the Scouts to obey, and we walked over.

They marched us to the town square. They seated us at a wooden table surrounded by Thracian soldiers and militiamen. The militiamen wore peasant clothes and carried old rifles and powder guns. Unshaven and with raggedy vests, they had the familiar appearance of our countrymen with the strong odor of garlic and rarely bathed bodies.

The three officers sat across from us and studied my uniform and epaulets.

"Are you the commander of your regiment?" The bearded officer asked.

"No, sir. I am an artillery officer."

"Why did you come here?"

"I came to negotiate a peaceful way out of this situation."

He stared at me. His red face burned with fire. His right hand rested over his gun holster.

"What do you propose?" His stern expression and threatening tone raised tension.

I studied his resolve, and thought of the words I should use. I prayed that I would get a chance to speak before his temper exploded. A wave of uncertainty rolled over my unwavering confidence. Was I in the footsteps of a glory-bound foolish young man? Stuck in the mud of an unfamiliar path, I gathered my last sense of reality. I took a slow, deep breath. A beloved voice of tranquility overcame me. I spoke in a role of a monk encouraged by the Holy Spirit of Mount Athos

"Brothers," I said. "Until yesterday, we were allies. We fought for the centuries-old idea of freedom from the Ottomans. We are Slavic people, with the same religion, tradition, and customs dating back a thousand years. Our people are farmers and traders, and..."

The bearded Thracian officer interrupted. "Come to the point," his voice sounded impatient, but no longer threatening.

"Our army has surrounded this town from all directions. Our heavy artillery is aimed at you and ready to fire. We are given less than two hours to negotiate a peaceful solution. Our commanding officer will not give us more time. I've come to ask you to surrender the town and leave your prisoners to us."

"You came to our town, and you dare ask me to surrender? What if we don't accept your proposal?"

"Your army pulled out last night. Your infantry unit and this bunch of ill-equipped militiamen would not last but an hour or two. Why sacrifice your men if we can negotiate a peaceful solution?"

"We have four Biares' hostages. Go back and tell your commander if he attacks, we will execute them. We'll fight in defense of our homeland until the last man is standing."

"In one hour and thirty-seven minutes, our commander will start shelling your town. I urge you to consider our proposal and leave. I would like to see your prisoners now."

Anger filled his eyes, and he spat on the ground. His voice thundered. He called someone named Vasily and ordered that the four prisoners be brought out. A few minutes passed before the Thracians came out leading the hostages. Their arms and legs tied, hurried along by bayonets, they walked in small steps.

When they reached the square, the militiamen tied them to the poles. I strained to identify my brother, but all four stood in the shadow of a big tree that blurred and shielded them from my view.

I turned toward the Thracian officer. With an intense facial expression behind his heavy beard, he faced me. I spoke, "Before I go back, may I see the prisoners and talk to them? I would like to know their names."

Deep furrows wrinkled his forehead. He stood still for a while. Then he turned to his men and ordered one to take me to the prisoners. My legs trembled as I followed the man. Dark thoughts entered my mind. What if my brother was among the four? How would I save him? We passed a firing squad of eight men standing about ten meters before their targets.

In the shadow of the large oak tree, I stepped up to the first man, his face unshaven, swollen from the beating, eyes closed.

"What's your name, Brother?" I asked.

He gurgled and moved his head slightly up. With almost white eyes, he stared aimlessly for a second or two. His body jerked, and he passed into oblivion.

The next man had also been beaten. He was alert. I asked "What's your name?

"I am Semo from the village of Durnik in Biares, just across the border. I'm not a soldier. The Thracian militiamen crossed into Baires and captured me with my herd of sheep. They captured me before me the other prisoners. I don't know who they are. They won't let us talk to each other."

I walked to the next pole. The prisoner appeared alert but his eyes showed fear when I asked about him. He looked in the direction behind me. I slowly rotated my head and spotted the militiaman about six feet away.

"Tell your leader I need some privacy with these men." My voice rang loud, and he walked back to his superiors.

I stepped closer and asked, "Are you the army scout? Do you know my brother Petro Babic?"

He looked at me and whispered, "I am. I do. He's tied to a pole behind me."

My heart sank, and my mind spun with panic.

"Be careful Mr. Babic. You mustn't give any signs of knowing him. Colonel Petro won't recognize you. They beat him severely." He stopped talking abruptly.

The militia leader approached me. "Are you done?"

"One more." I stepped to my brother's spot and looked at his disfigured face, mutilated body, and blood stained shirt. My eyes watered as I ached, but I held firm. I gathered my strength and spoke. "Who is this man, and why was he beaten so brutally?"

"He was the strongest of the three soldiers. When we captured them, he never gave up. It took ten of my men to subdue and tie him. I have no idea who he is. They had no guns. We tried to beat the answers out, but none would talk." The militia leader concluded, a ruthless expression on his face.

I walked back to the town square, sat at the table, and stared at the Thracian army officers. As I pondered about how to approach their commanding officer, how to propose the release of the prisoners, and how to delay the shelling in time, I considered several options.

He spoke first. "Where did you learn our language? You speak Thracian without an accent."

My head lit up like a brilliant star and cleared my clogged mind. Desko!

Thank you, Lord, for bringing my memories back. Filled with confidence, I answered in a calm and composed voice.

"I had a friend named Desko who taught me your language. We were both student monks in Zograf and Lanhidar on Mount Athos. A year ago, our destiny defrocked us, and we became soldiers of the liberation war against Ottomans.

A few months back, I met Desko south of Pirin. He was commander of the fifth battalion of Varna volunteers. I wondered what became of him?"

"Commandant Desko was killed in the last campaign against the Turks in the battle for Adrianople. I also knew him and his family. We were from the same village."

I crossed myself and folded my hands. My prayer echoed across the square as I mentioned the name of beloved Desko and asked the Lord to take him in His kingdom and forgive his sins. The Thracians and their leader kneeled and prayed with me. I stood and addressed them all.

"Brothers, our two nations are at war, and we'll never know why. Many innocent people will die and we will not settle many of the conflicts, like neighbors and brothers, but by powers greater than ours. I beg you to let me take the prisoners with me so you may leave peacefully and go back to your homes and your families. There is no need to shed our blood over this abandoned town."

I looked at their faces with great hope. I checked the time. Fifteen more minutes. Lord, please help me. My heart pounded as if it were about to burst. My head hurt. I pleaded with my eyes, and my posture.

"I want you to know my name. I am Nikolay, captain of the First Thracian Army. I will let you go with the hostages in memory of our mutual friend, Desko. But we will not pull out. This is our town, our country, our homeland, and we will fight until the last man."

He ordered the release of the hostages. I bowed to him and crossed myself. I was only thinking about thirteen more minutes. Subconsciously, I recorded the words of this proud man. He was a patriot and the sacrificial lamb for the ambitious dreams of a foolish emperor.

"Savo, run back and advise Colonel Pavich the Thracians are releasing the prisoners to us. Wave the flag as you gallop up the hill to catch their attention. When you deliver the message, get the medic and send him here right away. Bring some clothes for these men. Run, man, run."

I took a small bucket filled with water from the well and rushed to my brother. His eyes were open in a dazed state. He murmured. I cut the ties on his arms and legs and lowered him gently. I poured some water into his mouth, washed his face, and put his head into my lap.

I called the other scout. "Marko, untie the rest of the men. Here is my penknife. Cut their ropes and help them lie down on the grass gently. When you are done, refill the bucket and give them a drink of water in small portions."

I opened my brother's bloody shirt and carefully pulled it from the wounds on his chest and stomach. The painful sight made me sick for an instant, but I clenched my teeth and gently wiped away the blood. He stared at me, at my unfamiliar face, and at my sad, loving eyes.

"It's Dino." The words from my quivering lips spilled out. "I'm your little brother. Little Mute. Remember?"

Mesmerized by his eyes, I fell into a daydream of my youth and whispered a melody from our childhood.

My scout returned.

"I brought some water, sir. The other men were able to move on their own to the well. They are hungry, and I told them the ambulance wagon will be here soon with food and medicine."

"Well done, soldier. Let me know when the medic arrives."

"Do you need any help with this man, sir?"

"No, we cannot move him until the doctor comes. He may have some internal wounds."

"Very well, sir. I will search through a couple of houses for a pillow and a blanket."

Time passed faster than wished. It had been over thirty minutes since Savo left. Someone should be here soon. How soon? The fading light in my brother's eyes burned my hopes. Please, Lord, don't take him. Let him live. He's my only brother, and he's the father of my beloved nephew.

I looked toward the hills in desperation. No rumble. No galloping. Only my unconscious brother and I were in a waterfall of anxiety. His body gave no sign of life. I couldn't feel the pulse from his neck. I panicked and laid his head on the grass, then took his pulse from his left wrist. A faint throb passed through, and I sighed of relief. "Stay with me, Petro."

"Sir, I found a pillow and a blanket." The scout's voice came from behind, "and I also found some towels and bed sheets."

"Very well, soldier. Let me have a couple of towels, a pillow, and a blanket, and bring some water."

"Right away, sir."

"Is the medic here yet? What's taking so long?"

"They're coming, sir. I've seen the ambulance coming down a minute ago, and they will be here any time now."

"Bring them here immediately."

"Yes, sir."

Driven by a young medic the wagon stormed into town square. Next to him, an older man descended from the bench and rushed over to me, a medical bag in his right hand. He leaned over my brother's mouth and felt the pulse on his neck. He pulled out his stethoscope, placed the tips in his ears, and carefully put the diaphragm on Petro's chest. He listened and then stood up.

"This man is dying. His vital organs have collapsed. It's a matter of minutes or hours. Nothing can be done."

His words hammered through my head. My mind froze. Enormous fury erupted from my mouth. "What do you mean? He cannot die. He is my brother!" I screamed at the doctor in a threatening pose. "I won't allow it. You must save him. You must do something now!"

He stepped back and said in a low voice, "I'm sorry, son. Nothing can be done. We cannot move him. He needs our prayers and a priest now. I'm very sorry."

I looked at him in disbelief and sobbed. I murmured prayers.

"Stan," he called the driver, "Go fetch the priest."

I shook and wept. Then, I turned to him and said, "No need for a priest. I'm a monk from Lanhidar, and I always carry my cross. He's my brother, and I will give him his last rites."

The sun illuminated the sky, its rays forming a halo, bathing my brother's face in divine light. Lord, please watch over my brother Petro. I stood on my shaky legs, pulled a cross from my back pocket, and as if summoned by the Holy Father, I said the Lord's Prayer.

Dear Heavenly Father, with a heavy heart I come to you. My brother Petro is without sins, and he lies before of us in the shadow of death. Please, Lord, take his hand and let him find peace and joy in your grace.

Amen

My beloved brother opened his eyes, as clear as the blue Aegean Sea. He slowly inhaled and whispered his last words.

I dropped to my knees and placed my ear near his mouth. He was gone.

The roar of my painful cry echoed across the Thracian lands. I held tight to my brother's body. A sudden breath of heaven lifted his soul, and light from the brightest stars illuminated the holy pathway of ascension.

I screamed one more time, one last cry, one last goodbye. Darkness fell upon me and the rest of humanity. The weight of tragedy increased with a flood of guilt born and nurtured by my heritage. A constant battle raged between the impossible wrong and the impossible right. In my futile attempt to rekindle memories of the value of living, inside my human psyche, an evil force assaulted the goodness of life. Revenge, hatred, envy, and murderous instincts formed and created a henchman. Inside of me, fury boiled an untamable source of lunacy. Within me, arrows of lightning spewed the fire of damnation. At the border, I stopped to say goodbye to my brother, on his last return home. My salute to him lingered behind his coffin and disappeared in the last light of sundown.

FIVE

The courier from the Biares High Command caught up with my squadron on the way back to our regiment. He delivered the orders to our commanding officer in a sealed envelope.

"Sir, General Kundra, the Chief of Staff, has dispatched specific orders for your newly appointed commanding officer," the courier informed me. "Brigadier General Mandich is due to arrive from Gotin in four hours, and the orders must be delivered directly to him."

"What happened to Colonel Pavic?"

"I don't know, sir. I'm merely a messenger. Do I have your permission to withdraw?"

"You may go, Sergeant."

He turned his horse around and galloped away. I considered the changes, the urgent orders, and the new commanding officer.

Our regiment had taken a position near the border. When we arrived, I inquired about Colonel Pavic.

"The Third Army summoned Colonel Pavic and placed him in command of the Una Infantry Division yesterday. He left right away. Brigadier General Mandich of the Elite Reserves Battalion was appointed in his place," Captain Birgo reported.

"Do we know anything about this general?" I asked.

"He's a member of the old guard. In the liberation wars of 1878, he fought alongside King Tarpe, and retired with a chest full of medals. The old tiger was wounded seven times. He led the fearless charge on his horse against the overwhelming enemy force in the last battle, despite being wounded. His cavalry broke through the front lines, causing the Ottoman infantry to panic. He was then known as the Immortal General."

In the late afternoon, General Mandich arrived and gathered all of the commanding officers in his tent. He introduced himself and turned to the map posted on a makeshift stand. He focused his attention on the border, highlighted in black. The six of us stood behind his tall, corpulent figure. Our shadows danced in the light of a flickering lamp, while outside voices, horses neighing, broke the silence in the tent.

"Do we have someone who is familiar with the roads in Northeast Thracia?" General Mandich inquired.

"General, there are two men who traded goods across the border with Valachs and Thracians before the war. They are gunners under my command. Should I send for them?" Captain Birgo responded.

"Yes. Bring them in."

A few minutes later, the two men reported. Short, stocky, and fitted into tight uniforms, they looked like adolescent boys out of middle school. But their masculine bodies and rough faces suggested men of age, already worn down by a harsh life.

"They'll be perfect," General Mandich said as he studied the two soldiers and twitched his long mustache.

For almost an hour, General Mandich emphasized the surprise. He insisted we move tonight and get to our positions before morning. The move was quick and undetected by our enemy scouts, over a dusty road. The cavalry squadron rode through the balmy night, guided by lamp signals from the two scouts.

The muffled rolling of our artillery in the background, and the rhythmic padding of hoofbeats on the soft grass, lowered the curtain on my tired mind.

Deep in my thoughts and sorrow, I strayed from the main path and became separated from my cavalrymen. My horse had wandered off into the countryside, and I could no longer hear or see our artillery division. I paused to reorient myself. Without a map, I took out my compass and read the needle's position. For an instant, the soft moonlight sneaked through the dark clouds, and I read east. I turned around and looked for a road to get back. In total darkness, I lost my way. This eerie silence confused me. Should I go west or north? I remembered Venus rising before the sun from early geography and astronomy books, and it was somewhere north or northeast. I used my compass to point north and rode through the night, guided by the stars.

I traversed hills and valleys for three hours. The summer night was hot and humid. The sounds of a waterfall, the call of a coyote, and the hoot of a night owl interrupted the stillness, but there were no signs of human beings.

Fatigue finally caught up with me. I stopped and set up camp under a large tree. I tethered my horse and spread out my blanket on the grass. I sat down and closed my eyes.

Distant horse snorting and muted voices woke me. I shook the sleep off and opened my eyes to the rose and pink light of dawn. The noise came from somewhere below my location. I stood up and examined my horse. Undisturbed, he nibbled at the grass. The dense forest made it difficult for me to find my bearings.

I listened. An interrupted murmur came again. I crouched and moved slowly across the soft grass. Two men stood and talked about a hundred yards away, on the edge of the shrubby vegetation. They were dressed in Biares army uniforms.

I lifted my arms and was about to cry out overjoyed to see my countrymen, when a third man appeared from behind the two. He wore a Thracian blue uniform. I dropped to the ground.

My mind was racing with questions. Why were our scouts communicating with the enemy? What is happening? Was there a peace talk? It had been very possible that people could have come to their senses before the war. However, it didn't lead to peace because no one could follow the logic of the Balkan people. My grandfather used to say that we were the only people on this planet who lacked logic. It didn't matter. None of the Biares people knew what this word meant, anyway.

Should I reveal myself and join the pow-wow? One of my silent advisors appeared on my shoulder and put his finger to his mouth. "Pay attention," he said.

I heard nothing.

"Keep your mind open and concentrate."

I tried again very hard, but there were no sounds. "I can't hear. I need to get closer."

"You can't do it. They'll notice you. Wait. You'll be able to hear them when they return."

I stopped questioning. My imaginary advisors had no logic as well.

The scouts walked their horses up the hill and passed about twenty yards from me, a few minutes later. They talked loudly, and I could hear what they were saying. They appeared to be having a disagreement.

"Gute, what's the matter with you? Don't you recall? We just spoke with Captain Gavrov who brought the instructions for us." One of the men was chastised by the other.

"We are to inform General Mandich that the Thracian army will pass through the Robin Canyon tonight and will attack the Biares First Army in the morning. But instead, the Thracian Infantry Division will set a trap and await the arrival of the Biares Morava Division with heavy artillery tonight. It will be a splendid surprise and victory for our Tsar Ferdinand."

Everything was crystal clear. They were both Thracian spies. I crawled back to my horse and mounted it. I followed the two scouts to our camp from afar.

We arrived two hours later. Exhausted, I slid off the horse by the two soldiers standing on guard. They helped me to General Mandich's quarters. Before I entered the general's tent, a guard handed me his canteen, and I gulped down cold, refreshing water. Invigorated in mind and body, I stood up and walked into the general's tent unannounced.

General Mandich and three other officers hunched over the table studying the map, turned toward me in complete surprise.

"Lieutenant Colonel Babic, where did you disappear?" General Mandich asked. I saluted, expecting his reprimand. He studied my worn-out appearance, then raised his eyebrows and said, "Son, your legs will give out unless you sit down and tell us what happened."

A sigh of relief swept through my trembling body and down my shaking legs. I stepped to the table and, like a tired old man, squatted down onto a wooden folding stool. I gripped the edge of the table.

"Fetch him a drink and something to eat," General Mandich ordered. "Bring the doctor as well."

He sat across from me and waited patiently. I opened my eyes and whispered, "General, sir, I have located the Thracian army. But first, please arrest the two scouts who returned to our camp before me. They are Thracian spies instructed to lead you into a trap."

My voice quivered, and I took a deep breath. He watched me but said nothing. The orderly returned with a bottle of plum brandy and a plate with hot stew.

General Mandich poured a glass for me and said, "Drink it, son. You'll need some energy."

I hadn't tasted brandy since childhood when my grandpa taught me how to grade its age and strength. It was my first and last time grading twice-distilled plum brandy. I grimaced in an effort to crack a smile and gulped down the scorching drink. Fire stirred up in my mouth, throat, and stomach, but luckily, no one lit a match. An instant joy of a drunkard's debility rolled out of my mouth in loud, idiotic laughter.

When the taste of food lured me, I exhibited no table manners. I ate with dirty fingers, and with my mouth, I siphoned all the food the orderly delivered. A few minutes later, I turned to General Mandich. My mind floated while all I wanted was sleep.

"Thank you, son. You have done a great service to your country. We have arrested the two scouts, and they have talked. The surprise will be for the Thracians. We will set our artillery on each side of the canyon and close the escape routes. Tomorrow morning, with our guns at their throats, they'll plead for a truce."

Alcohol found its course quickly. My mind didn't respond. A medical assistant tried to pour some coffee into my mouth, but my tongue was a piece of dead meat. I couldn't say a word. Where was I? Was I sick? Faceless doctors and nurses passed by without a single reply.

I woke up in a canopy-covered ambulance to the clattering of metal buckets and cooking utensils attached to the sides of another wagon. I lay in the bed of an ambulance with the back canopy open. Two soldiers on the front bench of the mule wagon behind the ambulance swayed side to side on the bumpy road. The morning light slowly crept up over the eastern mountain peaks.

I tried to sit up, but my head weighed a ton. Wide awake, I realized I had slept in my uniform. Why was I in the ambulance? Was I wounded? I checked my head and body but found no bandages and no injuries. The motor was not running, but the vehicle was still moving. I got into the front and opened the back window of the driver's cabin. No one was inside. Up front, a set of mules pulled the ambulance cart. A soldier walked alongside, urging them on with a whip.

Ahead, a long line of supply wagons meandered over the hilly terrain. At a higher elevation, our artillery guns were lined up pointed in the other direction.

Doctor Milic climbed in, checked my pulse, asked me how I felt, and before I could answer he stepped out.

I yelled after him, "Hey, Doc, I'm hungry."

"I'll send the orderly to bring you some food."

A few minutes later, a soldier with a medical insignia on his sleeve brought hot food for me. He served it on a round platter and poured me a glass of white wine. The Soldier's Stew, flavored with southern spices, tasted pretty good. I quickly gobbled up the food, and he added some more.

With the morning sunshine, the surrounding scenes changed from gloomy to bright. Our invigorated soldiers pushed harder, animals moved faster, and the Biares Army regained its military strength before the battle.

At the entrance to the canyon I stepped out of the ambulance and mounted my horse. Our cavalry battalion stood blocking the east side, while several cannons aimed at the only way out, the narrow path west.

I rode up to the top of the canyon. Darkness melted away as sunshine entered with its long rays reaching the west end. It lit the stage for the ensuing battle. The canyon's majestic view revealed no movement. A dozen Thracian vehicles stood abandoned in its narrow passage. The lookout guardsmen threw long ropes over the steep cliffs and descended silently. A minute later, their voices echoed above the canyon. No one was there! They'd moved out.

"Damn! They must have had a warning. We may still have spies in our regiment. Damn. Damn. Damn!" General Mandich fumed.

"Colonel Babic, send one cavalry squadron in pursuit of enemy troops. When they locate them, report their position to our quarters and send another rider to headquarters in Gotin. Order the road cleared through the canyon, and if it's at all possible, let's get our artillery through today. When you're done, come to my quarters."

The enemy had left the canyon in haste. However, they left a few supply wagons and two army trucks perpendicular to the road. The cussing and blaspheming by our soldiers increased as time for clearing the passage extended to midnight. A seed of ambivalence planted by General Mandich about the infiltration of enemy spies within our army brought additional pain to my heart. My brother, Petro, was a spy—a brave patriot and a hero. The Thracian spies were also patriots to their homeland. Who would be the judge of their fate?

It had been three days since I sent my brother's body home. The thoughts of a terrible shock to my family of Petro's death increased my guilt for not escorting my brother. "I should be home. I should be home," a voice echoed in my head.

The next morning we were chasing the ghost in Biares. Our advance unit reported no enemy troops north or west. General Mandich asked, "How is this possible? We have all roads under surveillance."

They must have been invisible. How could they vanish in broad daylight? We passed through a small village, but no one there saw any Thracian soldiers or an army anywhere near. The villagers were not aware that we were at war with Thracia. The panic struck them, and after we drove away, a line of oxcarts, horse wagons, and people followed at a distance.

"Lieutenant Pervic," General Mandich addressed his staff officer. "Send two cavalrymen to advise the villagers not to follow us. We may soon turn back to Thracia. Advise them to take the next road west and go to the Starigrad garrison. They'll be safe there."

Passing through more villages with no sign of our enemy, we continued our course north. We didn't spread the news to other villages. They were so isolated and hapless, why should we make their life more miserable? I nodded. A fine man, our general. He could be a father of this army.

After two days of moving at the speed of an ox, we reached the Second Army Headquarters in Gotin. When General Mandich reported that we had lost track of the Thracian army within our borders, the chief of staff Four-Star General Tubin exploded. He screamed and spit out fire. He called our entire regiment incompetent nincompoops, all our officers degenerated cowards, and all our artillery battalions stupid fools, insults that were not easily digested. There ended my chance of a short leave to attend my brother's burial. A big lump in my throat prevented me from screaming back at him. I walked away from the army garrison and sat on a stump near my horse. His big eyes reflected the beauty of the land with its summer colors and a sense of animal curiosity or compassion for his master.

He nudged me and snorted softly. I pulled out of my pocket a small bag of dry apples and gave him his treat. He nudged me again.

"I love you too, brother." Subconsciously I also found the notepad, and wrote the letter to Galia.

After two days of tracking the Thracian army, our scouts reported another border passage. It was heavily guarded by enemy artillery.

"We must make a breakthrough." The message from the High Command came in the afternoon.

"Call the officers to my tent," General Mandich ordered.

The twelve of us reported promptly.

"Gentlemen, this is a true test of your military skills. The scouts reported that eighty artillery guns are pointed at the entrance of the passage. There is no close by crossing into Thracia. The nearest one is fifty kilometers from here. I have received an order to break through and proceed toward Fyaso." General Mandich's eyes turned dark. A cloud of concern hovered over his somber face. He took a deep breath under the weight of apparent indecision.

"What say you, men?" He challenged us.

"General, sir, do the scouts know how long and how deep the gorge is?" Major Gus inquired.

General Mandich and everyone else turned to the young officer.

Major Gus stood determined with a genuine glare of confidence.

"What's on your mind, Major? The scouts reported the passage to be one kilometer long. The gorge has a narrow entrance with high walls almost three hundred meters on each side. At its end, it tapers down to a lower elevation where enemy guns on both sides are waiting for us. The road through the gorge crosses the river multiple times. It would be a trap for our army to go into. Do you have a better plan?"

"No, General, I don't have a plan. But we have a platoon of mountaineers who could climb the canyon walls in an hour and survey enemy's position. The report would be in your hands three hours after nightfall."

"Nightfall will arive in two hours, so I will order the move at 10 p.m. You better get ready."

"Yes, sir, General, I'm off." He saluted and walked out.

"That young man is very confident. He means what he says. Send a platoon to protect him and his mountaineers in case they get spotted before the climb." General Mandich spoke absent-mindedly. His eyes peered at the exit as if he was following Major Gus to his destination.

I interrupted his thoughts. "Yes, sir, General. Shall we also get ready for the attack?"

"Right. If we should go, it must be tonight."

We moved into a position to enter the canyon. Silence fell upon the regiment. My tight nerves strummed to tunes of anxiety. In the twilight, I stared at the gate of hell and the thousands of imaginary Thracian eyes staring back at me. The mountaineers moved in. One by one, they climbed and disappeared into the crevices. Steep sides, almost reaching the stars, rose to the top.

The night swept away the remaining daylight and reigned in a dreadful silence. Around nine-thirty p.m. General Mandich summoned the officers. His face showed fatigue and anxiety. In the dim light of a lantern, he studied the map of the Thracian border.

"We are going in. We cannot wait for the report from Major Gus. We must break through tonight. The entire Second Army depends on our success. We will enter the canyon and create an element of surprise when we storm through. The Thracians won't be able to see us in pitch darkness, and we may get through undetected."

Undetected? With artillery and heavy wagons? I stared at him in disbelief. Had he gone mad? We'd be slaughtered like cattle in the canyon's narrow passage. No one spoke. I, the only idiot among us, choked by my thoughts, made a feeble effort, but only a gurgle came out.

"Something on your mind, Colonel?"

"No, sir," the coward in me replied.

"We must carry out the orders. You're dismissed! Tell the bugler to be ready," General Mandich said and waved us out. I stayed.

He turned and faced me. "Colonel Babic, speak up."

"General, sir, I beg your pardon. Could we give our scouts another hour?"

"No!" His loud bass startled me. "Here, read the dispatch. It says, 'Proceed immediately. Must cut off their third army.' Satisfied? Get out!"

I could almost feel his boot on my ass as I turned and walked out of his tent.

In the last minutes before the move, I stood by my horse with a cavalry squadron. The bugler, ready to blow, waited in front of the echelon of troops and artillery guns lined up a mile behind him. A quarter of a mile from the canyon entrance, I stared in the darkness for any signs of our scouts. Nothing. Fear crept up. A horseman with a long shadow rode by and took the lead. In a flash, I recognized General Mandich. He emerged in his ceremonial garb. The shining cavalry helmet adorned with a horsetail, and the sword in his right hand flashed in the moonlight.

"Christ Almighty, I hope he won't order a charge?" I whispered to Captain Iko.

"He might. He polished off a bottle this afternoon. You see how calm he is now?"

My new mischievous friend and confidant, Captain Iko, chuckled.

"Get your men behind him now. You will ride left of him, and I'll take the right side. We are under his command. We are soldiers of the Royal Biares Army, and we obey!" I whispered in anger.

In a few minutes, my elite squadron of thirty-six cavalrymen lined up behind the general. I, on the right, and Captain Iko, on the left.

General Mandich turned his horse around. Sitting tall and majestic, he addressed the regiment.

"Sons of Biares! We are forced again to defend our country. We must never fall to another conqueror. We will face the mighty Thracians and crush them. Long Live our King Tarpe." His words had a profound impact on our regiment.

"To war, to war," they sang and cheered.

A powerful echo bounced off the hills and trailed into the night. The fighting spirit of our countrymen awakened. The invincible Brigadier General Mandich raised his sword pointing forward, and to war we marched.

I thought of his words and the weight they put on our fighting men. The character of the Biaresen soldier may be described by saying simply that he was a hero, a born fighter, and a fatalist. Or it may dwelled it upon in an account that would fill many pages. I decided to leave this to our historians and follow the command of our superior officer. I knew that in battle, and in the hour of pain, the courage of the Biaresen soldier was above all praise.

My hometown drunks often claimed that we were the chosen people, and that God would find a place for us. If not in heaven, there would always be room in Helladise. I was sure God had created another town named Koles for his special people. Where else would angels find their sacramental wine?

SIX

We crawled through the canyon all night and found no resistance. At dawn, the shapes of the valley and the surrounding hillsides spread from the east as if painted by the spectrum of morning sun rays. Our regiment, a tired column of men and animals, emerged from the mouth of the canyon into Thracia.

Captain Iko pulled out his binoculars. He scanned the area, yawned, and mumbled, "Where are these cowards?"

The general's adjutant, Major Kobran, pointed in the direction of a forested hillside to the north. He handed the binoculars to General Mandich. "Over there, in the clearing, sir. About half a kilometer from here."

I struggled to see through my binoculars. A horrifying scene appeared. A body swung on a hanging rope. Two men walked away in a hurry.

"Snipers! Get me the snipers!" General Mandich screamed. "I want the Thracians dead."

Four men lined up with their scoped rifles. One by one, they fired at the moving target, a mere fifty meters from the forest. The Thracians dipped in and out of sight. One more round was fired by the three rifles. The fourth waited. I watched. My hands trembled. Boom! The fourth rifle fired. One Thracian stopped and then rolled down. The second disappeared into the woods.

"Get the body down," General Mandich ordered.

Three cavalrymen jumped on their horses and raced up the hill. We followed.

At the site, the three soldiers cut the rope and laid the hung man down. On his chest, a handwritten sign read: "DEATH AWAITS YOU IN OUR HOMELAND!" Young Major Gus stared at me with bulging eyes. Ligature marks and protruding tongue twisted my gut. A surge of vomit rushed up my throat. I dismounted and pulled out the canteen. I drank some water and splashed my face.

"Are you all right, Colonel?" Captain Ike asked. I nodded and drank more.

"Captain Iko," General Mandich called. "Arrange the transport and the escort for Major Gus's body back to Nais. Colonel Babic, order the move. We are going into Thracia."

My lips quivered. I yelled subconsciously at this foolish old man, "We are in Thracia," but no words came out again. Who were you, Dino? A coward or a mute? I scrutinized my character under the magnifying glass of my seven disappointed advisors. "What was happening with Dino?"

"Leave me alone, fellows. I'm an officer in the Royal Biares Army. I listen and obey. You could not grasp the meaning of it, you rebellious bunch."

General Mandich interrupted my thoughts, "Colonel Babic, I've changed my mind. You will take charge of the escort to Nais. I have a report to hand in, and this will be a good opportunity for you to join your family at your brother's funeral."

"Thank you, sir, General Mandich." I was elated.

"You need this brief rest, son." His fatherly voice surprised me.

If I had wings… My mind dashed a thousand kilometers ahead. No time for jubilation.

Shortly after, we parted and drove back through the canyon in half the time. Two hours later, we entered the Roman Highway, and from there we turned south to Nais. In the late afternoon, we arrived at the Second Army headquarters.

The garrison commander, Colonel Karnec, received me cordially.

"Welcome, Colonel Babic. If you don't mind bunking with three other officers, we'll make your accommodations for tonight in the third pavilion, second floor."

"Not at all, sir. I'd be content to overnight in a barn with horses."

"That won't be necessary, Colonel. Later tonight, we have a small gathering in the officers' club. Please join us."

"Thank you, sir. I have a report from General Mandich for the Second Army Commander, General Tadic."

"I will send the courier immediately. May I have it?"

I handed the envelope to him and asked, "What would be the shipping arrangements for the body of Major Gus Benru?"

"The coffin will be loaded onto the train tonight. We will inform his family to expect it at noon tomorrow."

"One more thing, sir. I haven't had a bite all day. Is there anything I could get from the garrison's kitchen?"

"Of course, Colonel. I'll order dinner for you." He called his orderly and requested several dishes.

"If you would like to refresh, we have a lavatory on this floor. My orderly will serve your dinner here in my office. Please, make yourself comfortable." In his welcoming manner, Colonel Karnec guided me to the lavatory.

The officer's club presented a challenge for me. I had never been to one before and could not remember any scenes of similar gatherings except being among my hometown people. No, I would not envision the Royal Army officers as residents of Koles. I recalled my grandfather's favorite quote. "We are all transplants plants until we become natives." I never asked him how we became natives, and he never explained his doctrines.

In the crowded and noisy club, Colonel Karnec addressed the group of young officers at the height of their spirited debate. "Gentlemen! Gentlemen! Please allow me to introduce our guest, Lieutenant Colonel Dino Babic."

Through a cloud of smoke, some puffers extended their hands, shook mine, and continued loud discussions. A glass full of plum brandy found its way to my hand, and a round of toasts ensued.

"Welcome to the club, Lieutenant Colonel Babic." A voice somewhat familiar came from behind. I turned and faced a man in decorative royal attire. Colonel Karnec saluted, and I joined in. His face looked familiar, but I couldn't place him.

"I'm George's brother, Prince Stephan. You remember me. I flew the airplane over the courtyard during the Royal Guard's Parade."

"Yes, Your Highness. I remember it well." I stood at attention.

"Relax, Colonel. We're in the club, and no title or rank matters much among the drunken officers of Biares. Let's toast to our victory against the Thracians."

"To victory?"

A thundering chorus interrupted my question. Glasses clinked, cheers erupted, and then the noise subsided. Only gulping, guzzling, and burping ensued. The calm lasted only a minute, and the ruckus returned with a vengeance. I wondered what victory we were toasting. Our regiment was still chasing ghosts through Thracia.

Prince Stephan came closer to my face and yelled, "Did you ever fly, Colonel?"

"Yes, Your Highness. I did. Once."

He cheered up. "When? How fast?"

"About three years ago. We moved at the same speed until the winds picked up. We couldn't navigate and we landed at a high speed."

"Why? Did your engine fail?"

"We had no engine, Your Highness."

"No engine? You flew with a glider?"

"No, Your Highness, the two of us flew in a balloon. Fortunately, we landed on Mount Athos in the peat moss of Monastery Panteleimon."

"I see," he said. "It must have been an exciting flight."

"Very," I confirmed.

"What are your plans for the next few days?"

"I am heading home for the funeral of my brother."

"Ah, yes. I heard about it. My deepest sympathies to you and your family."

"Thank you, Your Highness."

"When you return, would you like to take a reconnaissance flight with me over Thracia?"

Stunned, I stood without replying.

"Fear not, Colonel Babic. I have the fastest plane in the Royal Escadrille. We'll zoom in and out."

Against my better judgment, I said, "I'd be honored, Your Highness."

"George would be pleased to hear this."

My good Prince George smiled at me from a corner of my memory. His words rang loud and clear in my head. "Don't be a fool, Brother Sam. Stephan has already crashed twice." But instead of finding an excuse to bail out, all I said was, "How is His Highness Prince George?"

The funeral of my brother, Petro, took a big toll on us. My father, a corpulent Balkan native, turned into a stooped old man. Dressed in black, my mother, my sister-in-law Mira, and my sister Anitsa, exhibited the traditional mourning of the Balkan women.

Ominous clouds hovered over my family. I stood close by with a strange sense of being distant as if attending the ritual from a faraway place. Silent and dazed, I searched my soul for endurance against pain.

A mile-long procession from the church to the cemetery included the entire Koles population, area residents, and a delegation of military and government representatives.

Hours passed in the customary order. Hundreds of unfamiliar faces extended their condolences. Our priests and bishops delievered sermons, and the young monks from St. Jacob's Monastery Choir sang the heavenly psalms.

From the cemetery's temporary stage for the visiting dignitaries, the Biaresen parliament representatives and two military officials gave their speeches, expressed condolences, and faded into the background of sadness.

My two beloved uncles stood at the gate. Tall, skinny, dressed in black suits, top hats, and shiny shoes, they looked like guardians of Purgatory. At the gravesite, the coffin lay on top of a marble base. Flower bouquets, wreaths, colorful printed ribbons, crosses, and lit candles were placed all around it.

People passed by dropping single flowers into the grave, nodding their respects to us, and walking away. The never-ending line stretched far and beyond. In the late afternoon, Bishop Karabeg approached the grave and gave a sermon about the purpose of living and dying. I paid no attention to the significance of his sermon. My mind floated between the age of youth and the age of maturity. Why do we live and die? Somewhere in the Biaresen book of wisdom, the explanation for our existence was written. It may not have been based on science and logic, but no one questioned it.

As our priest preached often, "God giveth and God taketh it away," my hometown people assumed it was the umpteenth commandment. They couldn't count beyond the number ten. There were no more fingers.

After the burial, our family, friends, neighbors, and overnight relatives gathered in our home, and tradition took over. A mourning lament performed by the local choir of wailing women blared all night. An army of local drunks polished off a barrel of twice-distilled brandy. The beggars ate most of the prepared food, and the Gypsy brass band played post-mortem marches. Through all this unbearable noise, my beloved nephew Yablan woke up once for his food and slept the rest of the night like a king. It was the only time I envied him.

Uncle Jonathan pulled me out after midnight and drove me to the vineyard in a fiacre. "You'll stay with me tonight. I have prepared your room, and we'll be alone there." Then he added, "Not quite, your old friends will be there too."

"What friends?"

"Your guardian angels. Your childhood advisors."

"How do you know about them? They're imaginary. They're my... I'm puzzled."

"Ever since you were born, I've known about them. They revealed themselves to me as your future advisors. As far as they were concerned, I was not a threat. As you grew older, they became your eyes, ears, and voice. You didn't speak until the age of fifteen, but you talked to them. I overheard you so many times in your sleep and from your room when you were alone. They are still your best friends, you know."

"Oh, Uncle Jonathan, they were my childhood's fictitious world. I've outgrown that period of my life."

"I don't think so. You still see them, don't you?"

"You're right. Andronicus showed up not long ago. He advised me to have patience in a very stressful moment."

"Well, they're back, and they're watching over you."

The bumpy road kept me awake most of the way to the plantation. I thought of my seven imaginary advisors, and let my mind wander about, but I didn't allow my curiosity to turn on the lights.

"After you left," he continued, "your father didn't want to do anything with your property. Your mom begged me to stay and take care of it. Well, here I am, the future wine producer, merchant, and no longer a Brahman. I guess my roots are too deep in this enchanted land."

"Enchanted land? Things have changed around here. Nothing is the same. The magic is gone."

"I think you're wrong. The magic is still here. Drunk or sober, the people of Koles have always been magicians."

My uncle and I spent a week together. I didn't go back to see my family. I worried that my father would resent me for not being in Petro's place. On parting, my uncle assured me he would work to mend the broken ties

56

between my father and me. I left him with my seven imaginary advisors. He needed them more than I did.

On the day of my arrival in Nais, I reported to the office of the garrison commander.

"Colonel Karnec is no longer in command," a young officer informed me.

"What happened?"

"Nothing, sir. He was reassigned to a new command in the Second Army, and he left immediately. Major Nikolin is the new commander here. He's arriving tomorrow."

"So, who is in charge of the garrison now?"

"I am, sir. Captain Dane Strugar at your service, Colonel." He saluted.

"Any orders for me?"

"Yes, sir. You are to report at eight o'clock tomorrow morning to the Royal Aeronautics Academy at Nais Aerodrome. A car will take you there. Tonight we'll serve your dinner in the main dining room, and tomorrow morning you'll have breakfast in your room." He stopped and hesitated.

"Anything else, Captain?"

"Sir, we have a gathering tonight at the officers' club, and you are invited."

"Thank you, Captain, but I'll pass. At the last club social, I volunteered to fly with Prince Stephan. I have no more skills to offer for other military adventures. Good night, Captain."

"Good night, sir." Captain Dane saluted. An orderly waited outside the office and took me to my room.

A hearty breakfast settled my stomach, and a glass of local cherry wine calmed my anxiety. The morning brought sunshine over the hills and valleys and highlighted the beauty of the land. The green and golden colors of nature joined the blue skies and painted the most beautiful landscapes.

The military vehicle arrived at 7:30 a.m. On our way to the aerodrome of Nais, hundreds of sheep blocked the road. Our vehicle crawled through the baffled flock. Senseless and disoriented by the vehicle's rumbling noise, the sheep bleated, jumped, and pushed, but stayed close together.

Two shepherds tried to move the flock off the road, but the frightened animals continued to pile up in front of our vehicle.

"Stop the car!" I ordered.

With the engine turned off, the car shuddered, edged forward and stopped. Two sheepdogs stood up from their snoozing spot in the grass. They yawned as if bored with their jobs and chased the remaining sheep off the road. Some sheep crawled under, a few jumped over each other, and most dispersed in other directions.

We drove past the frightened flock. They stared at our strange contraption. Did sheep have brains?

"They do. Lamb brains on the grill are the common delicacy of the Balkan people," Copernicus reminded me.

"I thought I left you all with my uncle Jonathan."

"The Great Counselor Andronicus assigned me to your consciousness. I'll be with you for a while."

I weighed his response and took it as a fait accompli. I'd probably need him for the unknown fate awaiting me.

We arrived at the main building of the Royal Aeronautics Academy. The airfield had one runway, one hangar, and one large barracks.

In front of the barracks, two men awaited us.

"Welcome to the Paletru Field. I'm Captain Gunbut, and this is Lieutenant Bale. His Highness Prince Stephan will be here at noon. He instructed us to give you a quick flying course in his two-seater Farman H.F. 20. We learned from His Highness that you have some flying experience. This should be no problem for you."

All at once, his words shattered my remaining hope that this was all a dream.

The two aviators walked me into the barracks. The large open space had no wall partitions. Instead, furniture, equipment, bunk beds, and classroom blackboards on the walls designated separate areas for all necessary activities. The two officers fitted me with overalls, boots, and an aviator's head cap. When I was dressed, they strapped the parachute around me, and exclaimed, "You are ready, sir."

"Ready for what?" I asked.

"For your training flight, sir." Captain Gunbut said. "Lieutenant Bale will take you up and teach you basic airplane controls."

"I won't be flying the airplane," I objected. "Prince Stephan is the pilot, and he knows how to do it. Right?"

"Yes, sir, he does. But just in case something happens, you must learn the few piloting operations about how to land the plane down."

An enormous screen of realities opened in my mind. A banner, most probably made by my accompanying imaginary advisor, Copernicus, read. "Got ya!" I recalled my beloved Dudo and his unbending desire to try anything exciting and extreme. "Here I come, Dudo," I whispered. "Your idiot brother Samuilo."

Lieutenant Bale and I walked out and turned toward the hangar. More like any big hay storage barn. The main hangar featured doors facing the taxiway. On its side, another door opened onto the grass-covered parking area where two lightweight wood and fabric bi-planes stood. The hangar's exterior had clapboard wood siding and a tin roof.

"Our aeronautical squadron has four airplanes. The French Bleriot XI one-seater, Bleriot XI two-seater, Deperdussin TT, and Farman HF.20. We'll use Farman HF for your training, Colonel." Lieutenant Bale talked as if he were in a classroom with his student pilots.

We stopped in front of the bi-plane that looked like a wooden tub with a propeller attached to its rear end. The two wings made of intricate metal and wood components wrapped with a tightly stretched canvas rested on two sets of dual bicycle tires. The tail with its own wing and a rudder rested on a single bicycle tire. The entire assembly of this flying machine, made of wood, metal, and canvas, brought to mind a giant kite looming over Hisar Hill. That giant kite, named the Sky Raider, crashed by an unfriendly wind gust. In our childhood minds, it would live on for ages. Thank God our childhood memory lasted only a week.

I admired Lieutenant Bale's enthusiasm for his assignment to take me up, but I wasn't very excited about the prospect of my first flight in an airplane. Some sort of ecstasy or inebriation persuaded my common sense to accept Prince Stephan's invitation. So I faced the test of courage and said, "Let's fly."

A brief lecture about cockpit controls followed.

"Colonel Babic, sir, this stick is the rudder control for left and right lateral movement. The small handle serves to control flap-type uplift and downstrokes. This indicator is the fuel gauge for the gasoline reservoir behind our seat."

A drum full of gasoline reminded me of how dangerous airplane flying could be. I retained my composure with a row of goosebumps crawling up my arse.

After a short lesson about the controls in the two-seater fuselage, Lieutenant Bale ordered the plane to be moved to the main runway. This mosquito-like aeronautical flying device rolled and bounced into its position with a slight effort by the two mechanics.

The two of us boarded. Lieutenant Bale in the right seat, I in the left.

"Are you ready, Colonel?" He asked.

"I am." Excitement rose in me like a tide.

"Please strap yourself to the seat."

I found the belt under my rear and wrapped it around my waist. I locked it as tight as I could.

He turned back and yelled, "Start the engine!"

The mechanic behind the engine grabbed the propeller and yanked it around. Nothing happened. He crossed himself, grabbed it again, and swung harder. The engine fired, and the propeller turned. It gradually spun faster and then settled into idle speed. The whining noise from the engine increased. Lieutenant Bale moved the shift forward and pulled the accelerator. The plane jerked, the engine howled, and we rolled over the grass-covered runway. The lieutenant increased speed. Our small biplane hopped like a rabbit. It bounced off the ground several times and climbed into the air. With every meter of gained elevation, more exhilaration entered my soul. My sense of dominance over the passing earth increased, and my confidence returned.

At about three hundred meters the hills and valleys flew by at the incredible speed of one hundred and fifty kilometers per hour. Calm and adapted to my new role, I inhaled and relaxed. Lieutenant Bale turned to me and pointed to the controls. He shouted, gesticulated, and moved his hands repeatedly over the controls, but I couldn't understand a single word. He made an expression that appeared like, "Oh, hell, I tried," then pulled the back wing cable. The engine revved and the plane climbed again. He held the wheel until the plane leveled. Then released it and placed his hands behind his head. The airplane decelerated and took a nosedive.

I panicked and looked at him. He brought his hands forward and pointed to the controls. I read his lips, "Take over, Colonel!"

"Are you out of your mind? I'm not ready for this." My words got lost in the air. Don't panic, Dino. The plane continued to plunge. A flicker of the lieutenant's devilish smile passed across his face and disappeared. He grabbed my right hand and put it on the steering wheel.

I instinctively grabbed the accelerator knob and pulled it back. The engine increased speed, the plane leveled, and it resumed its steady course. I was relieved. Pleasure filled my heart. I took over the flight controls as instructed. With my tiny confidence restored, we flew. The white clouds from above draped our vision in front and around. The ground below appeared and disappeared as we cruised over the hills and valleys. My fear of heights melted away, and my heart danced with joy with every new maneuver we made. Our little biplane shuddered in the face of the wind gusts, tore into the calm air with its brave wings, and ascended, then descended while the two of us screamed and howled. After several circles above the Paletru Aerodrome we landed on the runway and bounced like a mosquito over a shallow pond. Lieutenant Bale stepped down from the plane and addressed me.

"It's unbelievable, sir! You handled her better than any of my student pilots. If this was your first time, it was a remarkable exhibition of your talent. You are a natural flyer, Colonel. I salute you."

Captain Gunbut and two aerodrome mechanics arrived and joined in the salute.

"Fellows, please. This was sheer luck. I couldn't fly an airplane without Lieutenant Bale's supervision. My instincts took control based on his instructions. I'm the one who should salute you."

"Colonel, Babic, sir, I watched your flying maneuvers with binoculars and I was impressed. I didn't see Lieutenant Bale holding your hand. If I didn't know better, I would swear that you were a pilot before."

"You'd lose your bet, Captain. But I beg you not to convey your exaggerated impressions to Prince Stephan. He may ask me to fly the plane while he's walking on the wings. I'm not ready for his showman acrobatics. I've seen him flying in the capital. He scared my horse to death.

SEVEN

Prince Stephan didn't show up in the afternoon for our scheduled reconnaissance flight. While I discussed other details of the Farman biplane with Lieutenant Bale, Captain Gunbut walked out of the barracks and addressed me.

"I just received a telephone call from Prince Stephan's adjutant. His Highness is planning to arrive tomorrow morning and take an early flight with you, Colonel Babic."

"Good. That will give me enough time to learn more about the airplane."

"Very well, sir." Captain Gunbut saluted and turned to walk away. Then he stopped and said, "We'll have lunch served in the office. Sergeant Robi is cooking the local delicacy."

"Oh, what would that be?"

"Stuffed hot banana peppers with pig's liver and lima beans, simmered in Kukuma wine, and served over goats' cheese on pita bread. It's very pungent. This is why we serve it for lunch, while for dinner we prepare a milder dish. It gives our stomachs slight relief from the burning hellfire. We hope you'll like it, Colonel."

"I'm from Koles, Captain. The hot peppers capital of the world."

"Indeed, Colonel. My grandmother was born in a village neighboring Koles, and every summer her father and her brothers carted a load of hot peppers to our hometown in the north. My grandpa called it her annual dowry."

Our lunch caused a lot of sweating down our fiery red faces. As our appetites increased, we smacked our lips in delight. Hiccups followed, and we drank wine in helpless attempts to put out the infernos in our stomachs.

After a while, around our table, the merry intoxicated men's eyes sparkled with drunken stupor. Every time one of us tried to make a toast, an act of physical imbalance resulted. I maintained my balance by drinking less.

Unnoticed, I stepped away from the table and walked to the hangar where I found a bench. Laying on it, I drifted into my long delayed thoughts about Galia. I hadn't heard from her in two weeks. I miss her so much. Worries pecked my conscience. When would I see her? Was my fate taking me further away? This war was my enemy, and I was drowning deeper in it. Through a tiny peephole into my future, I could barely see the pathway to peace and happiness. A bitter cocktail of sadness and despair settled in my dream. As night came on, my afternoon daydream changed into a nightmare with war drums echoing across the Balkans.

At dawn, an oncoming ruckus of honking horns, automobiles screeching to a stop, and some loud male and female voices woke me up.

I went into the barracks, dressed up, and walked out.

Drunk as a skunk, Prince Stephan staggered out of the first automobile.

"Howwwww do you dooooo?" He addressed two mules on the other side of the runway.

Too late, his driver rushed to help him stay on his feet. Prince Stephan fell, face down, into a pile of warm mule dung.

Two academy officers from the second car made giant leaps and lifted the giggling Prince Stephan.

"Brrrrr." He shook his head and spat excrement out of his mouth.

"Your Highness, let us wipe your face," the tall officer said and pulled out his kerchief.

"Give … some… wa… wa… wash me mouth," the prince blabbered.

A petite woman staggered out of the third automobile with a bottle in her hand.

"Have some bubbly from last night." She swayed and came closer. "Hey, Stephy, have you got a new mask? Oh, you're so cute. Let me kiss you."

Prince Stephan turned around and searched for her. His vision seemed blurred. He stuck his tongue out, rolled it around his mouth, and puckered his lips. "Where are you, my beauty?"

Eyes closed, she came near his face. A whiff of a stench stopped her. She pulled away. "Pee-yew, Steph. You need a bath."

Prince Stephan nodded, inhaled and exhaled quickly, spat, and declared, "Men, you heard Obry. Let's go."

Lieutenant Bale assisted Prince Stephan and his escort to the shower cabin.

Captain Gunbut invited two women and one academy officer from the second automobile into the barracks.

The four guardsmen stayed outside.

I joined the guests in the small dining room and introduced myself.

"We're delighted to meet you, Colonel Babic. Prince Stephan told us you will be his co-pilot today. I'm Lieutenant Agir; this is Miss Kosa Livada and her sister Rubelina Livada. Miss Obrina Belica is with His Highness Prince Stephan and my two colleagues," the third academy officer reported.

"At ease, Lieutenant," I said. "Would you like some coffee?"

"Thank you very much, sir. The night was long and boisterous. Coffee would be a welcome change."

The two young ladies sat on an old, worn-out sofa, and quickly fell asleep. Lieutenant Agir turned to call them to the table, but I stopped him.

"Let them rest, Lieutenant. They seem exhausted."

"You're right, sir. We're all exhausted. It's a formidable task to follow the thrilling tests of courage His Highness Prince Stephan seems to encounter daily. He invited us to some flying aerobatics this morning."

"I doubt that he'll be flying anywhere this morning," I said.

"I beg your pardon, Colonel, sir, but after I saw Prince Stephan dancing on top of the Orient Express on our way down from the Capital, one would assume he is fearless, indestructible, or daring."

"I would say all three describe him. It runs in the family," I replied, facing his puzzled look.

A motorcycle rumbling to a stop alerted our attention. The door opened and a burly sergeant stepped in. He saluted and walked over to Captain Gunbut. "Sir! Sergeant Gorki reporting. Brigadier General Kosic is on his way here. He's bringing directives for today's reconnaissance flight. Did Prince Stephan arrive?" He looked around the room.

Oh, Lord! This didn't look right at all. I walked over and introduced myself. "How much time do we have before the general arrives?"

"He could be here within the next hour."

"You must be hungry. Our cook is preparing a delicious breakfast. Go to the kitchen and order something to eat." I practically pushed him out of the room.

"Lieutenant Agir, we need your help. General Kosic from the high command quarters is coming on an official visit. I want you to take the ladies out of the aerodrome and drive around to avoid the general. Your academy colleagues will follow you later."

"Yes, sir, Colonel. We'll leave right away." He saluted and rushed to wake up the women sleeping on the sofa.

"Captain Gunbut, go get Miss Obrina and take her to the lieutenant's vehicle. I'll take care of Prince Stephan."

I rushed to the other corner of the barracks where shower stalls and toilets were lined up along the wall. In the last stall, Prince Stephan was showering and singing an incoherent marching tune. The two academy officers, facing each other, sat on a bench in a heated discussion.

I passed them and stopped in front of the shower curtain.

"Your Highness!" I called out. "It's Colonel Babic. May I talk to you?"

"You may," he answered cheerfully. "I'll be out in a minute."

Stark naked and white as snow, he walked out of the stall and grabbed a towel from a little fellow who appeared from nowhere. Where did he come from? Did they keep him in a trunk?

"What's going on, Colonel? Are you ready for today's flight?"

Amazing! He was sober now? How could that be?

"Your Highness, General Kosic is arriving in the next hour with directives for today's reconnaissance flight. I have taken the liberty to order your party out of the aerodrome premises. I hope you won't be offended, Your Highness."

"You've done the right thing, Colonel. General Kosic is like a brother to my dad. They grew up together and fought in the two liberation wars against Ottomans in the eighteen-fifties and eighteen-seventies. I bet my father sent him to prevent me from flying into Thracia. How much time did you say we have?"

"About fifty-five minutes, Your Highness."

"That's plenty of time. Let's put on our suits and fly out of here before that old fart arrives."

I was stumped. I questioned his sobriety, but I deduced from my kindergarten wisdom that sober and drunk are always together.

The morning illuminated the green hills and fields around the Paletru aerodrome. The crisp air with its refreshing fragrance swept through the valley and washed our faces with the remaining morning dew.

Our Farman bi-plane was waiting on the runway. The two mechanics and Lieutenant Bale stood by when the prince and I approached, dressed in flying attire with strapped parachutes on.

"Your Highness, may God protect you and Colonel Babic on this important mission. The plane is ready for takeoff. Here is the canteen with hot coffee as you requested." Lieutenant Bale saluted and handed the canteen to the prince.

"Well done, lieutenant. Let's get started," Prince Stephan replied and climbed into the cockpit.

As I struggled to get up, he gave me his arm. I grabbed it, and he pulled me in with the strain shown on his face. "My, oh, my, you're a husky, big man." He puffed a little.

"No, Your Highness, it's probably your lack of sleep and the loss of energy from last night's exploits," I said, smiling. "Shouldn't we strap ourselves in?"

"Yes, you're right, we should." He searched for his belt while I strapped myself tight. He wrapped it around his waist and locked it. A loud yawn, then a brrrr with a stretch of his arms, followed. "Let's hope this coffee will keep me awake." He took a long swig out of the canteen, turned back, and ordered. "Start the engine."

The mechanic crossed himself and cranked the propeller. The engine fired, and the plane shuddered. Prince Stephan grabbed the shift and moved it forward. The two of us sat snugly in the tiny open cockpit. Our plane rolled forward as the engine revved. The speed increased. The plane bounced off the ground, kissed it a few times with its miniature bicycle wheels, and ascended. The engine revved increasingly louder as we climbed into the air. The yellow-white-yellow bar of color at the end of the runway disappeared as our plane approached the colonnade of cedars and oaks rustling above the pale stones that marked the road to and from the Paletru Aerodrome.

Prince Stephan pointed down and then lifted both arms in jubilation. I read on his lips, "The Old Fox is late. Let's give him our welcome."

In the distance, a column of vehicles rambled across the dusty road.

The plane nose-dived, leveled at about five hundred meters, and made a pass over the coming vehicles. Prince Stephan then made an aerobatic turn to the right, circled in a wide arc span, and lined up to face the oncoming vehicles. He lowered the altitude to three hundred meters above ground and revved the engine at full blast. The biplane went into a steep downward plunge. In panic, I watched the earth coming. I glanced at Prince Stephan's wacky behavior. He was laughing like a lunatic. There was no time for other thoughts or decisions. From a tiny cell in my blank mind, Copernicus waved goodbye to me and vanished. I froze. And just when I said my last prayer, God, or this idiot prince, extended his arm and lifted the plane up, a few meters away from the column.

I caught a glimpse of an old man in the first vehicle. In a fit of rage, he threatened with his arm and spat fire from his mouth.

Way up in the air, where the forests and meadows below looked like a map of parcels with rivers and creeks like tiny arteries, and all other geographical forms like the body parts of mother earth, we flew east into the sunrise.

"Take over!" Prince Stephan said and pulled a notepad out of his inner pocket.

I took the controls and maintained altitude. The engine hummed at a lower intensity. At the far distance, the edge of war appeared behind clouds of explosions, black smoke, and artillery gunfire.

"Get lower." Prince Stephan pointed downward.

I reduced the speed and pressed the rudder paddle. The plane lowered its nose and descended at a suitable angle for a low-level reconnaissance. The engine ran smoothly, and the noise lessened. Prince Stephan leaned over the edge of the cockpit. We flew above our artillery batteries. The Howitzer cannons blasted the enemy lines. The Thracian's artillery pounded our positions. I couldn't detect the movement of infantry on either side. We maintained an altitude of about eight hundred meters. Thousands of small craters decorated the no-man's-land. Sections of forests were blown away and nearby hills leveled. This part of the earth, observed from above, gave the impression of being a giant checkerboard. One tiny church sat in the middle of the battlefield, its round cupola roof bathed in the morning sun. It reflected the sunrays and stood defiant like the Olympic torch. The church bells rang loud enough to be heard. Sadly, God had no ear for us.

A few minutes later, the first line of Thracian Army trenches appeared. From the top of the two adjoining hills, the Thracian artillery shelled our positions. Four observation platforms behind artillery batteries were occupied by flagmen who signaled the shelling distances. The Thracian infantry lay in trenches and waited for that imperial order embedded in every soldier's mind: Attack!

"Lower!" Prince Stephan yelled.

"We're already very low, Your Highness. They could shoot us down."

He kept his thumb pointed down, and I obeyed. At five hundred meters, I increased the speed and leveled the plane. A dense rain cloud came from the north and obscured the view below. Prince Stephan leaned forward and said, "I'll take over. Let's get above the clouds."

The engine accelerated into a full-scale surge. Our small biplane shuddered, squealed, and creaked, moving through the heavy curtains of rain. The compass needle swung violently in all directions. The airspeed needle oscillated beyond its normal rate. The plane spiraled down, and all efforts by Prince Stephan to pull her up failed. He tried the rudder, and the air speed went back to zero. An uncanny feeling of being detached from the tumbling airplane stayed with me until we emerged from the cloud in an upside down position. The prince regained control of the flight again. And, as if it were a training maneuver, he turned the plane upright and smiled at me. I collected my remaining traces of courage and looked down. The Thracian soldiers were firing at us. The bullets whizzed past. A few pelted the bottom of the cockpit, and one caused a loud pop in the back of us.

"Damn, they snapped the rudder cable. We're going down. Hold on." The prince shouted over the noise of a loose cable pummeling the engine cage. "Take the accelerator and keep it steady. I'll retrieve the cable."

He unbuckled, and like a cat, stood up, stepped on the trusses of the wing, and slid out of my sight. The plane was dragging us down. The treetops were nearing. I held on as tightly as I could. "There was no need to pray now. I asked for it."

Prince Stephan returned to his seat. "What did you say?" He pulled the broken cable from behind and wrapped it around his right hand.

"Let's try to land in that field yonder." He pointed at an opening about three kilometers away. "I'll keep the rudder tight. Pull her up a bit."

Jointly, we landed on an open field behind enemy lines.

"Let's turn this bird around and try to lift her off the ground."

"But, Your Highness, the rudder...." The rifle shots from afar interrupted me.

"I'll jump out and push the tail around. You keep her running. When I tie the cable, we'll taxi back to our army position."

Before I could ask or say anything, he was down. He grabbed the tail and lifted it off the ground. He set the rear wheel at ninety degrees and pushed the tail around. With the engine running, the plane moved easily. The shots whizzed over my head. "Go!" He screamed.

I shifted, and the plane moved forward. He ran alongside and jumped onto the wing. I slowed down. "Don't stop!" he yelled as he moved up to the cockpit. He let a painful cry and rolled over into his seat. His right leg hung over the side of the cockpit. Blood oozed out of his boot and dripped onto the floor.

"Your Highness, you're wounded. We must stop and look at it."

"No!" He yelled. "Don't stop. I don't want to be captured. But if we do, remember that I'm Stephan George, the pilot of the Biares Escadrille."

"Yes, Your Highness."

"Stop addressing me as Royal Highness. Get used to Stephan. You out-rank me now."

We rolled and bounced over some rough terrain, and taxied through meadows, and sparsely forested areas until we ran into the camp of a widely spread Thracian army.

"Oh, crock!" Prince Stephan exclaimed. "Well, we have no choice. Plow right through and pray."

Miracles do happen. We taxied right through the center of the camp and passed by the over-awed Thracians who gazed at the strange contraption without urgency or panic. Their lunch break was interrupted, and they stared in disbelief. Mesmerized, some held a spoonful of food before their open mouths. Some intently watched our incredible parade from the entrance in the east to the exit in the west.

When we crossed the no-man's-land, the front was quiet. No artillery shelling nor machine guns rattling. I maintained the same speed and maneuvered our crippled plane over a small elevation and down a dry creek bed until we came upon the first row of our army trenches. Cheering erupted, and the bugler announced our arrival. I stopped the plane and looked at the prince. He lay motionless in his seat. Oh, Lord, I hope he does not die.

"Get an ambulance! His Highness is wounded," I hollered at the two soldiers coming our way.

A crowd of other soldiers gathered around.

"Help me get His Highness down," I said.

Three men came to the fuselage and formed a step-down platform with their bodies. Two other men jumped up and gingerly lifted the prince out of the seat. They put the blanket on the grass and laid him on it.

"Colonel, His Highness is alive," one soldier said.

"The doctor is coming. Make some room, men," a heavy-set sergeant ordered from behind.

The soldiers stepped away, and the doctor approached. He cut open the prince's trousers on his right leg. The wound was large–a hole below the right knee. Shattered bones protruded from the calf. Blood ran freely from the severed vein.

The doctor pulled out a piece of cord, wrapped it tightly around the prince's leg above the knee, and tied it into a knot. Blood stopped flowing.

The Doctor turned to his medic. "Let's get him on the stretcher and put him into the ambulance. We must operate immediately."

"Doctor, how serious is it?" I asked.

"Very. If we don't operate immediately, gangrene will start, and the prince may lose his leg."

The medics picked up the prince on a stretcher and gently placed him inside the ambulance. They left in a hurry. I watched the vehicle until it disappeared.

The heavy-set sergeant spoke, "I sure hope young Prince Stephan will be all right." A cluster of sun rays passed through the clouds and illuminated the path uphill. "My dear prince, someone is watching over you," I whispered.

Three days later, I learned that Prince Stephan had undergone a complex surgery. He was recovering at the hospital in Nais. Three of the best army surgeons had saved his leg, but healing could take a long time. The royal family had come to visit him.

"Colonel Babic, you're summoned to report to Major General Kosic at the High Command Headquarters in Nais," an officer on duty at the garrison informed me.

"Is there any mail for me?"

"No, sir! Not here, but you may try the Royal Army post distribution center at headquarters. All military mail goes through them."

"Can you arrange for a driver to take me to the Nais hospital?"

"No need for it, sir. The hospital is across the street from us, a five-minute walk. I'll take you there."

"Thank you, Major."

In front of the hospital entrance, four royal guardsmen stood at attention. We saluted and walked in. Inside the large lobby, three separate hallways led to the interior of the hospital complex. The center hallway had additional guardsmen on each side and a desk with a receptionist seated behind it. As we approached, he asked, "Could I help you, sir?"

"I would like to visit His Royal Highness, Prince Stephan. I'm Colonel Dino Babic, his copilot in the last reconnaissance flight."

"Colonel, sir, the royal family is visiting Prince Stephan now. Major Suza informed us that the prince was expecting you. Please take a seat in the waiting room. I'll announce your arrival."

The escorting officer saluted me and returned to the garrison. I walked into an empty waiting room and sat by the window. I was musing about the past few weeks of inconceivable current events when the door opened wide, and Prince George entered.

Uncertain if I should salute him or rush to hug him, I stood up and waited.

"Brother Sam," he exclaimed. With arms spread out, his face bursting with joy, he rushed towards me. "Look at you! My Lord, Brother Sam, you have no trace of a monk in you anymore. Army feeds you well. You're beefed up like a wrestler."

Our hug lasted for a few seconds. We separated, looked at each other, and burst out laughing.

"Your Highness, you have changed a little. I'm so happy to see you."

"Same here, Brother Sam, except that now I'm looking at Colonel Dino Babic. It's hard to adjust to maturity when our youth runs out. It always happens before our dreams come true. How is your lovely wife?"

"Your Highness, I haven't seen her since our marriage. My soldiering has taken me away, and I'm worried about her."

"Oh, Lord, that is not right. We must do something about it. But first, let's visit my brother, Stephan. He is very eager to see you."

In the rehabilitation room, Prince Stephan was resting on his bed with his right leg bandaged and elevated on a large pillow. Members of the royal family surrounded him and were chitchatting when Prince George and I entered.

Prince George announced my arrival affectionately. "Hey everybody, look who is here. Our hero, Lieutenant Colonel Dino Babic."

All heads turned toward me, and I bowed to Queen Ariel. I straightened up and saluted Prince Stephan and three other high-ranking officers who sat near the queen. The two princesses, along with several other young ladies, sat at the round table on the other side of the room and stared at me. I bowed to them as well. They giggled. The other royal family members, aunts and uncles, nieces and nephews, grandparents, and closest cousins filled the room except for His Majesty King Tarpe and Crown Prince Kasander. Their absence was noticeable.

I walked over to Prince Stephan's bed. Exhaustion and fatigue showed on the prince's pale face. A drastic change in his cheerful disposition had taken place. His eyes, empty of expression, searched aimlessly. He attempted to talk, but the doctor standing by his bed stopped him. Prince George put his hand on his brother's forehead and whispered, "Don't force yourself, Stephan. You need rest. Colonel Babic has come to wish you a quick recovery."

I observed Prince Stephan's sorrowful state and wondered how much damage the bullet did to his soul.

"Lieutenant Colonel Babic." The soft voice of the Queen Mother sailed my way like a breath of wind. "Please join us before you return to your quarters. George can take you to our summer residence." I bowed while she stood up and motioned for everyone to leave. A minute later, the room was empty. Only the doctor and his two nurses remained.

Prince Stephan motioned for me to come closer. He took my hand and squeezed it lightly. A streak of emotion trembled across his face. A raspy whisper trickled out of his mouth. "Dino, you are here." A tear rolled out of his left eye. "I'm so glad…"

"Please, Your Highness, don't exert yourself. You'll recover soon, and you'll be back in the air." I spoke cheerfully.

His eyes lit for a second. A near smile quivered, and then his face turned somber. He muttered, "Maybe."

Prince George stepped in. "All right, Stephan. Rest now. We'll leave you now and come back tomorrow. Get well, Big Brother."

Prince Stephan held my hand. I waited. His eyes closed and his dream took over. I parted with thoughts about my future. What if I were wounded?

How would my Galia know?

Built at the turn of the 20th century, the royal summer residence with its towering palace stood in the center of Nais. Surrounded on three sides by canals, linked to the mighty Deva River, it offered a picturesque view of its grandeur through the palisade of tall iron railings and the magnificent arched gate.

Evergreens on each side of the cobblestone road to the royal palace overshadowed the long boulevard with its colorful flower gardens. They gave the residents of Nais enchanting promenades every summer night under the silvery moonlight.

Prince George and I arrived in a motorized carriage driven by a chauffeur dressed like an airplane pilot. A white scarf around his neck, a leather headcap, and a pair of goggles with tinted lenses made him look like he'd come from the Paletru Aeronautics Academy of Airplane Pilots.

The reception by the queen was more intimate than ceremonial. I enjoyed her motherly approach and her natural ability to open the hearts and minds of those around her. Despite her graceful and venerable demeanor, it was difficult to determine her age. With children my age and older, she must have been in her early forties, as my mother was.

"How is your family coping with the loss of your brother?" She asked this in a delicate manner, leaving all formalities behind.

Her direct question was too abrupt for my painful and haunting memories. I gathered my thoughts, then allowed my emotions to flow unencumbered.

"Your Majesty, losing my brother Petro was a terrible shock for everyone," I said vividly shaken. "My mother and father, from the moment they heard about his death, withdrew from everyone. My sister-in-law, Mira, cried for days in disbelief, and my little sister Anitsa, dressed in the Balkan mourner's black, locked herself in the room with the coffin and sobbed all night. At the burial as the earth swallowed my brother into eternal darkness, I couldn't cry, nor could I scream or summon Jesus to resurrect him. My silent prayers couldn't be of any help. I left to rejoin the war, but my heart stayed behind. I don't know how my family is handling the passing of my brother, but I miss him more every day. This war is taking a terrible toll on all of us."

Prince George came to my rescue. "Mother, Lieutenant Colonel Babic is married. He hasn't seen his wife Galia since the day he parted from her hometown, Chestnut, in Maradonia, and he hasn't heard from her in weeks."

"My dear child, life has had no mercy on you," Queen Ariel said, dismayed. "Let us pray to our Lord Jesus Christ. He will give us guidance."

She opened her arms and motioned for all of us to come. The two princesses scampered to her embrace. Prince George and I stepped closer and kneeled down. The Queen of Biares assumed the prayer posture on her knees. She crossed herself and raised her eyes toward the ceiling. Four painted frescoes of the virgin birth of Jesus, the crucifixion, the divine revelation, and the divine ascension looked down upon us.

Dear Lord,

Help us amid these trying times and declare peace for our humanity. Please, Lord, give us a tangible reminder that our hope is an unbreakable spiritual line. Help this child, our favorite son of Biares, Lieutenant Colonel Dino Babic, to find peace and joy in reuniting with his bride in Maradonia. Lift him out of despair and place him on the road to happiness as he had done for our royal family by saving the lives of our two sons.

Amen

The prayer of our queen struck me with her candid way of addressing our Lord Jesus Christ. Her motherly voice gave the impression of a normal conversation between the divine and mere mortals. I may have underestimated the royals. They could be descendants of our saints. I should know better because my grandpa told me they were.

For a moment during my silent wonderment about the royal family, a pair of beautiful eyes peered at me from under the arms of Queen Ariel. It was the older princess, Rina, whose curiosity burned with the same familiar flame my beloved childhood friend, Rudy, exhibited so often.

In the afternoon, Prince George and I accompanied the young princesses on their walk through the garden.

"Mother summoned Brigadier General Kosic to the palace. I asked her to get approval for your furlough to bring your bride home."

A slight tremor passed through my heart, and I heaved a sigh of relief. Galia my love, I'm coming. I glanced at Prince George. His eyes searched for my reaction. The two princesses stared at me. How should one react when surrounded by royals? Back in Koles, I would scream with joy and jump all over George. He wouldn't be prince there. No one would recognize him.

I poured out my words of happiness. "Thank you, Your Highness."

"On one condition," he said. "I'm coming with you, and we're taking the Royal Guards Cavalry Squadron as our escort."

I couldn't say anything more.

He seemed to understand, and we strolled through the garden. Lost in my thoughts while prince George and princesses chattered, giggled, and played their childhood games, I wondered how long it would take us to get to Chestnut? Why were there no letters from Galia?

EIGHT

The confrontations between the invading forces and local guerrillas delayed our train another day from crossing into Maradonia. We stopped about thirty miles from Chestnut. The train conductor advised that the rail tracks were blown away by the enemy.

"Let's mount," Prince George ordered.

We rode along the railway tracks on a narrow pathway. A line of train passengers formed behind us. About fifty or sixty men and women, loaded with their personal luggage, huffed and puffed, and slowly fell back. An hour later, only a few, mostly men, followed.

"Your Highness, should we wait for the rest?" I asked.

"It's up to you, Dino. You are in command."

"With your permission, Your Highness, I'd like to wait. There were mothers with children. Perhaps we could help them."

At dawn, the long hay wagon with four mules and a driver, loaded with older women and children, waited for my command. The squadron stood ready with Prince George at the helm, while civilian men and young women from the train lined up behind the wagon. I galloped down the line to check if everyone was set to go. The bugler sounded off my command through the crisp morning air. Slowly, the column moved down the hill. A few minutes later, I caught up with Prince George at the head of the squadron.

The riders sent an hour in advance to scout Chestnut were on their way back at flying speed. Their horses galloped in rhythm with merciless whip lashes. Urged by spurs, their strides across an uphill meadow lengthened. Their hoofs dipped in and out of the tall grass as if swimming through water. The horses' bodies glistened with sweat and foam. The groaning increased. The hollering of riders swept across with unclear words, "fire… town… janissaries… attack."

Sergeant Ninko yelled, "Colonel, smoke and fire is coming from the rooftops!"

I looked through the binoculars and shuddered. A dozen homes burned in the center of town. Shots echoed in the distance.

"Mount up!" Prince George ordered.

The squadron waited at the ready. I stood dazed.

"C'mon Dino. Let's go and get Galia," Prince George urged.

The name of my beloved woke me out of the doldrums. I jumped into the saddle and stormed in a furious gallop. We passed the exhausted scouts, and a few minutes later, entered the outskirts of town.

Sporadic gunfire came from nearby houses. Children's cries and screams mixed with harsh voices. We moved closer from behind and faced the horrific scene. Five janissaries were raping young girls tied to a hitching post.

A bizarre, soul-piercing neigh roared from my horse. The janissaries turned around. Their blurred eyes and twisted facial features showed their abominable human nature.

"Untie the children and take them away," Prince George commanded.

Many thoughts ran through my head. Fear darkened their clarity, and I fought to overcome the panic. "How many are you?" I asked.

No answer. Only drunken, bewildered eyes stared back at us.

"Line them up against the wall!" I ordered.

Sergeant Ninko selected the firing squad and waited.

"One last time. How many?"

A short man waddled forward one step, "Officer, there are twenty of us." He spoke in the Sanjeck dialect.

"Fire!"

Shots rang through town. The five janissaries lay dead. The howling and screaming stopped.

"Sergeant, take your men and sweep town. Shoot the marauders on sight. We will check the burning structures and look for casualties."

Sergeant Ninko saluted and rode off with the squadron. They split into four groups and searched through backyards.

We entered the main street.

Ahead of us, a few Chestnut residents looked left and right, then ran across the street. As we approached, some stopped and gazed at us for a second, then crouched and disappeared. Gunshots came from the other side of town. We trotted faster and came upon the burning church. People ran with buckets and poured water over the flames. Cries intensified from inside.

Someone hollered, "Break the door open! There are people in the church."

I dismounted and ran to the entrance. A big log propped against the door held it closed. I grabbed the log with all my strength and moved it to the side. We opened the door. Smoke poured out as if from a locomotive chimney. Blinded, I covered my mouth and rushed in. The fire was raging on one side. The draft between the broken windows and the door sucked out the smoke, and visibility increased. Prince George and the guardsmen walked in.

Behind the iconostasis, a group of women and one man lay on the floor gasping for air with painful cries and moaning.

When I approached, they screamed and ran behind a small curtain. The man stayed down, immobile. He groaned. In the flickering light of the fire, I recognized the priest who officiated my marriage to Galia. He lay wounded and unconscious.

"Let's get them out of here," I said.

Prince George and I lifted the priest and carried him into the front yard. The guardsmen and the women followed. We laid the priest on an outside bench, and I pulled out the first aid kit out of my saddlebag. I removed his shirt and found a deep wound caused by a yataghan. The cut was large and blood was oozing out. I cleaned the wound, sprinkled yellow sulfate powder, placed a gauze pack, and wrapped a wide bandage around his upper torso. The priest moaned and opened his eyes.

"Father Naydan, how are you feeling?"

He attempted to rise, then shrieked, turned pale, and fainted.

I looked around, searching among several women standing by. Prince George came over and put his hand on my shoulder. "She is not here."

A little girl, kneeling by a woman sprawled on the grass and sobbed. "Mama! Mama! Wake up." She shook her mother's lifeless body. Another woman stretched out her arms and hugged her. "Don't cry, Savelina. Your mom is in heaven now."

I approached.

Gunshot bullets ricocheted off a nearby wall. The women screamed and dropped to the ground. Two men with water buckets ran into the church. The gunfire subsided, and an ugly, deadly silence took place.

Father Naydan opened his eyes. His lips moved, but no sound came out.

"Don't exert yourself, Father. You are wounded, and you need rest."

He coughed. I wiped his face and poured a few drops of water into his mouth. "More," he whispered. I poured two spoonfuls and waited. He motioned for more and I obliged him.

I had a burning desire to ask where Galia was. My prayers came through when he opened his eyes again and said, "You are Dino?"

"Yes, Father. It is I, Dino. Galia's husband. Do you know where she is?"

He summoned his strength, and with a painful effort whispered. "The Sanjack Janissaries, on their way back to Turkey, attacked our defenseless town. They killed old men, dragged women and children out of their homes, and set the town on fire. Some folks escaped into nearby cornfields and forests." He gasped for air and continued. "I gathered a few women and children, and we barricaded ourselves in the church. Old man Jovan stood in front of the church entrance with a pitchfork to defend us. They killed him and butchered his body. Then they tried to break in. The door held. Thanks to the Almighty for sending you...." He stopped. His eyes opened one more time. His head rolled to the left, and his last breath expired.

"What about Galia?" I questioned the dead priest.

He didn't answer. His eyes stared somewhere in the distance as if pointing.

"Yes, yes. I must go to the cottage. She must be there."

I closed his eyes and blessed his journey to heaven.

"We killed four, and we trapped twelve other janissaries in a barn. They are well armed. In the initial attack, two of our men were wounded. We have surrounded the barn and are waiting for your orders." Sergeant Ninko reported.

"Offer surrender," Prince George said.

Sergeant Ninko took a white flag and rode toward the barn. About one hundred meters from the barn, he yelled, "We're giving you a chance to surrender. You'll be taken as prisoners of war and judged for the war crimes you have committed in this town. Drop your guns and come out with your hands up."

"Go to hell! We are not surrendering."

As the shots whistled over our heads, sergeant Ninko galloped back, out of their range. Our guardsmen returned fire.

"It's a waste of ammunition. Let's burn the barn and force them to surrender."

"But, Colonel. How?" Sergeant Ninko asked.

"We have everything here, Sergeant. We have ash for arrows, maple for bows, and dry hay for torches. I'm sure many of our soldiers have made them for their childhood games."

He seemed puzzled but turned to his guardsmen and pointed to each group of soldiers. "Men, let's make some bows and arrows. The six of you cut maple branches for bows. The four of you find straight ash branches for arrows, and the two of you get some dry hay for torches."

"Colonel Babic, I must talk to you." Prince George moved closer. "An enormous pot of anger is brewing inside of you, ready to blow up. I have the same fears as you do, but may I remind you we're Biaresens, people with compassion and understanding. God teaches us to forgive. Although the janissaries' acts are unforgivable, we cannot be judges and executioners. If we take revenge by burning and killing them, we would be the same as they are, cold-blooded killers."

"What do you propose we do, Your Highness?"

"Let's give them another chance to surrender. If they refuse, light a few torches on the roof and wait. The smoke will force them out. If they resist and shoot at us, we'll order to shoot back. Do you agree, Colonel?"

"Yes, sir."

At that moment, anybody's reasoning was better than mine. Prince George had matured. His stately considerations and decisions sprang from the centuries-old wisdom of the royal dynasty. He had detected a drastic change in my monastic soul, and assumed the role of my guardian. Since my mind deserted me at the most challenging time of my life, I accepted his guidance.

A few minutes later, he called Sergeant Ninko. "Are your men ready with bows and arrows?"

"Yes, Your Highness. We already tested eight."

"Get four men and circle around the barn at a safe distance. Light the torches and shoot the arrows near the barn, then yell this message to the janissaries. 'You have two minutes to surrender, or we'll burn you alive!' If there's no reply after two minutes, shoot the torches at the barn and wait."

Sergeant Ninko saluted and gathered four men with bows and arrows. They crouched and crawled until they reached shielded positions about fifty meters from the barn. The first set of torches dropped a few meters away from the barn walls. The janissaries fired their guns at our guardsmen.

Sergeant Ninko's powerful voice conveyed the message. More guns were fired in reply. Four arrows with lit torches landed on top of the barn roof. The fire burned quickly. A minute later, the front roof collapsed and opened a big hole. Huge flames spread onto the walls and quickly rolled down. The first screams came out of the back. More piercing cries sounded from inside. Three janissaries ran out. Their turbans and clothes burned. They collapsed and rolled on the ground. A few more, with blazing guns, ran out of the barn.

The prince ordered, "Fire!"

Six of the raiders fell to the ground. The barn, now ablaze, crackled and popped. Its rafters and wall studs collapsed. The wood, piled in the center, added more fuel and burned with fury.

A cow mooed from within the barn. The fire subsided. We moved closer. The remaining janissaries lay on the grass. Their faces, hands, and arms, scorched with flame, glowed in the afternoon sun. Their stomachs heaved with the last breath of air. One by one, they expired.

"Sergeant Ninko, have our men throw the bodies into the fire. If anyone survived, we will take them with us," I ordered in a calm voice.

"There are no survivors, sir."

We swept through town and established peace and order. The residents returned from their hideouts and filled the town square. Prince George and I inquired about Galia's fate, but no one had any knowledge.

"What about her parents and her younger sister?" I asked (a person).

"They could all be at the lake cottage," someone suggested.

"Could you show me the way to the lake?" I asked a young fellow.

"I'll take you there, sir. It's only ten kilometers from our town."

In my subconscious, horrifying images danced in a circle of bloody madness. The awful thoughts passed at lightning speed and dragged my hopes into an abyss.

It was already getting dark, and my horse was in a hurry to overtake the shadows.

"This way, Colonel," our guide called. I sped up the hill, my horse galloping like crazy towards the lake settlement. From a distance, a light flickered in one of the lake houses. My heart pounded like a bass drum as I glanced over the dark shapes of the house where my Galia lived. We stopped at the front gate of the house where the lamp flickered. As we dismounted, the lamplight went out. Our young guide called to the occupants.

"Grandpa Blashko, this is Dimche Petrovski. Open the door."

No one answered. The guide and I walked through the gate and knocked on the door. "Don't be afraid, Grandpa Blashko. We are friends. We brought Makarov's son-in-law, Galia's husband."

The silence lasted a long minute, and then the door opened a small crack. Someone behind them whispered, "Dimche, is your father here?"

"He is in the village with my mother and my sister. Can I come in with the colonel?"

"Come in, son. I'm alone in the house."

Dimche and I entered. Old man Blashko stared at the two of us. His eyes were full of fear and uncertainty. He finally gathered some courage and stepped forward. When he recognized Dimche, he hugged him and sobbed. He greeted me warmly and didn't let go of my hand until he calmed down. Old Blashko tried to hold back his tears, but his pain seemed too deep.

I was rapidly losing patience and anxiously waited to ask him about Galia and her family. My eyes searched desperately around Makarov's neighboring houses. My thoughts came out of Dimche's mouth, "Is there anyone in Makarov's house?"

Again, an eternal moment of expectation. In the glimmering light of the lamp, Blashko's eyes watered, and tears rolled down his wrinkled face. In a trembling voice, he described the gruesome events of yesterday.

"Late in the afternoon, screams and gunfire from the upper stream excited everyone. Makarovs and Draskovs came out of the house and soon realized that they were in danger. They rushed back to get their guns and stood bravely against the attackers. A wounded shepherd ran down from the hill and collapsed a few yards before our men with his last word, 'janissaries'.

"The wild horde stormed in, fired their guns, and howled like a pack of wolves. They first killed Lenko Makarov and his brother Ben, then grabbed young Galia's brother and butchered him with knives.

"I stood at the gate of my house and watched as if hypnotized by this inhuman act of horror.

"The women came out screaming and crying. The janissaries gathered them inside the house, and the unthinkable ordeal took place. My Brena took the pitchfork and stabbed the first man who entered our house. A knife flashed. She grabbed her throat and gagged. Blood squirted and ran between her fingers. She collapsed on the floor. I stood silent. Non-existent.

"They passed me several times. Their glassy eyes searched through me. Uncertain if I were dead or alive, they passed me by. Saliva ran down their beards. The beastly thirst for unholy pleasures drove them in and out of Makarov's house. The remaining screams and an occasional death rattle sounded weak and faded into the night.

"Late that night, a drunken horde lined up on the road and marched to Chestnut. The silence allerted me out of my stupor. The unbearable outcome of this horror struck me hard. Hapless and distraught, I found three women barely alive. The panic in their eyes spoke the silent screams. Two other women lay on the floor dead in a pool of blood. Each held a baby in her embrace. All dead. I couldn't think of what to do. I couldn't help them. Then an angel spoke to me. 'Go to St. Mary Magdalene Monastery'.

"It took me until midnight to climb five miles up the mountain and alert the sisters of St. Mary's order. The rest of the night, they buried the dead and moved the wounded souls up to the monastery. I stayed home and prayed."

"Was Galia saved?" I couldn't wait. "Is she still alive?"

"Yes, son. She is alive, but she is now seized by the Moon."

"What do you mean, Old Man?" I yelled.

He didn't speak anymore. He stared somewhere beyond me.

Dimche spoke softly, "Colonel, sir, he meant to say that Galia is not herself now. I'll take you up to the monastery, and we'll talk to the sisters."

I was exhausted. I couldn't think or talk. In my chamber of horrors, I blamed myself for leaving Galia behind. A load of guilt weighed me down. I hyperventilated on our way up. My loud gasp alerted Prince George.

He stopped the squadron. "Let's get him down."

The two guardsmen dismounted and helped me down from the horse. Sweat trickled down my face and neck. Prince George pulled out a small towel and wiped the perspiration off my face. He poured a few drops of water from his canteen into my mouth. I calmed down and drank more.

"Take it easy, brother. We'll rest a bit here."

"No! No rest. We must keep going. Galia needs me."

Cloaked in total darkness, the monastery appeared before us like a ghost castle. We announced our arrival with a bell hanging from a wooden post on our side of a deep moat.

Ten long minutes later, a woman's voice called out, "Who's there?"

"God be with you, sister. Dimche Petrovski is at the gate."

"If you are Dimche, what do you want at this hour of the night?"

"Have no fear sister. The murderous janissairies are no more a threat to us. They were surrounded and killed by the cavalry of our allies, led by Colonel Babic, the husband of Galia Makarova."

A murmur and soft outbursts of exclamation passed through the gate. The nun spoke again. "We must talk to Mother Superior for permission."

I couldn't control my patience. I yelled back, "Sister, I have come a long way for my wife Galia, and I will not wait too long. Please open the gate or I will order my squadron to break it down."

"God will punish you for crossing the threshold of His shrine with force."

"Then you better hurry, and bring Mother Superior down."

In the following few minutes, my neurotic behavior prompted my to jitter and neigh. He was an offspring of an Arabian and Mongolian line, bred mainly for horse racing. I leaned and whispered in his ear, "Calm down, Brother. It will be all right." These soothing words relaxed both of us, as if spoken by someone else.

The clouds dispersed, and the shapes of the monastery appeared in the glimmering moonlight. This wooden structure built on top of a rugged cliff face, well hidden by tall thick conifers, had survived through centuries unharmed. The gate stood ten feet high between two cypress trees. A narrow drawbridge over a wide ditch protected the convent from intruders.

Wooden clugs announced their return. The gate crept open. A nun stepped out. "Mother Superior Christophora will see you now. We will allow only two men in the courtyard."

I dismounted and signaled Prince George to join me. The two of us walked across into the monastery. At the end of the narrow courtyard, two other nuns stood waiting. The taller one had a long prayer rope tied around her waist with a wooden cross hanging down her dress. I knew she was the abbess.

"Your Highness, follow my greeting gestures." I whispered and lifted my hands with palms up, and walked toward Mother Superior.

"Bless us, Mother, we have come in peace." I bowed and Prince George followed.

She put her hands on our heads and murmured her blessings and prayers.

"May the Lord give you peace, my sons."

My anxiety returned, and my eyes burned in expectation.

"You are Dino. I heard your name many times in the last twenty-four hours from Galia's screams and cries. She has suffered so much..."

"I must see her, Mother Christophora. Please take me to her."

"She has been through an ungodly expereince. Her mind is permanently altered. The harmful implications will have a long-lasting effect on her future. She is not the person you know and remember."

"No! No, you are wrong. She will recognize me. I am her only salvation. You must let me see her. Gaaaalia!"

A moaning echo came from one of the wooden hallways. I stepped between Prince George and Mother Superior and tried to pull away, but the prince held me firm. I pleaded and kneeled, begging Mother Superior.

She put her hand over my head, "Oh, Lord, give me your strength, your wisdom, and your guidance to be the judge of their destiny. Help me find the path to their salvation and peace for their tortured souls. Bless us, oh, Lord, and shine the light of reverence for your devoted servants. Amen!"

She turned to me and said, "I will take you to Galia, but you cannot go in as a soldier. You must put on a robe with a hood and swear to me now that you won't say a word while we are in her room, no matter what you see or hear. The presence of a man could trigger the suppressed horror and may drive her deeper into the abyss. She's surrounded with eternal fear in her darkness. Only God knows if she will ever recover after the terrible shock she suffered. Galia almost died from bleeding and the delivery of a dead fetus. Her screams echoed for hours among the Holy Hills of Upper Chestnut."

Mother Superior's words slashed through my hopes. I shut my eyes in anguish. An inners burst of panic pounded in my chest. My head ached and my heart trembled, "I won't give you up. I will never leave you."

Inside Galia's room, three nuns stood by her bed when Mother Superior and I entered. Two candlelights flickered revealing Galia in bed. Under the blanket tightly wrapped around her, her mummy-like face peered out from under the blanket with eyes wide open.

Her whisper floated to my ears. "My baby is sleeping. Please don't wake her up. She is so tiny." Then the screams erupted, like a howling wind from the chapel of wailing mothers fro all their dead sons.

My body shook, and my pain threatened to overwhelm me, but I kept the cries inside and let the tears cascade down my face onto the black robe. I fell to my knees sobbing. Mother Superior pulled me out of the room and walked me back to the entrance hall.

NINE

Prince George led the squadron back to town. I rode behind him in a daze.

"You've suffered a great shock, Brother Sam."

"No, My Prince. I failed Galia. I should have never left her behind."

"But you could not..."

I shook my head and gasped for air. "I acted in our traditional way. I came home to tell my family about my marriage and my new bride, but I broke the ties between my father and me. I walked out angry and instead of taking care of my new family, I rejoined the army. It is all my fault."

"I don't agree with you. You can't blame yourself for all the casualties of war. Atrocities done to the innocent and defenseless are the highest price paid. Humans will never stop killing each other, or else they self-destruct."

I pondered his words and the reasoning behind them. Prince George's statement was powerful. Our destinies collided with an unavoidable storm of events before we gained maturity. He had taken the path of royal education while I chose common sense and morality. We, the people of Biares, had always claimed to be students of wisdom. But wisdom could never stay in line with us.

At 3 p.m., I joined our Third Army in the capital of Maradonia and said goodbye to Prince George. My new assignment under General Lugar put me in command of the 7th Artillery Battalion. Our orders led us into a confrontation with the most powerful and battle-ready Thracian army.

Both sides dug in and shelled the invisible positions of the attacking forces. For days we made no progress. Both armies, firmly entrenched, spewed hellfire in a battle for more territory. Death and life crossed their swords and called for victory. The signs of the coming Armageddon shone in the sky. There was nothing offered except death. The slaughter of infantrymen with machine guns and artillery continued. There were more bodies in no-man's-land, and the cries of the dying echoed in a continuous flow of screams, death rattles, and frenzied calls.

Night descended on the battlefield like a dark cloud from the heavens. A sudden burst of flares lit the ground and vanished into the darkness. Machine guns rattled. No movement. The occasional glow of dead eyes reflected the spirits of the night.

The soft voice of Lieutenant Gavrilo roused me out of a snooze on my feet as I stood against the trench wall. "Colonel, sir, General Lugar would like your presence in the bunker."

I walked behind him into the temporary quarters of the Third Army. General Lugar and several high-ranking officers were studying the map when I entered and saluted.

"Colonel Babic, I will get straight to the point. We're at a stalemate, pinned down by the Thracian long-range artillery and well-positioned machine-gun nests. Our losses are mounting. Our only hope is a daring surprise attack on the Thracian Second Army." General Lugar pointed with a stick at a place on the map. "About two kilometers southeast from here, a steep gully has a very narrow passage that leads into Lower Komer Valley. It's protected by Thracian howitzer cannons and one infantry platoon. They have guards on both sides. At exactly 10 pm, our artillery will open fire on the Thracian positions around the gully. The shelling will end at 10:05 pm. Under your command, Colonel, the cavalry regiment will cross into the Komer Valley and circle around the Tarak Hills. You will have enough time to slash through the artillery batteries and disable their firepower. If you pass through undetected, it will be a total surprise for the Second Thracian Army. Three flare signals from you behind the enemy lines will start the all-out attack by our infantry and unleash a barrage of our heavy artillery across the entire front. We are counting on a moment of confusion from the surprise attack by your cavalry regiment. Our chances of succeeding are very slim, and every detail of our plan must be flawless. The five hundred highly trained riders of the Divagora Cavalry Regiment are waiting for your orders. Major Stolar and Captain Vuksan will be under your command. You have only two hours to study the passage and prepare everything before you depart. Let's synchronize our watches and get you on your way. Any questions, Colonel Babic?"

"General, sir, I'm honored, and I thank you for your confidence in me and my squadron. If I may suggest, my experience in battle is very limited, and it would be more practical to put a war-seasoned officer in command."

"Son, our wars, throughout the history of Biares, forged the fighting men of the strongest army in the Balkans. The beaten path left by your family's brave men is a trail of courage and sacrifice. I had the privilege to fight shoulder to shoulder with your grandfather Spiridon in the liberation wars of 1876, and I have no doubts about putting you in command of this daring attack. May God protect you and your cavalry."

I saluted and walked out. Orders were orders, and in war, you did not ask questions.

Outside the bunker, a slender officer greeted me. "At your command, Colonel Babic. The Divagora regiment is ready for our mission. All horses' hooves were fitted with soft boots. The saddles were removed and replaced with field blankets. The riders will carry sabers and pistols as their only weapons."

"At ease, Captain. In one hour, the royal squadron will join the cavalry regiment. Leave one man to guide us to the meeting point."

"No need for it, sir. Your squadron has already merged and is ready to move. Colonel, follow me, please." He turned around and walked through the main trench between the idling infantrymen on the way out. I followed.

The exit led to a downslope of a barren orchard and wild shrubbery. The mellow light of distant flares created shadows of men and horses about five hundred meters from us. We descended over the soft ground and came upon two guards, who led us to the only tent surrounded by horses and trees.

A short cavalryman approached. "Major Stolar is waiting for you, Colonel." He opened the tent flap, and we entered.

"We're ready for your orders, Colonel," Major Stolar reported.

"Major, before our shelling begins, we must disable the Thracian sentinels guarding the gully crossing. In my estimation, this is the weakest point of the Thracian army. I will lead the twelve royal guardsmen and neutralize the defense. We have one hour and forty-five minutes. I count thirty minutes on foot to the top and ten minutes to remove the sentinels and disable the two howitzers. We should have the gully under our control by 9:50 p.m. I'll send a flare in your direction, Major, and you make sure you're near General Lugar to stop the shelling at 10 p.m. We don't want to draw any attention of the Thracian Second Army to this point."

"But, Colonel, you cannot risk…" Captain Vuksan tried to talk me out of it.

"I speak Thracian fluently. Any of your soldiers?"

"No, sir!"

"Then I'm your man, Captain. Move the regiment up the hill at 9:10 p.m. If you don't hear any shots by 9:55 p.m. the passage is clear. We'll be waiting for you at the top."

I selected twelve of my men, and we rushed up the hill under the cloak of darkness. On the steep climb, we used a long rope and a stealthy approach to the first guard position. My men disabled the Thracian sentinels, and we moved up the gully to the next observation point. My two scouts reported a squad of Thracians guarding the passage. On each side, two howitzer canons pointed at our army's position.

"We have twenty-five minutes only," I whispered the commanded that was sending us into a minefield of uncertainties.

I didn't allow my common sense to sway the dreams of glory. Balkan pride and the military mentality had no place for reasoning. At that moment, I couldn't think of anything other than the breakthrough ahead.

Through my binoculars, I spotted four first-line guards around a small fire. They sat and smoked. Rifles leaned against the rock behind them. Their leisurely strolls showed no signs of caution about the immediate dangers. The Thracians had relaxed their alertness.

Out of the darkness, four shadows emerged. The cloaked figures fell upon the Thracians, and in an instant, the enemy sprawled dead on the ground.

We moved the entire cavalry regiment into the gully undetected in the night's silence. I checked my pocket watch at 9:35 p.m. About a hundred meters separated us from the main enemy position.

"Mount up!" I ordered. "Pull out your swords and get ready. We'll ride to the top in pairs. When we reach the camp, I'll wield the sword. At that moment we'll attack, slashing through the camp and then onto the cannon's crew. There will be no yelling or screaming. Those Thracian soldiers who surrender will be tied and escorted back to our army quarters. They will be treated as prisoners of war. God is with us. Let us pray for our victory!"

I said a quick prayer and asked the Lord to protect us. In a split second of my eternal questioning of right and wrong, I wondered whose side He was on.

The plan of attack worked. The Thracians surrendered without firing a shot. We gathered twenty-three prisoners and escorted them to our army lines. My guardsmen pulled the two cannons and dropped them off the cliff. My pocket watch showed 9:45 p.m. I sent a flare in the direction of General Lugar's bunker. We took the hoof boots off our horses, and I ordered the move.

We crossed into the Komer Valley, and I checked my watch again. At 10:00 p.m., silence prevailed. Major Stolar had conveyed my message to General Lugar. The Tarak Hills were in front of us. At the foothills about two kilometers from us, four artillery batteries lined up one after another facing our army positions. We had to circle the hills. General Lugar assured me we would be undetected if we waited for the moon to hide. Dark clouds danced around the moon's face. Light white clouds drifted by, but the moonlight stayed on our path. Then a big dark cloud swallowed the moon, and we darted across the soft summer grass.

The moon came out again, and we slowed the run at the back end. Cautiously, we crossed the valley and came in front of our target. The closest artillery battery had six cannons pointed up and over the Thracian army frontline. With my binoculars, I observed the gunners standing by. A hundred meters ahead of them, the first line of infantry appeared from several parallel and crisscrossing trenches, followed by the machinegun nests before the no-man's-land. We were about five hundred meters away, still undetected and as vulnerable as a flock of birds out in the open. God help us!

The distance between our cavalry and the first battery had no woods or shrubs to conceal our attack. I pondered if I should shoot the flares now or after the suicide run. Both decisions would have a significant impact on the outcome. I knew many of us would die.

"Captain Vuksan, what would be a greater risk? To attack under the bright moonlight and sacrifice half of the regiment, or shoot the flares and get killed by our own artillery?"

"I would rather be killed by our own than by the enemy," he replied decisively.

"Then, let's shoot the flares."

Three flares were fired over enemy lines. Our cavalry moved forward at a slow trot. The Thracian's battery crew raised the alarm. They turned one of the cannons toward us. I screamed "Gallop!"

The fury of our horse stampede spread across the open field, and caused panic among the Thracian gunners who ran in all directions. Bullets whistled above our heads. Some found their targets, and horses with riders tumbled behind us.

We had slashed through the first and second artillery battery when the cannonade of heavy guns from the Second Biares Army exploded all around us. The firing of a Thracian machinegun decimated the right wing of my regiment. I ordered an attack on the third battery position. Two of their cannons slowed our attack. The remaining cavalry of my regiment was split into two lines. We avoided direct cannon fire and fell upon their crew with swords and revolvers. With our wounded carried on their horses, we stormed through the fourth cannon battery.

The Thracian's artillery ceased firing. Our mission was accomplished. I surveyed the casualties, and a sense of grief and guilt entered my Christian soul. How easy it was to kill a man. All you needed was hate and a weapon.

The sound didn't arrive before the explosion. The muscles of my horse trembled and his ears stood up. He neighed while the wave of force from the grenade lifted us in a cluster of flashes. We flew up, he in pieces, I in my saddle. Humming entered my ears, and the smell of death entered my nose. A crash into the hard earth knocked me out of consciousness. Silence choked the war drums, and all was quiet in the land of eternity.

I lay in warm dirt. Blood crawled over my face. My heavy lids stayed shut as if glued. Darkness lingered within and all around me. The sounds returned and brought painful screams, voices calling. The dying responded, and their souls marched into purgatory, or through heaven's and hell's gates...

I awoke to the sounds of painful cries, steps rushing over a wooden floor, soothing female voices, and the chime of a melodious church bell.

A woman near me called out, "Doctor, this one is awake. You said I should call you when he comes around."

"I'll be there shortly," a man's voice replied. "Take off his bandages and put on cold compresses."

A caring embrace from a soft-breathing woman helped me sit up. She murmured some kind words, patted me on the back, and secured my seating position with a gentle rubbing of my back and neck. I relaxed.

"I will take off your bandages now," she whispered. "Please relax. The doctor is coming to examine you next." Her caring voice lessened my anxiety as she unwrapped the layers of gauze around my head. Uncertain, still in total darkness, I gathered the courage and asked, "was I disfigured, was I without a face, was I blind?"

"There, there, Colonel Babic. When you fully recover, you will be fine." She replaced the bandages with a cold wet compress and laid me down on my bed.

I sat up and threw it away. "Tell me–am I blind? Am I disfigured? I cannot see!"

"The doctor is coming, sir. Please calm down." She held my hand and stroked my palm. With her soft fingers, that invisible woman entered my soul and crushed my anger.

"What's happening to me? Help me, please."

Strong hands took my head and through a breath of stinking tobacco, a man spoke in a raspy voice, "I am going to check your eyes, soldier. Can you see the light from this lamp?"

"No, Doctor. I don't see anything. Have I lost my sight? Am I wounded? I don't feel any pain. Please tell me."

"No, sir. Your eyes are still in their sockets. You have suffered temporary vision impairment, and it may last awhile before you regain sight. You'll receive daily treatment with chamomile dressing pads. It will ease your pain. Nurse Emily will care about you, Colonel."

TEN

In my unbearable state of blindness, scenes from the past appeared in my dreams. Despair and guilt conquered my soul.

I dreamt of Galia. I talked to her in both my conscious and delirious states. Sometimes, I felt her presence.

Nurse Emily accompanied me to the sanatorium for wounded soldiers in the hills of Vala, where an eye specialist would see me. My rank provided officer's accommodations in a single room. It provided a quiet and healing environment.

I was enjoying the fresh air coming through the open window when Nurse Emily entered.

"Are you ready for a walk, Colonel?

"Yes, Ma'am, my legs are ready. I'm not sure about my body and spirit."

"Oh, is anything wrong, sir?"

"Do you know when the doctor will see me?"

"He is arriving tomorrow afternoon, and you are his first patient."

"I must know the truth. I can't sleep anymore. My life is a nightmare."

"The fresh air will do you good, sir. It'll keep your mind off your worries."

She was right. I needed to get out. I stood up and extended my left arm. She took my elbow and led me out of the room.

The birds chirped, and the wind blew over my head.

"Tell me what you see, Nurse Emily."

"We're leaving the courtyard of the sanatorium. The front faces the hills, and the back overlooks a small village. Ahead of us, a chapel stands on the left, and a flower garden on the right. A narrow road, leading uphill and downhill, cuts through tall oak trees. Thick treetops cast a shadow. On each side of this forested ridge, vineyards cover cascading down slopes as far as one can see. We could take a walk uphill through the forest or downhill through the vineyards, sir."

"I'm in your hands, Nurse Emily."

I couldn't see her smile, but I sensed a current of joy from her. Her soft squeeze of my arm confirmed my assumption.

We walked uphill, and every summer flower released fragrant breath. The morning sunrays sent heat through the giant trees, and the evaporation of the remaining dew on the ground reached my nose. The bees hummed on the pollination road, and the birds chirped above our heads. Somewhere nearby, water from a small creek rushed downhill.

The soothing sounds of nature brought a vision of my estate near Koles. I murmured a few words and stopped.

"What is it, Colonel? Why did we stop?"

"In my dream, I saw the grapevines of my vineyard in Pukovo. My father is pruning the plants, my mother is weeding, and my sister is cleaning the alleyways. Little Yablan is napping on the balcony, and my sister-in-law Mira is sweeping the cottage. What an idyllic scene. I wish I were there."

"Perhaps soon, sir, you'll be going home."

"Not blind. I won't go anywhere until I can see."

"God willing, sir."

The sound of a flute came from behind. I turned around and said, "Would you take me closer? I love shepherd's music."

"Yes, Colonel."

The melody spread through the crisp morning air and resonated with nostalgia. Emily led me to a place where sheep moved around us.

The flutist stopped. "Good morning, sir. Good morning, nurse. I hope I'm not disturbing you."

"Not at all," I replied. "I wanted to come and hear you play. Do you know 'My Hometown is not Far'?"

"I think so, sir."

"Play it for me, please."

The flute opened with a soft sound and summoned deep, evocative lyrics. Every note, linked to familiar verses, moved my lips along until my muffled humming sounded out in a raspy voice. Tears wet my bandages and drained down my face. I choked, but I continued to hum until the music stopped.

"I'm sorry, sir, but I don't know the entire song," the shepherd said.

"You did good. Thank you."

"Goodbye, sir. Good bye, nurse." He gathered his sheep and walked away. Another melody from his flute spread its wings over the area.

"Colonel, I must wipe your face. Please sit here on this log." Nurse Emily guided me to a large tree trunk.

She cleaned my cheeks and beard with gauze, then dabbed the bandage over my eyes.

An hour later, we returned to the sanatorium, where she took off the bandages and replaced them with dry ones.

She left me and said she would return later.

I ate a hearty breakfast and sat by the open window, enjoying the mountain breeze. I fell asleep.

The orderly brought lunch. He cleaned up the table and told me it was 2 p.m.

"Do you need anything else, sir?"

I waved him off and picked up a cup of tea from the table. The warm, sweet liquid calmed my anxiety.

A whispered conversation came from under my window. I awoke from my slumber and listened. The voices were not far, but I could barely understand the words of a woman and a man.

At one point I heard the woman say, "I don't know…," and then the man raised his voice, "You must…"

"Is he ready for it?"

Of the two voices, I thought I recognized Nurse Emily. What did she not know?

Who was the man? Why was he urging her? What must she do?

I waited.

Late afternoon brought rain and lightning. A strange sensation of lightning bolts appearing in my view alarmed me, and I was sitting in bed listening to the rumbling thunder. Nurse Emily rushed in and closed the window.

"I'm so sorry, Colonel. I should've come earlier."

"It's all right, nurse. I'm used to thunder and explosions. Any news about my doctor?"

"Yes, sir. He is coming tomorrow morning to examine you. But I have other news of importance to you."

"What? What is it?"

"I have a letter for you, sir."

"Letter? Who is it from?"

"It is addressed to you, but it doesn't show the sender's name. The stamp on the envelope indicates it comes from Maradonia."

The name rumbled through my head as if the rolling thunder had found its way in. My anxiety rose. "Open it, please. It must be from my wife, my Galia."

Silence stepped between us.

The sounds of an envelope tearing and a letter unfolding ended. With a calm voice she read, "To Colonel Dino Babic, Second Army Artillery Battalion, from the office of the Mayor of Chestnut, Maradonia.

Honorable Colonel Babic, We regret to inform you…" Nurse Emily's voice stopped. She took a deep breath.

My heart sank. I whispered, "Go on, please, don't stop."

"…We regret to inform you that your wife, Galia Makarova Babic, passed away on June 22nd, 1913, at 1 a.m. in the monastery of St. Mary Magdalene. She will be buried in the Chestnut Cemetery in her family lot. May God open the windows of heaven and let Galia Makarova Babic and her family rest in peace. Acting Mayor of the city of Chestnut, Honorable Stanimir Ilijevski, Republic of Maradonia, June 24, 1913."

With the sound of the letter being slowly folded, desperation sat in my soul. I tore my bandages and shouted, "Lord, take me, please."

Nurse Emily rushed over and held me tight. Her calming embrace had a healing effect on my soul. Her steady, rhythmic heartbeat reminded me that I'm a soldier, and I should act like one.

ELEVEN

The tragic end of my Galia triggered a sudden fever. I lay in bed and bathed in the hot sweat of my exhausted body. My spirit drowned in delirium and floated above my tormented self. Cold compresses brought me back to half-consciousness. I strained my eyes through the darkness. I heard a whisper of urgency. Hushed words mixed with despair echoed the sounds of fear.

"Doctor, he is melting away. What little food we forced him to eat he rejected. His pulse is fading."

"Prepare a double dose of serum."

"But, doctor, that could kill him."

"If we wait, he'll die overnight. He's young. We must try."

His last words added dismay to my boiling kettle of uncertainty. My unspoken soliloquy ceased. Somewhere on a path of separation between my spirit and body, I asked, was I dying? Then Galia appeared under the beam of a shining star, her hand waving, her image quickly fading.

"Galia, Galia, stop. Wait. I'm coming, my love." In my semi-consciousness, I cried out the whispers of anxiety. Her subtle voice came with the lightness of a non-being and urged my soul to follow her path.

The silent walk under the starry sky led me closer to my beloved. Yet, far, far away, unreachable, she vanished into eternal whiteness.

She was in heaven; I was still on earth. The solar wind blew away the remaining words of hope, and my dreams joined the wandering ghosts of the universe.

A sharp needle in my left buttock caused enormous pain. I screamed. Now awake in this world of gloom, I struggled with breathing. I gasped in quick breaths, but my lungs had no energy to recover.

A rubber cup was placed over my mouth, and forced air entered. A nurse kept pushing something that pumped air, and my normal breathing resumed.

101

"Good," she said. "He can now breathe on his own. I think the medicine is working, doctor. His pulse is higher, and his blood pressure is stabilized."

"He must be watched overnight, Nurse Emily. Would you stay with him until midnight? I'll send Nurse Marisa to replace you."

"I'll stay with him all night, doctor. No need to remove Marisa from the intensive care ward. Our nursing staff is already stretched to its maximum."

"That's very commendable, Nurse. Good night, and God bless you."

"Thank you, doctor."

I was fully awake during this noble conversation. Dedicated professionals serving in the medical field were no different from soldiers in war. They were in a constant battle with death. They shared the same tragedies and triumphs as we did.

The serum worked, and my vitals showed signs of recovery. I slept peacefully. Youth was a magic gift from God. Nothing could destroy it.

Nurse Emily's soft snoring woke me up.

I slid from under the bed cover and stood on my wobbling legs. Fever exhausted my muscles, and I couldn't walk. I held onto the wall and dragged myself out into the fresh morning. I sat on the bench and soaked God's heat from heaven. Vigorous molecules of life reentered my veins, and spread vivacious currents through my body. The rising sun brought more heat from the east, and all living creatures joined the chorus of nature. My heart increased its rhythm. All my senses awoke, and I wanted to shout, "I'm alive."

"Colonel, where are you?" Nurse Emily called.

"Out here, nurse. I'm outside in the garden."

She came out.

"Colonel, sir, a miracle happened overnight. You have won the losing battle. We thought the fever would take you. Thank God, Doctor Momir was right. I must run and tell others about your recovery. Will you be all right here, by yourself?"

"Yes, Nurse Emily."

"Great, I'll return in a couple minutes."

"Please, I'm starving."

"Me too." She chirped with delight. "I could eat an ox."

Two weeks later, accompanied by my new medical guardian, Nurse Selma Medova, and my adjutant, Lieutenant Korda, I was released from the hospital. Doctor Momir had arranged my visit to the eye clinic in the capital, where I was to be examined by a specialist. The attention and urgency given me by Nais Hospital's medical personnel exceeded normal care. The bits and pieces of communication and special services on the train ride north made me realize I owed this to a higher authority than the army. Was my future closely linked to the galloping destiny of our small kingdom?

In my blind state, I could not foresee the coming changes, but I could sense the coming of another war. The long columns of the royal army marched north and south on both sides of the train tracks. At every stop, people celebrated the victory over the Thracians in the last Balkan War. Mothers wailed for their young sons returning home–limbless, blind, or dead. Old women asked "Soldier, are we at peace now? Blame our tradition. Blame those foolish old men who celebrated their kids going to war. Oh, God, do we have to suffer for the sins of others? Do we have to fight these senseless wars?"

Nurse Selma returned from the train restaurant with a tray of dishes emitting the captivating aroma of roasted meat, hot peppers spiced with garlic and cumin, freshly baked bread, and Leepa flower tea, flavored with honey.

"You must be hungry, Colonel. Your face is following every move I make with our lunch dishes as if, pardon me, you could see."

"I cannot, Nurse Selma, but my nose can. I'm really hungry. But I wish I could see your smile."

"Sir, you're making me blush.

"I'm sorry, nurse, but I really mean it. Soon I hope."

Lieutenant Korda opened the door. An air of anxiety poured in. "Colonel, sir, I have a cable message for you. His Royal Highness, Prince George, and the entire Royal Guard Cavalry Regiment are awaiting your arrival in the capital this afternoon."

A moment of silence prevailed over my emotion. Why? I was going there for a medical reason. I didn't need excitement. "Read the message, Lieutenant."

Lieutenant Korda took a deep breath and stepped closer. "Honorable Lieutenant Colonel Babic." His voice thundered through the compartment coach, and I raised my arm to stop him.

"Calm down, Lieutenant, I'm not deaf."

He apologized and continued in a lower tone. "The Royal Family and the entire kingdom of Biares are celebrating the victory over the kingdom of Thracia. It is our duty to honor the fallen and celebrate the living heroes of war in defense of our freedom. Their Majesties, King Tarpe and Queen Ariel, will attend the Victory Parade on the morning of July 2nd, 1913, and the celebration will continue with the reception of our heroes at the royal palace. It is a special honor to have you as our guest, Lt. Colonel Babic. Your outstanding courage and commanding leadership in a surprise attack won a crucial battle for our army. May God protect you and provide a clear path for your triumphant arrival in the capital." Lt. Korda stopped, inhaled aloud, and concluded, "signed by the secretary of the royal home office, Mr. Barko Ciric."

A quiet, awkward moment spread throughout the cabin.

Lt. Korda coughed and said, "I have another message for you, Colonel, from His Highness Prince George."

"Please, read it."

"Brother Sam, our destinies seem to conspire again to bind us in future encounters. I'm happy, and I look forward to our reunion. The victory celebration will bring pride and joy to our nation. I'm delighted to inform you that your family is also invited to the victory parade and to the reception at the palace. You will be riding next to me and Crown Prince Kasander during the procession. I can assure you no one will know about your temporary impairment. Young Doctor Timic has prepared a special pair of sunglasses for you. Praised be the Lord, Brother Sam.

His Royal Highness, Prince George III."

"The Lord be with you," I whispered.

"Colonel, sir, we're scheduled to arrive in the capital by 4 p.m. A short rest before lunch would get you ready for the events. I have your ceremonial uniform hanging in the closet. We'll have you dressed before the arrival."

"Well done, Lieutenant. I'll take a short nap."

Lieutenant Korda walked out, and Nurse Selma prepared my bed.

"You didn't touch your food, sir. It's cold now, and the tea is lukewarm. Should I go back for a warm teapot and another dish?"

"No, nurse, I am fine. Thank you."

"Well, I'm in the next cabin. If you need me, just knock on the wall. Sleep well, Colonel Babic."

I couldn't sleep. My thoughts were with my family. How would they react when they saw me? I doubted my father would be there. He could never

104

forgive me. Even now in my state of blindness, would he change his mind? But I must be there for my mother, my sister Anitsa, and Mira with Yablan.

Lord, lend me your hand. Open my vision and allow me to see my people, my family, and my friends. This fate that leads me through turbulent times doesn't open the gates of happiness. The path is covered with blood from the many battles of foolish wars. Heavenly Father, let us have peace and humility.

TWELVE

A solemn atmosphere welcomed the arrival of our train into the capital. Different from comings and goings at other times here, when crowded, boisterous citizens of Biares elbowed their way out of or into the moving iron contraption. The train stopped, the doors of the passenger cars banged open, and the locomotive's deafening whistle announced the end of our journey.

"Take my hand, Colonel Babic." Nurse Selma touched my shoulder, and I stood.

"No, Nurse Selma, I will descend from the train without your help."

"My orders are to always walk in front of you. For your safety, Lieutenant Korda will follow you." Her voice carried a tone of command.

"All right, nurse."

My legs wobbled on the first step down. I almost extended my hand to hold onto her, but I caught my balance.

"You are doing well, Colonel."

Her encouraging voice sounded close. Was she walking backwards? Steady, Dino. Two more steps. The second step seemed easier. Her deep breath, and her slow exhale of relief affirmed her anxieties. She whispered, "One more step, sir."

My confidence returned. I straightened up and took a step forweard. My foot hit the platform hard. I cringed and stepped down.

A thundering command broke through the station. "Attention! Salute!"

The chorus of soldiers responded. "Long live our hero. God save the King!"

"Welcome, Brother Sam," the heartfelt voice of my prince greeted me.

I opened my arms unconsciously, and the two of us fell into a firm embrace. I responded to the gentle royal hug with the bear hug of a battle-seasoned soldier of Biares. He stepped into the boots of my brother Petro, and our destinies were linked forever.

Both of us stood speechless for a few seconds, then he said, "Did you travel well, Brother Sam?"

"I have, Your Highness. My guardian angels took care of my needs, and the four hours passed by quickly."

"I have a surprise for you, Brother Sam. Put your hand under my arm, and I'll lead you to the waiting room."

I focused my thoughts on one person. "Is my family here?" I couldn't wait to ask.

"Yes, they are. I wanted you to have some private time before we go to the palace."

"Is everyone here?"

"Not everyone."

I knew he wouldn't come. He'd never forgive me. My heart was sinking, my strength was waning, and my legs trembled.

"Are you all right, Brother Sam? We're almost there. Should we stop and rest?"

"No, Your Highness. I will be all right."

A few steps later, we stopped. Someone opened the door, and we entered. The joyful screams of my sister Anitsa and my mother erupted. I counted every step of their running until we embraced, and kissed. We whirled around in a circle of happiness. Then came the sobbing and crying. A creeping sadness invaded my heart, and I realized Mira and Yablan were not with us. I whispered, "Where are Mira and Yablan?"

Anitsa, her arms around my neck, lifted herself closer to my ear and said, "She left us after Petro's burial. His death broke Papa's heart, but when Mira and Yablan left, he lost the desire to live. Papa has aged. He talks to himself. He carries guilt about that awful clash between the two of you, and he curses the day that took you away from him. Dino, Papa is a shadow of the father we used to know."

I kept her close in my embrace and let her calm down before I asked, "Where is Papa now?"

"He is here," she whispered.

"Here? Where?" Then I opened my heart and in a loud voice called him. "Father, embrace your son! I ask for your forgiveness. I cannot see you, but my heart can feel your pain. I'm here, Father. I've come home."

Muffled footsteps resembled the sound of an old person shuffling across the church floor. Not far from me, it stopped. My mother whispered encouraging words, and he moved closer. I could almost touch him. I opened my arms wide and imagined his huge bear hug, his thundering voice enveloping our reunion.

My mother embraced me. Her body shook. She wept. "Dino, your papa asks for your forgiveness. In God's name, son, take the burden off his beaten soul."

"But, Mother…"

A very gentle voice whispered in front of my face. "Son," he stopped and gasped, "I have done you wrong. Please forgive this old foolish man."

I extended my arms and searched for the corpulent man I knew. When we embraced, a skinny, shivering body fell into my arms. I gathered my courage and suppressed an avalanche of pain. In the dungeon of my blindness, I summoned the spirits of the past—my beloved grandpa and grandma, my uncles, my childhood friends, and all others from our world of smiling faces—to share the joy of our reunion.

THIRTEEN

The royal adjutant, commander Simon Dinich, informed me that during our visit to the capital, my family and I would reside at the Academy. Before departing, Prince George invited everyone to the palace after the victory parade. He stepped close to me and whispered, "Brother Sam, your sister is a beautiful girl."

Unprepared for his open admiration of my little sister, I said, "She is only fourteen, Your Highness."

He stepped away and addressed my family. "I bid you all goodnight. Rest well until we meet tomorrow. Commander Dinich has arranged transportation to the hotel for you and your escort."

"Thank you, Your Highness."

The ground floor accommodations in the left wing of the old Academy Hotel consisted of large rooms where dignitaries and their families customarily resided. A whiff of the atrium garden brought back memories of laughter and giggles, kids running through the hallways and stairways of the old Academy Hotel. These were sweet remembrances of long ago when Mr. Andrew's middle school choir from Koles performed for the royals.

Nurse Selma and Adjutant Korda had adjoining rooms, and my family shared a room next to Lieutenant Korda.

Before we entered my room, Nurse Selma said, "Colonel, sir, your father wants to stay with you. I explained to him that Lieutenant Korda and I are assigned to care for you night and day, but he won't leave. He's sitting in a chair next to your bed."

"I will speak with him, Nurse Selma. Go fetch my mother, please."

"Papa, I'm in good hands. Nurse Selma and Lieutenant Korda provide all the help I need. Please go to your room and rest. Tomorrow will be a big day for all of us."

"No, son, I will stay by your bed. What do they know about your needs?

I have carried you and your brother on my shoulders since you were born. Your mom and I raised you to be healthy and strong. I won't let anyone take care of you, and I won't leave you this time."

None of my arguments persuaded him otherwise. My mom attempted to reason with him, but all she could gather was that he missed me very much. "Tell your nurse to cover him up when he falls asleep. Goodnight, son. Sleep well."

Lieutenant Korda found a better solution. He said the hotel located a wooden wheelchair with a seat and back cushion, and he convinced my father to use it and sit in greater comfort. Soon after, the loud snorer was wheeled into another room. A peaceful night provided much needed rest until the lieutenant brought my father back at dawn.

"Colonel, sir, your father spent the night sawing lumber in his sleep, snuggled in comfort with a warm blanket. I'm sorry he woke you up, but we didn't want to upset him about the change we made."

"Please, don't mind my father, Miss Selma. He was known in Koles as the Bear, who hibernated every night until five in the morning. He always woke up before the roosters. For many of our neighbors, the silence at dawn was a wake-up call. The roosters moved out because they couldn't sleep next to my father's snoring."

Nurse Selma giggled. "As soon as your family is up, we'll have breakfast in the Atrium restaurant. I'll head over and help the ladies. It will be a glorious day, Colonel. I only wish you could see it."

In her voice, I detected a touch of hope. A peculiar woman? Despite the war tragedies around her, she showed courage and optimism. She was a seasoned nurse. She was trained to keep her emotions within herself. How could one judge her personality by her voice alone?

The glorious day arrived with a loud roar from our victorious kingdom. And I could swear it was the loudest celebration human ears could tolerate for a short period unless they were destined to lose their hearing.

Prince George and I rode together in front of the procession. He described the spectacle of the city's mass celebrations in detail. The gun salutes from canons and rifles echoed around the seven hills of the capital. The marching bands competed with the pounding boots, cheering crowds, and rumbling wheels of artillery guns and horse wagons.

"Brother Sam, how are you holding up?" Prince George shouted.

"I pray that God doesn't deprive me of another of my faculties. My eardrums are about to burst."

"Very soon, we'll be leaving the parade and going to the summer palace where the victory celebration will continue. There will be speeches, medal-of-honor presentations for our war heroes, a banquet luncheon, and finally, circle dancing and ballroom waltzing will take place. The Queen Mother has invited you and your family to sit at the royal table. She has a fond memory of you."

"Your Highness, I'm honored and touched by Her Majesty's invitation. Would my family and I, the simple commoners from Koles, match the particular standards of Biares high society?"

"Brother Sam, our ancestors were pig farmers. I don't expect our countrymen to reach upper class status any time soon, as long as they eat pork and drink plum brandy. No other culture could have such an effect on the character of our nation. We like what we are. Besides, we're used to each others' scent."

I didn't dispute his common sense. He was always smarter than me when sober.

The royal squadron departed from the cavalry brigade. We entered the courtyard and dismounted in front of the main entrance. An orderly led me up the long stairways into the reception hallway. A deep voice announced the arrival of the palace guests.

As we stepped closer, the voice of Prince George broke through the soft chatter, and silence fell over the festive ambiance.

"Your Majesty King Tarpe, Your Majesty Queen Ariel, Crown Prince Kasander, Prime Minister, and honored guests, may I introduce our nation's hero, Lieutenant Colonel Dino Babic, who led our cavalry battalion into a surprise attack against our enemy. Facing overwhelming enemy odds, the royal guardsmen under the command of our hero, Lieutenant Colonel Babic, stormed the unsuspected Thracian's heavy artillery, and disabled the main threat to our ground troops' offensive."

Prince George's words floated by as if I were in a dream. Battle scenes appeared and disappeared. The fallen comrades died in the lands of no return, and the centuries-old painful wailing of mothers echoed across the Balkans. What were we celebrating and why were we glorifying our victory when tomorrow we'd go to another war? My internal vision revealed our kingdom embroiled in another endless conflict. I shook my darkness off and turned on the light of hope and happiness to rejoin the speech of Prince George.

"I'm very proud to have Lt. Colonel Babic as my friend and my family's favorite son of our nation. Sadly, in his act of bravery, while trying to save his wounded cavalrymen, Colonel Babic was wounded by enemy fire, and he lost his vision. Let us pray for the successful recovery of his eyesight."

The attending bishop led a prayer accompanied by the palace chorus and guests in a uniform plea to God.

Prince George took my arm and said, "Hold on, Brother. The audience with King Tarpe and Queen Ariel is next. Your family is already there."

"I wish I could see everyone. I feel like a blind goat ramming my way through."

"We have scheduled your appointment with the eye surgeon for tomorrow. Your anxiety will soon be over. Our young doctor is highly praised by Zurich University of Medicine, Vienna School of Medicine, and London Ophthalmological Clinic. He is touted as a miracle eye doctor, and we are very fortunate to have him."

"I won't be able to sleep tonight, Your Highness."

"The royal brandy is 160 proof. After we toast, you'll be counting sheep."

The victory celebration in the royal palace brought faith and great hope to our nation. The young people of Biares expressed happiness and delight with songs and dances that echoed across the Balkans until the morning hours. Old King Tarpe and Queen Ariel quietly departed for their quarters, and soon after, most of the invited guests left the palace. I was troubled by a sense of uncertainty tied to tomorrow's visit at the eye clinic. Questions about my vision floated unanswered through my mind. Thoughts about a future as a blind person challenged my courage. A sleepless night prevailed.

At 8 a.m., a vehicle came and took Nurse Selma and me to Dr. Timic's office.

The ride didn't take long. Judging from my position, we climbed uphill and came to a stop. Nurse Selma guided me through the entrance door, where a soft-spoken man greeted us.

"I'm Dr. Danbog Timic. Welcome to our clinic, Colonel Babic. Please, come into my office."

Inside, Nurse Selma guided me to a chair.

"Could you remove the bandages and gauze from his eyes, Nurse Selma?"

"Yes, doctor." She came from behind me and carefully unwrapped the dressing.

"Colonel Babic, I will point a small light at your pupils from various distances. If you see anything, please tell me."

"Doctor, his eyes have no apparent injury nor any change of color. All dressings were clean," Nurse Selma said.

"Thank you, nurse. That's very encouraging. Do you have headaches, Colonel? Any irritations? Scratches? Dry eyes?"

Confused, I searched for answers. Time passed. I heard his motions in front of me.

"How long has it been since you lost your vision, Colonel?"

"I was wounded in the last offensive, on July 20th, 1913."

"That makes it almost a month. Did you experience eye bulging, burning, or bleeding?"

I shook my head and waited. Seconds ticked like hammers in my head.

"We'll schedule a clinical examination to find out the extent of the damage. Then we'll decide on a course of action. Our clinic will be ready for you tomorrow at 10 a.m. It's a long procedure and requires preparatory measures. When someone is thrown in a blast, they can sustain retinal damage called Purtscher's retinopathy, which causes a sudden loss of vision associated with head and chest trauma. I have read the letter from Doctor Momir, delivered to me by Nurse Selma, where he described his findings about your loss of vision. He believes your condition may not be permanent. However, our examination should determine if the injury is from the blast wave, or from the undetected minute fragments carried by it."

Silence had no mercy on me. My chest heaved. My heart pounded with anxiety.

"Colonel, sir, I wish to prepare you for unexpected consequences. If the results of our examination reveal primary damage to your retina, it may take a long period of time for your vision to return. I suggest you pray and hope God will shine a light on your future."

His words stunned me. My buzzing head must have blocked my vocal pipes. I could not speak.

The doctor waited a few more seconds for my response. He cleared his throat and said goodbye. Nurse Selma walked me out. Our driver took us back to the hotel.

The next day, the same driver arrived in the morning and drove the two of us to the eye clinic. A woman greeted us and introduced herself as a nurse. She led us into a room and instructed Nurse Selma to remove my uniform. The two women dressed me in some kind of sleeveless coverall and seated me on a stool.

Two men entered and introduced themselves. "We are Dr. Timic's assistants, Colonel Babic. We will prepare you for the examination. You will lie down on the exam table during the entire process. The doctor will be with you soon."

"Is my nurse in the room?"

"I am with you, Colonel," Nurse Selma whispered. A gentle touch of her soft hand assured me.

One assistant unwrapped the bandages and washed my face with warm water.

"Drink this, Colonel," the second assistant said. "It will relax you during the examination."

"What is it?"

"A mild sedative to allow painless stretching of your eyelids."

"I'd rather have a glass of high-proof homebrew."

"Well, sir, this is just what the doctor ordered. Pure and chaste, brewed by his own grandfather. Here, have a sip."

"Hmm, it's very good. Almost as good as the brew from the Holy Mount of Athos."

"This one is also blessed by Father Naidan. To your health, Colonel. Bottoms up."

I drank the rest of the medicine, and to my utter surprise, nature's sleeping pill took effect immediately.

I woke up with sore eyelids. My head, as heavy as a cannonball, rolled from left to right on the pillow. I moaned loud enough for Nurse Selma to rush into the examination room.

"Colonel, are you awake? Are you in pain?"

"Woooold…" I attempted to ask for a glass of water, but my heavy tongue and swollen mouth couldn't make sense.

She ran out and called the doctor. Then she returned and put a cold, wet towel over my eyes. I sucked the water dripping out of it.

"Oh, my Lord. I'm sorry, I'm sorry, Colonel. Here's a glass of water."

I drank it in one gulp. She brought the pitcher, and I poured the cold, refreshing mountain spring water down my throat. I said, "More."

"Right away, sir." Nurse Selma rushed out.

The door opened again. The doctor and his assistant walked in.

"Are you all right, Colonel? Nurse Selma told me you were very thirsty and your tongue is swollen. Can you speak?"

I opened my mouth, rolled my tongue around to test for the obstruction, and said, "I think I can, now, doctor."

"What happened?"

"When I woke up, I felt like I was choking. My tongue blocked the airflow in my mouth. I couldn't call for help. Everything in me was like a furnace, with clouds of dryness fuming through my mouth. I don't know what caused it, but thank God for water. It took care of the swelling."

"You had an allergic reaction to the anesthetic compound. We should've tested you prior. I'm sorry, Colonel Babic."

"Your findings, doctor? I'm anxious. Please tell me."

"Well, sir, I'm afraid it will not be an overnight cure. There are some retinal complications that will require an extended period of treatment."

"How long, doctor?"

"I don't know, Colonel Babic. We will try all the available topical solutions. If we make no progress, our last option will be a surgical procedure previously performed eight times in France, three times in Great Britain, and twice in Switzerland. The risk is much higher with surgery since only three patients have fully regained their vision."

"That doesn't sound very promising, Doctor Timic. How long would it take for the topical solution to work?"

"It may take several months or longer. We don't understand the curing characteristics of the herbal and chemical compounds in this experimental medication, but we know it's harmless, and it helps."

"Do I have to stay here?"

"No, Colonel. It would not be necessary since the Ministry of Defense assigned Nurse Selma to care for you. She can administer the medication as prescribed and keep a daily journal. We'll supply the medication for three months, and if no changes are noticed, we will re-supply it for an additional three months. Should this treatment fail, we'll consider surgery."

I listened and digested his numbing summary. Difficult times were ahead of me again. Being mute was much easier than being blind. Oh, God, I didn't want to live in darkness.

"Colonel Babic, it's your decision where you wish to stay in the capital or at home in Koles. Regardless of where you are planning to be, I'll schedule my weekly visits and check on the treatment status."

"I will probably stay home with my family, and Doctor, you're welcome to visit anytime."

"Goodbye, Colonel. May God be with you."

"He's very busy now, doctor. Not too long ago, I was His servant. But now that I'm a soldier, He has no time for me. Good bye, and God bless you."

FOURTEEN

August sunrays tickled my face through an open window. The fermented grapes awoke my memories and brought back remembrances of Grandpa's vineyard. Every year, he would announce the annual wine-making festival. He had brought an idea from the north and built the first grape-stomping vat in Biares. Loads of harvested grapes were dumped into this huge wooden vessel, and at first, the invited Pigskin Kolo dancers crushed the grapes. But when the testing of unfermented wine released a strange aroma, my grandpa replaced them with young maidens whose legs they thoroughly washed before grape stomping. His wine, Young Maiden, became the household name for all local winos. It could've been the scent of maidens' happy tears, or an occasional mismatched load of grapes that gave a special flavor. My Grandpa never discovered the mystery behind this refinement. He simply didn't care. For him, this was just another nectar from God for long, gloomy winter nights when he could not play chess.

Every time I thought of my grandpa, I smiled. He was my happy angel.

A knock on the door roused me out of my daydream.

"Colonel Babic, are you awake?"

"Yes, Nurse Selma. I am."

"May I come in?"

"Yes, please."

The door opened, and she walked in. "I brought you some tea, sir. Your mother is making a hearty breakfast. When you're ready, we'll eat. After that, your father will take us for a walk through the vineyard. He wants to show you… Oh, excuse me, sir, I meant he wants to tell you about the changes he plans to make."

"I'll have tea after I take a shower. Would you be kind enough to pull out my clean underwear from the chest of drawers and place it on the stool by the bathroom door?"

A quick wash rejuvenated my body, and I dressed joyfully. Excitement rushed through my body. I drank the hot cup of tea, extended my hand to Nurse Selma, and said, "Let's go outside for some fresh air."

We walked out on a warm, sunny day. Life twirled around us. Goldfinches and canaries chirped, a flutist nearby played an old tune, and church bells rang for the valley's morning service.

"Colonel, sir, your cottage reminds me of the many Ottoman plantations I've seen in Southeast Maradonia."

"Oh, have you been there?"

"During the Liberation War, I was attached to the Third Army Ambulatory Nursing Care. At one time, we occupied a Turkish vineyard that we used as our field hospital. Its cottage had construction elements similar to those I see in your house."

"You have a sharp eye, Nurse Selma. The previous owners abandoned this property and fled Biares with the defeated Ottoman armies. His Majesty, King Tarpe, issued a decree to give ownership of all Turkish properties in the liberated parts of our kingdom to the Biares national heroes. Although this is our country, and we fought to liberate the remaining territories under Ottoman occupation, I'm saddened when I think of the previous owner. He dedicated his life to raising his family and living in peace with his Biares neighbors. Alas, with the defeat of the Ottomans, he was uprooted and forced to flee to the unfamiliar homeland of his ancestors."

"But, sir, the Turks conquered and ruled our lands for four centuries. Our people suffered but always maintained their religion, identity, and hope for freedom. The liberation wars achieved our dream."

"You're right, Miss Selma. I am still a monk in my heart. Let's change the subject. Could you tell me something about yourself?"

"I've been a nurse from a very young age. My father was a country doctor in a small town in Northwest Biares. From the age of fourteen, I tended to my bedridden mother and helped my father raise my younger brother and sister. When I was seventeen, my mother died. My father enrolled me in the Royal Academy of Nursing School in Prague. This is where I met my late husband Chaslav."

"I'm very sorry, Nurse Selma. I didn't mean to pry into your personal life."

"It's all right, sir. We were young and full of ideals. An ambitious doctor and a nurse on a mission to save the world."

"When did you lose your husband?"

"He died in 1912 from rampaging malaria in East Africa, just before we were to return home."

"Oh, Lord, you suffered a tragic fate. How old was he?"

I didn't know if my question provoked thoughts about the similarity of our personal tragedies.

"He was twenty-two, a wonderful doctor, a devoted husband, and a remarkable human being. Everyone loved him. I miss him so much."

Soft and restrained crying reminded me of Galia. Subconsciously, I extended my arms, and she fell into my embrace. I don't remember whether I was trying to calm down Galia or Nurse Selma, but thank the Lord, in my soothing words I didn't use their names. A storm of emotions accompanied our embrace, but it was cut off when my sister called, "Dino, breakfast is ready. Come into the dining room."

We weren't too far from the house. Anitsa probably saw us in an embrace. I wondered what she thought of it. "It doesn't matter," I mumbled. "We're coming, little sister," I called back.

The aroma of Mom's cooking aroused my appetite, and my stomach grumbled.

"Nurse Selma, my father is a first-class gourmand. Please, do not be alarmed by his loud grunting sounds, lip-smacking, suckling, and bone-cracking. His fondness for mom's cooking provokes such noises with every bite he takes."

"My father also enjoyed tasty food, but he hummed, and my siblings and I imitated him. He loved our mom's cooking, but mostly he loved his family. He's so lonely now."

"I guess loneliness is a trait of our nation. Well, breakfast is waiting. We better get in before my father comes."

We carried our laughter into the dining room, where my mother greeted us with a cheerful voice.

My mother danced around us, served the house delicacies, and asked if we had enough, or if the food was to our taste before we had the first bite.

The inborn virtue of every Biaresen housewife was to serve and to wait for praise at the end of every meal. The Turks taught us to express our gratitude with a loud burp after a delicious meal. Our ancestors, the delicate pig farmers, acquired the thousand-year-old tradition to articulate the pleasure of feasting with grunting, squealing, munching, and mumbling sounds, with an occasional exclamation. 'To please a man, feed him well.' These embroidered words hung on the walls of every kitchen in Biares.

My father's entrance brought in the spirit of happiness, and joy in his voice as he prayed, "Blessed be all who are in this house, and blessed be the mother who prepared this heavenly meal, Amen."

He came to my side and said, "Rise my son. My heart is aching to hug you. Welcome home, Dino."

He sat next to me. "Anitsa, bring my surprise for Dino."

My sister ran out and returned with something she handed to my father. Unpacking noises were followed by a ping against a glass. She poured the liquid into a wineglass.

"Get a whiff of this, son."

A pleasant but unfamiliar aroma reached my nostrils. I inhaled again and half-lifted my arms in a sign of expectation.

"Well, my boy, what do you say? But wait. First try it, and then tell me."

The wine had a floral and grapy taste. "Sweet, fruity, and smooth. It's wonderful, Father. Nothing I tasted before. What is it?"

"It's called Muscat, a white grapevine. Our cousin from Montevero brought the seedlings that I planted this spring, and they love our soil. God willing, in a few years, we'll make our own Muscat wine."

The feast continued with the traditional noisy gratitude of the men, and was enhanced by the women's delightful laughter.

The afternoon brought more joy into our lives. The unexpected arrival of Mira and baby Yablan surprised everyone. My father clapped his hands and tried to call his beloved grandson. His voice wavered. Behind me, my mother sobbed.

Mira walked over to me, and whispered, "Dino, welcome back." She hugged me. Her warm tears rolled down my face.

Anitsa brought Yablan and placed him on my lap.

I panicked.

"Don't worry, Dino, I'm holding him," she said.

My light touch on his head awoke his vocal cords. He screamed at the top of his lungs.

"There, there Yablan, it's your Uncle Dino." Mira picked him up and walked away. A few seconds later, he stopped. His happy gurgling sounded as he nursed at his mother's breast.

My father pushed away from the table and said, "Well, this is a good time to take a tour of the vineyard. It will help us digest our breakfast."

"Yes, Father. It's a good idea," I agreed.

Anitsa said, "Dino, I would like to come with you. Let Nurse Selma stay with mother and Mira."

"Of course, my darling angel." I hugged my sister. "You wouldn't mind, Nurse Selma?"

"No, Colonel, I wouldn't. You are in good hands now at home. If you need me, I'll be here."

"Thank you, Nurse.

While my father talked about the new plants, his work on the old parcels, the expansion of the winery, and the equipment he was planning to buy, Anitsa and I walked slower. Soon the growing distance between us diminished the sound of his voice.

Anitsa stopped. "Dino, I must talk to you. I have so many questions, I don't know where to start."

"What is it, little sister?"

"Am I a woman at fifteen?"

"But you're not fifteen yet."

"I'll be in two weeks, a full grown woman?"

"I don't know, my little angel. I haven't seen you in several months. Although I can assume from your voice that you are maturing sooner than expected, I think our mother would be a better judge. Why are you asking me?"

"I cannot talk to our mother. She would not understand."

"Understand what?"

She paused, took a deep breath, and said. "Ever since Prince George and I met, we have fallen in love with each other secretly. No one knows. Only you. We correspond almost every day. His private courier delivers and collects our mail. After the victory celebration in the capital, we met once for a brief time in Nais. I made an excuse to visit Mira and Yablan, while mother and father were planting the new grapevines here."

"Does Mira know about this?"

"No. I didn't visit her until Prince George and I met."

"But how…?"

"He arranged for the Royal Daily train to pick me up from Koles, and take me to the meeting point outside of Nais. There were no passengers, and we spent an hour together in the royal car."

"Alone?"

"Oh, no. Don't worry, Dino. It was all proper and courteous in the presence of his adjutant, Captain Neven."

This shocking development made me speechless. I couldn't process everything Anitsa was telling me. George must be out of his mind. I recalled his first impression of Anitsa. I paid little attention to his compliments, but this occurrence overwhelmed me. In my mind, she was too young. Or is she? How old was my mother when she married our father? Fifteen or sixteen?

"Oh, my sweet little sister. You are confronted with the big, complex issue of adolescence. You are in love with a prince of our nation who is probably spoken for."

"No Dino, he loves me and he wants to marry me. He told me so several times. In his letters and with his words."

"But my dear, he cannot decide for himself. He's a royal, and royals do not marry commoners."

She fell into my arms and cried. I held her tight and let her endure the bitter taste of reality. I didn't have the heart to tell her to forget her dream, Prince George, and the unreachable vows. I must stop all this at once.

Our father called from the lower end.

"You must stop crying now, dear. Wipe your tears and take me down."

"I'll be good, Dino. I'll cry later when I leave you with father."

We proceeded down the slope. I had no consoling words or advice. Prayer would help, I thought. Lord, please don't punish my little sister. She is too young and naïve to step into the heavy boots of life. I'll take the blame.

My father stepped in front of us. "Holy Archangel Michailo, you two must've had a lot to talk about?"

"Well, father, I haven't seen my little sister in a while."

"She's grown up, son. She now looks like your mother when we met for the first time."

Anitsa interrupted. "Papa, I need to go back and help mother with lunch. Nurse Selma will come down to take Dino and change his dressing."

"We'll be under the big birch tree, sitting on the stone bench and talking. You tell Nurse Selma not to rush."

Days passed by. I learned from my daily visits with my father that our vineyard would have a very good year. He had purchased a brand-new gear-driven press and planned to process six cartloads of grapes a day. "Ten times faster than that from Grandpa's vat batch," he exclaimed. "Isn't that so, Mother?"

My mother's soft approval followed, "Yes, dear."

I doubt she understood any of his embellishments, but she was his muse, and everything he did or planned required her candid support.

Dr. Timic came one afternoon and examined my eyes. The prescribed treatment didn't show any progress, and he departed with encouraging advice to be patient and stay out of the sun.

The next morning, the royal courier delivered the letter to me.

"Nurse Selma, please read it to me," I said.

"It's from Prince George," she opened the seal.

"Dear Brother Sam,

I'm writing to ask for your forgiveness. I don't know where to begin since you are unaware of the events that transpired during the Victory Celebration." Nurse Selma stopped and said, "Colonel, sir, this dispatch from His Royal Highness Prince George is addressed to someone named Brother Sam. Should we stop and return the letter?"

"No, Nurse Selma, it is for me. I'm Brother Sam, the former monk of Lanhidar monastery on Mount Athos. Please continue."

"Meeting you and your family at the train station in the capital filled my heart with joy. Our reunion brought many wonderful memories and rekindled the adventurous times of our youth. On the turbulent path of our destinies, we became close friends. We learned from each other the wisdom of faith in God and man, and from our brave soldiers, we acquired respect for leadership in the Liberation Wars. But our close bonds were strained when I met your sister and fell in love with her at first sight. She is the most beautiful young lady of Biares, and I set out to win her heart. Instead, she conquered mine. Her smile, her eyes, and her melodic voice lured me into her enchanting web. I broke the rules of tradition, and I expressed my feelings for her in

125

a brief moment of privacy during our dance in the palace.

"On parting, I promised to come and visit. Two days later I wrote my first love letter to her. I dreamed of your beautiful sister every night and every day. I used my private courier to deliver and pick up our daily mail. I arranged our first meeting in complete privacy inside the Royal Daily. Our love has grown at a very rapid pace, and we gave each other our first vows. I couldn't think of anything else than Anitsa. They say that first loves are eternal.

"In one of my letters, I promised to marry her. How foolish of me to make such a commitment. Two days ago, I gathered the courage to inform my mother, the Queen, about my intentions and my vows. She listened, nodded, and said she would talk to the King. The stormy response and reprimand I received the following morning from the King and my brother Kasander, the Crown Prince, forced me to erase my dreams and vows. They confronted me with the reality of my royal family and my commitment to them. My father, His Majesty King Tarpe, raised his voice for the first time in my life. "Your marriage was arranged long ago, when you were eight years old. Do you want to break our tradition, the most sacred word in the history of our nation?"

"The telegram was dispatched to the Principality of Lodovia on the same day that I was coming to meet my future bride, and spend a few days getting to know each other.

"My will and dreams were shattered. I succumbed to the will of our tradition as I realized this was my greatest punishment.

"I beg you to forgive me. Please find a way to explain this misleading course of our fate to your beautiful sister.

"Goodbye, my beloved friend, my brother in Christ. May God help you to regain your sight.

Prince George Nathan Karageorge."

Nurse Selma folded the letter and sighed. She didn't comment.

I didn't know if I should be relieved by the turn of events, or if I should feel sorry for both Prince George and my sister.

"Should I leave you alone, sir?" Nurse Selma asked.

I nodded and said, "Please burn this letter in the kitchen stove."

The following day, at dawn, I found my way to the dining room terrace.

My mother brought some tea and biscuits, kissed my forehead, and sat next to me.

"Don't you ever sleep, Mother?"

She sighed, took my hands, and placed them on her face. Tears wet my palms. She whispered, "I couldn't sleep for the last few days. I'm worried about Anitsa. She seems depressed and absent-minded. I don't know what's come over that child."

I couldn't share the truth with her. I reasoned that Prince George had come to his senses by the forces of our customs and accepted the royal prerogatives. My mother walked back to the kitchen when she heard Yablan's crying. By God, that boy was the replica of my father. Feed him and he'll purr, stop and he'll roar.

I was alone on the veranda when my sister approached me.

"Dino, I haven't heard from him. Something must have happened. It's not like Prince George." Her quavering voice hung between the sobs.

"Sweet angel, I'm sure he is very busy, and he'll write to you when he gets a chance."

The Lord had answered my prayers, but the truth may bear brutal consequences, and it could break my sister's heart. In total darkness, I searched for light, for my sister's way out of this royal quagmire.

FIFTEEN

After the harvest, my father used the new mechanical press. It processed cartloads of grapes at an incredible speed. The town's curious crowd watched in awe. Unbelievers murmured words of doubt about the wine quality made without stomping feet, and proclaimed—it was the end of Young Maiden.

My father paid no attention to their foolish judgment. He knew, like Grandpa, these same prophets would knock on the winery door to stock up for the coming holidays. Our holiday season always started on St. Luke's day, October 18th, and ended on April 8th with toasting to St Gabriel, until the last drop of wine was consumed.

In my grandpa's promotional words, our wines were famous for their medicinal cure for ill temper, grumpiness, spitefulness, and underperforming married couples. That last one I couldn't explain, because in the year before the Balkan Wars, our town bore more children than the entire Kingdom of Biares. Was there any truth in it? To the drunks of my hometown, it didn't matter as long as the wine flowed through their veins.

"Miss Selma, would you take me to town in a horse buggy? My father will have the old mule hitched up and ready for us by 10 a.m. I told him I'd like to visit Petro's and my grandparents' graves and lay some flowers."

"There should be no problem, Colonel. I drove many horse-pulled ambulances. I should be able to handle a mule-driven buggy."

"Wonderful. We are only about eight kilometers away from Koles. An hour's ride."

At the entrance gate, my father was talking to someone. It appeared as an argument between my angry father and a soft-spoken person. Nurse Selma and I approached. I asked, "What's going on, Father?"

"This bum here claims that he has a message for you. He's dressed in rags, looks like a beggar, more like a skeleton, and he only wants to talk to you."

"Father, let him come in. It's ungodly to let him stand at the gate of our home without hospitality. We'll sit at the stone table and talk. Miss, please go back to the house and ask my mother to send some food and cold water."

My father mumbled and walked away. Nurse Selma escorted the beggar and me to the stone benches, then returned to the house.

"My dear fellow, I apologize for my father's manners, but he has always suspected anyone he doesn't know. Would you tell me what brought you to my house?"

A soft voice sounded distant, as if coming from a cellar. The stranger appeared to struggle with his breath. He inhaled slowly several times. He whispered some disconnected words between gasps. We heard about a long journey, God's mountains, prayers of hope, and other puzzling expressions.

"Take your time, Brother. Rest."

At that moment, my sister and Nurse Selma returned. They placed the food and drink on the table. The very slow movements by the man called for Nurse Selma's attention. She urged him to open his mouth, swallow, drink, and eat more. Small bits. Small sips. Sniffing followed the increasing noises of hunger.

I listened to his enjoyment and considered his predicament. From my father's description, this fellow could've been a monk or an unfortunate man bumming through life in search of happiness.

"Dino, he wants to say something," my sister whispered.

"Drink some more water," Nurse Selma urged the man. "Take a deep breath and slowly exhale. Don't exert yourself. Take your time. Lie down here on the grass and rest a bit."

She and Anitsa helped him off the bench. He moaned and passed out.

Nurse Selma said. "He is a very sick man. I don't know how he lasted so long. There's not a gram of life left in him. He is carrying a small pouch around his neck. It appears to be something he brought for you. In two instances, he pointed in your direction and at the pouch. I pray he lives to tell you about it."

"Whatever God has in store for me, it will come. Right now, he needs to rest."

"We need to get him into the hospital," Nurse Selma urged.

"We don't have a hospital in Koles. People around here live and die mostly of old age, bad moonshine, snake bites, duels, and wars. The nearest hospital is in Nais." I turned to my sister, "Anitsa, is the cottage used by our vineyard's guard furnished?"

"I think so. There is nobody there now. Papa discharged the last guard a month ago."

"Good. Please find Father, and tell him to bring a gurney for grapes. We can use it to carry this man to the cottage."

A few minutes later, my father and Anitsa returned. He didn't say a word. The three of them placed the man on the gurney. My father and nurse Selma carried him down the path. Anitsa and I followed.

On Sunday morning, the bells of St. Mary's church rang across the valley.

"It's time for Holy Communion," my father announced at breakfast. "Dino, would you like to come with us?"

"No, Father. I'm not ready yet. I'd rather stay home."

"I saw your guest sitting outside the cottage yesterday. Nurse Selma has done a remarkable feat of nursing him back to life."

"Thank you, Mr. Babic. He told me he was now ready to go back." She turned to me and said, "Before he leaves, he would like to see you, Colonel, sir."

"Maybe we can see him tomorrow. I'm also curious about him."

"I'd like to stay and keep you company, Dino." Anitsa said.

"If you wish, honey. Wouldn't you rather see your classmates?"

"No, I'll stay with you and Miss Selma. We'll play dominoes, and you can play your violin for us."

"Oh, it's been so long since I played. I don't think I remember any of the tunes. Besides, the old fiddle is probably all cracked up, with a hairless bow and no strings."

"You are wrong, Dino. Mother had it serviced every year, and it's like new. It's hanging on the wall and waiting for you in your study room."

"Well," my father spoke. "In that case, the three of you can fiddle, sing and dance. We're taking Mira and Yablan with us, and we'll bring you some anaphora from the church. By the way, if you've forgotten how to play, there's an old gramophone your uncle Jonathan brought back from one of his exotic travels. It's in your study room also, and it has a bunch of round disks with it. He never played it. It was for you, he said."

I couldn't believe my ears. My father didn't use any cursing or demeaning words about my uncle Jonathan like he always did. I even detected a slight melancholy in his warm voice. There is always a first time for everything. My grandpa's wisdom floated from above.

The three of us walked up to the second floor and entered the large room my father designated as my study room. I rarely entered this room full of hand-crafted furniture, Middle Eastern carpets, and decorative wall coverings with a strong smell of musk and presence of ghosts of the previous residents.

Anitsa brought my violin and placed it in my hands. This old instrument rekindled warm memories of my youth. 'Dino the Fidler' kids used to call me.

It didn't take much convincing for me to play the forgotten melodies of my childhood. To my ear the tunes seemed flawless, but the bow and the strings could not find the tracks. After a few screeching attempts, I handed it to my sister. "Please hang it back up. Let it stay in its place like all other antiques in this room."

The vivacious melodies from the gramophone, wound up and turned on by Anitsa, broke the melancholic atmosphere and restored the splendor of the past in this room. From my memories of furnishings, tapestries and pictures on the walls, one could deduce that life in this house had two faces. One for Eastern and the other for Western civilization.

Nurse Selma touched my hand. "Colonel Babic, would you be my partner for our first dance?"

"I'd be happy to oblige you, but…"

Before I could say the rest, she pulled me up, embraced me, and counting with rhythm she led us into a whirlwind of a waltz. The music re-entered my soul. The touch of a woman recalled in me a longing stream of desire. Dormant remembrances of unending sadness and incurable pain blended with lively dances. It changed into a cocktail of joyful awakening. We floated above the parquet floor, uncertain if our feet touched it or if the magic of our youth carried us over into oblivion.

My uncle's gift played its role. And if Uncle Jonathan became a prophet, he would know the purpose this musical wonder could have. Could he have foreseen my future?

With the next disk, I learned to dance the mazurka with my sister.

"It's easy, Dino. It's almost the same as a waltz. You count one, two, three, but put the accent on the second beat. That's the difference. And here we go."

The music was lively, and I stepped into it, holding Anitsa in my arms. She fluttered and squealed like a hawk flying over its nest, happy and enchanted by her dreams, so tiny and beautiful.

Dancing with the two, I gained a greater desire to step with my flying feet into the musical carousel of Straus, Chopin, List, and other famous composers.

The spring-driven music machine fell to a lower speed, and it wound down to a sniveling sound with the last light of sundown. With our energies spent, the timely rescue came when mother called from the dining room.

In a most surprising act, the following day my father brought our guest to the house for lunch. There were no introductions. My father overtook the podium and announced that he and the unexpected guest had shared a subject of great interest.

"The knowledge this man shared with me about growing grapevines is invaluable. In just a short time, I learned how to set a trellis so our vines can grow upwards and get full sun exposure. My old man taught me good practices, but Brother Desha has opened a world of ideas that will improve growth, prevent diseases, and produce good grapes. I'm very pleased and grateful."

My father hadn't sounded so enthusiastic since we obtained this plantation. It seemed that he wouldn't stop talking about the stranger and his superior knowledge of plants, his practical plant care routine, and his vast vocabulary of botanical terms.

I forgot to tell you something very special about my father. After exactly three glasses of wine, he would stand up from his chair, sway, and walk away from the room. Minutes later, you could hear him snoring behind the door to his bedroom.

In the peaceful atmosphere of the lazy afternoon, when our hefty meal settled, I summoned my thoughts and addressed our guest.

"I was told that you have a message for me. I would like to encourage to stay here with us, and free to go as you wish. It is our Christian custom to welcome you and share our table with you, but we have learned that you are planning to leave after you deliver your message. If you are a messenger tell us who you are and where you are coming from."

Our guest addressed me in the familiar manner of a seasoned monk.

"Brother Monk, beloved Dino. I bring you blessings from our Lord Buddha, and words of love from your Uncle Jonathan."

The name of my uncle Jonathan resounded in an exciting murmur from my mother and sister.

"I come from the peninsula–Agion Oros, where we have established the first Buddhist Sangha order. Your uncle Jonathan is the Trapa of the future Drepung Buddhist Monastery. My name is Desha Passang, the close follower and companion of your uncle. If you wonder how I know the Biaresen language so well, I was born here. As a young man, I worked for your uncle, and over the years I acquired a taste of the religious fervor he carried in his heart. He taught me many things before I joined the order.

In his powerful vision, he had seen the battle and the devastating tragedy your battalion suffered. But he couldn't find you. He could not see your face and your eyes that shone with smiles in his heart. That day, in desperation, he prayed loudly and called on Buddha to help him. He changed. From a true follower of Brahma– never asking, never wanting, never praying for–he reacted as an ordinary human being. All he prayed for was your salvation. However, your blindness prevented light from entering his heart.

"After two weeks of praying without food and water, the word from Buddha revealed your fate. Your uncle has reentered the living. He prepared the medicament, which I brought in this pouch, for you to apply as I will instruct you. He assured me it would cure your blindness."

This long, breathtaking, and heartwarming divine revelation touched everyone deeply. For a long time, we sat silently, letting our sighs out uninhibited. A ray of hope sparkled in my mind. Anxiety worked its way in, and I awakened my childhood curiosity with questions about the enigmatic cure from the mystery world of my beloved uncle.

In my realm of blindness, sky-blue eyes entered and gazed at me through the celestial sphere. I could clearly see and count the stars. I could feel the breath of air, and I could hear the whisper of a voice from within–"believe".

"I'm with you, Brother Dino." The close-by, soft-spoken words of Desha broke the spell.

"What's happening?" I asked.

"I opened the pouch and you inhaled the scent of Himalayan herbs. Your uncle's instructions are very specific, and you must apply the healing medicament as follows:

When you are ready to start your treatment, take a teaspoon of powder and dissolve it in hot water. Soak a piece of cloth and place it over your eyes. Then cover it with a dry towel. Do it early in the morning and late at night in a quiet room. You will experience some form of displacement, mild hallucinations, but after the first two days, you will enter the state of Nirvana. Treatment may cause a loss of appetite, but you must drink a lot of water to balance the effects of this transcendent state.

"After a week or more, the curtain on your blindness will begin to rise. The opening of the eyelids may be very painful. It will feel like the skin is tearing off. More light will shine as the vision increases, and one day, the world around you will become visible. Your sight will be back and you will try to keep your eyes forever open. But don't fret. The eyelids will get tired, and you'll sleep like a log. The following day will be bright and sunny.

"My mission here is complete. I leave blessings from Buddha, your uncle Jonathan, and our brothers. I bid you all farewell."

"Desha, my brother in Christ, my heart is with you. I'm forever grateful to you and my uncle. If, God willing, I regain my vision, I will take the journey back to the Holy Mount to join you in prayer for humanity. May you travel in peace and safety, and may God lead you back to your compound."

"Believe, Brother Dino, believe."

SIXTEEN

My body and mind reacted strangely to the use of Himalayan wet compresses on my eyes. I couldn't sleep for more than a few minutes. Mild depression had set in. The occasional fever that kept me in bed sapped my energy. Nurse Selma advised me to discontinue the use of this remedy, but I trusted my uncle and followed his instructions exactly.

Two weeks later she confronted me with the sobering reality of the promised cure. "Colonel, sir, we haven't seen any improvement with this medication. In fact, you've lost a significant amount of weight and are completely exhausted. Everyone is concerned about you, and we need to put an end to this nonsense right away."

Sounding the alarm, her words rang in my hazy mind. In the last two weeks I had been confined to my bed. She fed me liquid nutrients, watched over my hallucinogenic state, which was accentuated by constant shivering, and slept next to my bed. Hell had engulfed me. Dreams took over my sanity. In my sleep, I screamed, but no one heard or responded to me.

Our priest came by with a censer spreading the incense smoke around my bed. He performed the last rites on me and placed his cross on my lips. But how could I have seen him? Was it all a dream? I couldn't even open my mouth to speak. I struggled to keep the air in my lungs.

While holding her finger on my pulse, Nurse Selma rubbed warm brandy onto my torso. She removed my Himalayan compress and draped a wet towel over my brow.

Images flashed before my eyes when I opened them. My mother prayed kneeling in front of the Virgin Mary icon. At the foot of my bed, Anitsa sobbed. Nurse Selma stood over me, rubbing a warm, damp cloth over my slender arms. My father sat in a corner with a cross in his hands murmuring a prayer. Little Yablan crawled around his legs, attempted a few times to stand up, gurgled baby sounds, and rolled to his mother Mira as the scent of her milk lured him to her.

The evening brought peace and calm. My sleep, long and uninterrupted, provided the necessary boost of energy. Then, the first miracle in my life occurred at dawn. There was no compress over my eyes. My hibernating eyelids slowly opened. The stream of early daylight entered my vision and I stared at the open window thinking, it must be an apparition. But it was not. Two sparrows landed on the windowsill. The wind swayed the wooden shutters and they flew off.

I lay motionless. Nurse Selma came in with a tray of medicines and breakfast for me. Anitsa and my mother followed.

"I will take his temperature and pulse, Anitsa. You might feed him with the soup. Also, I brought some warm tea. Try to give him as much liquid as possible."

I was ready to talk. No, I was ready to scream, but I could not. I had no voice. No whispers. Nothing. No wonder they thought I was dying. My father, Mira and Yablan entered. Amazingly, from the corner of my eye I was able to follow every move. Then the priest came in with the smoking censer. Was this my last hour on this earth?

Good morning everyone. I can see! I can see! With my restored vision I tried to make eye contact with anyone, but their eyes remained closed in a deep trance of prayer. I couldn't convey my calls. Maybe I wasn't alive anymore. My hapless mind wandered. Nah. They would have stripped me naked and bathed me in holy water. A heaven opened where the sun dappled over the gleaming grapes, and life was simple and blissful. My heaven thrived in a world where today and tomorrow followed in the footsteps of yesterday.

My father appeared before my eyes. As he sat on the edge of my bed, his large hands concealed his face. Sobbing shook his body, while his hushed prayers to God pleaded for me.

"Father," I murmured quietly, "Father."

My second call drew the attention of my nurse. Her tear-filled eyes twinkled. She shrieked. "He can see us all. Look into his eyes."

My family encircled me and leaned in like four angels from heaven. God Almighty, I made it back to Earth. The gentle colors of a sunny afternoon entered my room, bringing with them the sounds of everyday life with the scent of mother nature.

With the rising sun, happiness returned. My vision has broadened.

Horizons have expanded. I walked around with my eyes open, touching everything in sight. The greatest challenge, however, was reuniting with my family and Nurse Selma after such a long period of darkness. My lovely mother had grown older. My husky father had shrunk, Anitsa had the striking beauty of a young woman, and Mira, my late brother's wife, showed signs of loneliness and depression.

The biggest surprise came from Nurse Selma. Her Hellenic beauty surpassed my expectations.

"We are overjoyed with your recovery, Colonel. You will no longer require my services, and I will depart for Nais this afternoon."

I was speechless, but my sister came to my aid and said, "Ah, Nurse Selma, you're not leaving us. My brother needs you, and we all want you to stay. "

"But I must depart, my dear. I received word from my cousin that my father is dying, and I'm leaving from Nais on the train tomorrow."

The news shocked me. So soon. I cringed when she told me that my adjutant was on his way to take care of my needs. I had to think about that. I needed to consider what I would say. She was not my servant. She was only here to care for me while I recovered. It was all over. I had to let it go. The resentful me told me that I didn't need my adjutant. I required Nurse Selma's assistance. I was still in the healing process. But the rational part of me said, of course Nurse Selma must return to be with her father in his final days.

"Say something, Dino." Anitsa insisted.

I gathered my senses and repeated my rational words, "I wish you a safe trip and the best of luck in your future endeavors."

"Please write to us," my sister said.

Early in the afternoon, the horse-drawn carriage arrived. My father brought her luggage down and waited with my mother. I stood on the balcony and watched Nurse Selma, my sister Anitsa, and Mira walk down the stairs.

The late-afternoon sun glistened off Nurse Selma's scarlet gown. She was a woman of exceptional beauty. Her uncovered, loose, silky blonde hair fluttered over her shoulders. With her sun-kissed lips, she waved one last goodbye to me.

I've never been unfaithful to Galia in my dreams. However, daylight images and sounds eroded the shields of yesterday, and ushered in the inevitable drowning of memories and promised vows. With the departure of Nurse Selma, another breath of hope faded. God, am I a pilgrim of your faith, or a soldier of misfortunate destiny?

SEVENTEEN

Nurse Selma's departure was a temporary emotional setback for me. I tried to accept the reason for my melancholy state. Did I miss her presence already? Several months of care, sweet words of encouragement, and her alluring presence helped to trigger challenging emotions in my wounded soul. Her departure opened another door to an unpredictable future looming on my horizon.

However, the return of my vision increased my appetite for my mother's delicious meals. The desire for physical work with my father on the plantation restored my mental strength and military fitness.

My father's enthusiasm increased, and as a reincarnated patriarch of the family, he did everything he could to get me involved in the workings of the winery. I listened and followed every step of his enormous wealth of experience, his love for winemaking, and his audacious plans for the future. But my heart was not in it. It was marching with the armies of my small kingdom into an unknown future. My father had always wanted me to dedicate myself to this winery. However, without my brother Petro, the five hundred acres of land was a very big responsibility for me. I did not wish to disappoint my father, nor did I try to explain the ongoing military developments in my career.

The arrival of my adjutant, with orders delivered to me, clarified my status and prepared me to face the coming duties. My time with the family on the plantation was a temporary escape from reality, while my military pilgrimage had already been pre-established.

Anitsa grew out of her unrealistic dreams and didn't ask me about Prince George anymore. I had no news about him, nor any sources of information.

At dawn, lower-pitched sounds, of ruff-ruff and woof, awakened me. Scratching at the door and whining followed. Waking up early Sunday morning was not my plan. Manual tilling and weeding the previous day tired my body. I rose in bed to determine the source of this noise. Nothing moved in my room. The soft voice of my father and the muffled barking came from outside. Then the door screeched, and a shadow of a small dog barking and running to my bed appeared in the twilight. His small front legs pushed against the side of my mattress and his hind legs attempted to jump high and get to the top.

I leaned over and lifted him up.

"Hello, little one. Where did you come from?"

He looked at me with big brown eyes.

A stream of pleasure ran through me as I held the trembling tri-color puppy in my hands. I brought him to my chest, and he calmed down. He licked my cheek and woofed again. Perhaps he made his sign of love at first woof.

I laughed and placed him on top of my bed. He covered his head with his paws. With big eyes he watched my movements. I got up and patted his head. He jumped to the floor and rolled over several times.

As I approached the armoire, he ran, sliding on the floor. While I dressed, he ran around my legs and barked. I lifted him up and carried him out.

"OK, boy, we are off to eat. I hope you're as hungry as I am."

For a moment, I thought about the origin of this morning's surprise, but I assumed my father had an answer. The warmth of this natural exchange between a man and a dog reminded me of the book The Call of the Wild, by Jack London. It brought feelings of joy into my heart.

We entered the dining room where mother and father were already sitting and talking.

"I see that you have met our new guard dog," my father said.

"Papa, I'm overjoyed by our new member of the family. He will be a splendid companion to our Yablan. It brought back memories of our early childhood when Petro and I wrestled and played with Grandpa's German shepherd. I was five and Petro was seven. He was our dog. We loved him so much. I never found out what had happened to him. I knew that he had vanished, and Grandpa told us that he had returned to his own homestead. What homestead was that, Papa?"

"Well, son, telling the truth to the two small boys would have been a horrible shock. After Grandpa's dog, Orkan, disappeared, we pondered how to explain it to you. The truth would hurt, and if revealed bluntly, it could have caused childhood trauma."

I couldn't wait. I interrupted my father, "What truth, Papa?"

"Be patient, son. I want to tell the entire story. Now that you're grown up, you'll understand Grandpa's state of mind caught between two alternatives. In those days, Grandpa had a herd of sheep in the hills. Shepherd Boban, and our dog Orkan, guarded the lot. The two were inseparable. Every time Grandpa brought Orkan during our summer holidays, after a tiring chase with the neighborhood dogs, a game of fetch, and hide and seek with the kids, he would disappear at night and return at dawn."

"Where did he go?"

"Back to the mountains. As if he didn't want to leave the old shepherd, Boban, and the sheep alone."

"I don't remember the dog, Papa. I saw once a small picture of Grandpa and his dog, but I couldn't figure out what breed he was. Petro claimed he was a wolf."

"Petro teased you, and tried to scare you, but you showed no sign of fear. The dog was a German shepherd. Playful as a puppy, but he was a very strong animal. Your grandpa tested him first with an empty horse-drawn buggy. Orkan pulled it. So he added four fifty-pound bags of grain. The dog strained, muscles tightened to a breaking point, but the buggy moved. The wheels rolled forward and Grandpa jumped with joy.

One day, he didn't return. Your grandpa and I hiked up to the cottage and found half of the herd slaughtered. The mutilated body of shepherd Boban lay on the ground. It was awful. His last word was Orkan."

"What happened to Orkan?"

"Boban couldn't give us an answer. We searched the area and found the rest of the sheep in a crevice nearby. After blocking the exit, our search for the dog continued, but he was nowhere. We returned and buried the old shepherd, then walked back to town to gather more help.

The following day, our search party of eight returned. Your Grandpa and I had shotguns. Others had machetes and clubs, and your uncle Miladin had an old rifle with a scope. Our assumption led us to believe that a pack of wolves surprised Boban and killed him and half of the flock. But questions poured in after our thorough investigation. Bodies of dead sheep were intact. A bite to the throat was the cause of death. If the wolves had attacked, they would have been killed for food, and their bodies would have been torn apart and eaten. This looked like an orderly, submissive slaughter.

What could have killed them? And why? No signs of sheep scattering or running away. All in one place. All stood by and waited. Like Christians in the Roman Coliseums.

Someone said, "He is rabid!"

"Let's go to the gully and check the remaining sheep," Grandpa ordered.

"About a hundred yards from the crevice, our dog circled in front of a pile of branches used to close the entrance. I stepped forward and called out, "Good boy, Orkan." He turned and growled. He was squinting and trembling. His legs were unstable, but his crouching showed a beast ready to kill.

"Stand aside," Grandpa yelled. As the dog leaped into the air, he raised his shotgun and fired. Orkan fell and sprawled on the ground. The cloud cast a shadow across the sun. Grandpa's tears glittered and rolled down his face. We buried the dog next to the shepherd's grave.

"Oh, Dear Father, what a sad ending. My poor grandpa."

"You know what, son? You should name this puppy Orkan. Your grandpa would like that."

"I'll do that, Papa. Come on, Orkan, let's eat.

Puppy Orkan and I spent a lot of time walking through the vineyard until orders arrived for me to report to headquarters in Nais. In the last few days of my preparation for the return, he discovered his new companion, my nephew Yablan, who appeared to be his true match. My nephew was already walking, and the two of them chased each other, tumbled and rolled, pulled and barked. This caused tremendous delight for everyone, but mostly for my father.

Release by my eye doctor was required, and I patiently awaited his arrival. Most of the time I spent with my father, who seemed preoccupied with thoughts about the threatening winds of war between the world's empires.

"The wars are over, Papa. Europe needs peace."

"I'm concerned, son. Our king is old, and our kingdom is small. Every time the storms of nationalism blow over the Balkans, our people are ready to fight. Swayed by the talks of our radical prime minister, Crown Prince Kasander is intoxicated with dreams of expansion. Our nation is too tired to fight another war, and I'm too old to lose another son."

My father fought in the Liberation War in 1878. The loss of his two brothers left a permanent scar in his heart. Although my grandma often wept alone in the corner of her kitchen when no one was around, my grandpa relied on the stoical upbringing of the Babic forefathers. These forefathers never shed tears.

My mother and Mira were busy preparing dinner the last day before my departure. Anitsa was setting the dining room table for more people than we normally would have. My father brought out of the cellar the six remaining bottles of Grandpa's finest white wine.

The two little buddies slept on the ottoman, exhausted from their play. Through the window, I watched my father put the wine inside a wicker basket. He tied it to the bucket rope and dunked it in the cold spring water of our twenty-five-meters deep well. It dawned on me that they were preparing a feast in my honor.

At four o'clock, a carriage arrived in front of our house.

"I had no idea we had guests for dinner," I asked my mother.

"It's a surprise for you, Dino," Anitsa said and ran out to meet the guests.

The view from my window showed an older couple, stooped and walking with difficulty up the stairs. A younger couple followed. Although the features of the young man seemed familiar, the glaring sun prevented me from discerning his face. I walked into the hallway to greet them when the young man shouted my name and rushed over to embrace me.

"Rudy! My dear Rudy," I hugged him and held him tight. Within that split moment of our reunion, there were many gleeful words and childish affectionate exchanges. Our tears sparkled and we danced. Two young boys, sharing pure delight. It seemed as if we'd stepped back into the twilight of our childhood reliving the precious moments of our lives.

A few minutes later, Rudy turned to my parents and said, "Allow me to introduce my fiancée, Danica. We received blessings from our parents, and we are planning to get married on St. Nikola's Day, December 19th, at our church, here in Koles. You are invited to our wedding, and I would like Dino to be my best man."

"I'd be…" Overwhelmed by emotions, my voice choked up. There was no hesitation between us. I opened my arms and hugged Rudy. Endearment flooded us, tears ran freely, and we were one again–children of the happy springtime of life. My father saved our dignity as grown-up men.

"Rudy, my son, it will be a great honor for our family to share the brotherhood of love anointed by God between you and Dino. Let's toast to our sons and their future families."

We toasted, drank, and chattered like birds in the spring. The merry-go-round of my mother's finest gourmet delicacies and Grandpa's delightful wine made our carefree conversation a remedy for worries and uncertainties about our future. While Rudy and I tried to catch up on all the details of our past, my father suggested that we, the men, go on a vineyard tour.

After a few minutes of walking behind, we separated from our fathers and their lively discussion about winemaking. We sat on a bench and listened to the sounds of nature.

"I have received my orders. The eye doctor is coming tomorrow to release me from sick leave, and in the afternoon I'm going to headquarters in Nais. I don't know what my assignment will be, but I'm ready wherever they send me. How about you? What are your plans?"

Rudy studied my face, attempted to respond, then covered his mouth with his right hand, and turned his head away. "My God, Dino, you've been blind for months. Now that you have your vision back, you are eager to rejoin the army?"

"I'm a soldier. It's my call, Rudy."

"I'm also reporting in a few days to my newly assigned command quarters in Porit. I'm the captain of the first motorized Royal Ambulance Corps. We have received fifty-six motorized vehicles from France and only two instructors to train twelve hundred drivers and medics in thirty days. "

"Congratulations, Rudy. That's a great assignment. The first motorized ambulances for the Royal Biares Army. What a challenge! I'm so happy for you."

"Don't be so sure, Dino. A year ago I was a second lieutenant performing diligently the duties of my rank to uphold the traditions and standards of the Royal Army. Today I'm a captain. No schooling, no training. What will my fellow soldiers think of me? Will they obey my orders? Or will they laugh at me?"

"Rudy, we are a young nation. But our will to defend and protect our freedom is beyond any doubt. Our army, hardened in values of our tradition, embodies our moral codes and is constantly learning in terms of leading, training, and motivating soldiers. Lead by example, maintain and enforce standards, and take care of your soldiers. They will follow you on every road to glory or defeat." My speech sounded like a pep talk, but it seemed to light a sense of hope in his eyes.

"You're right, Dino. I'll face the challenge and earn respect. The new motorized ambulance corps will be the pride of our army."

"That, my friend, is the spirit I know."

On parting, Rudy hugged me and held me tight. "You are my best friend. I miss you very much. I've learned about your tragedy and my deepest sympathies are with you. May God give you strength and the will to find peace and happiness again.

It was one of those moments when happiness turns into uninvited sadness, and thoughts of despair invade our defenseless minds. How crucial were these thoughts in my life?

Anitsa couldn't stop talking about Rudy's future bride. Our parents excused themselves and retired to bed. I kept yawning, and my sister kept pouring out the beautiful impressions she had gathered about Danica and their wedding plans. How exciting, how magnificent, how glamorous, how …. By the time her last praise reached my ears, I was sound asleep on the sofa.

Anitsa's persistent calling and pulling on my arm woke me up.

"You received a letter from Nurse Selma. It arrived this afternoon when you were walking with Rudy."

I fixed my gaze on the envelope she handed me.

"Good night, Dino. Go ahead read it, and have a wonderful dream." She kissed me and walked away.

I opened the envelope and pulled out the letter.

October 29, 1913
Darvid, Kingdom of Biares

Dear Colonel Babic,

There aren't many words a wounded soul could scribble on a piece of paper. The ink flows according to the dictates of a woman's mind. It dumps emotional sediment into a sea of pain, loneliness, and fear. My father's final days brought back memories of losing a loved one. Reflecting on the positive times helped me get through difficult times of despair. My career and achievements were heavily reliant on the encouragement and support of two men I loved, my father, Ilija, and my husband, Chaslav. Now I'm alone, but their courage and dedication to the medical profession have stayed with me to inspire me in my quest for greater accomplishments.

I must admit that my assignment in the last few months, when I cared for you, restored my faith in human beings. Despite the fact that I am aware of how women are treated in today's society, the time I spent with you and your family reaffirmed my respect for men. Your actions, not only as a military commander but also as a kind and well-mannered human being, have left an indelible imprint on my soul. I appreciate it, and I hope our paths will cross again in the future. My military service with the Royal Biares Medical Corps has come to an end, and I received an honorable discharge from the army.

I'm pleased to inform you that my medical career is heading in the right direction. Dr. Negotin Deva, Dean of Bellcity Medical College, has offered me a position as an assistant professor in the newly established School for nurses. While I was considering this offer, I received an invitation to join the newly formed movement for women's rights in Prague as the Secretary of the International Suffrage Alliance. My late husband Chaslav and I were outspoken advocates for equality among us, and I have vowed to carry on our fight.

Dear Colonel, please accept my apologies for bringing up this taboo subject in our traditional society, however if we are to maintain our friendship, in all aspects of life, I want to share my thoughts and opinions with you. There will be no peace in my heart until civilized nations recognize women's right to vote.

We both share the human tragedy of losing someone we love. But my profession has taught me that time heals all wounds, and when the scabs disappear, our lust for life returns at full speed. This will be my struggle between the past and the future.

I hope your next assignment takes you to the capital. I'm undecided about the two offers I received, and I'm interested in hearing your thoughts on the presented opportunities. Please forgive me for opening my heart to you, but leaving you and your family has also left a part of me behind. I have fallen in love with your family, particularly your mother's traditional dignity and the inner voice of strength against patriarchal male dominance. Your father clings to her like a puppy. I declare with overwhelming joy that I have witnessed the power of love over bigotry.

I could write much more, but it will lead to a carousel of words created by aimless thoughts from a woman marching into the future without a compass.

Nurse Selma Medova, with deep respect and admiration for you and your family.

The letter prompted me to reflect on its contents. Nurse Selma conveyed a message in a subtle manner. What was she attempting to tell me? Words were missing in between, and the intimacy she was attempting to unravel struggled to be explicit. Was there something I'd unknowingly started? No, this wasn't a woman acting on a whim. Her strong character maintained professional communication skills acquired through years of correspondence with military and medical personnel.

As a teenager, whose brain matured slowly like pickled cabbage, I would've used my late grandpa's favorite expression from his vocabulary, "Women!" and the rest of his infamous idioms from his chess-playing days. However, maturity replaces innocence, and I let my thoughts stew for a little longer before responding to Miss Selma's letter.

Doctor Timic arrived the following day, and after a thorough examination, determined that my vision had fully recovered.

"Colonel Babic, you have a robust genetic constitution. Your body heals fast, indicating that your vital organs are well maintained. Fitness and a healthy diet are the foundation of good living. Your release form is signed, and you are ready to report for duty. Good luck, Colonel. I wish you all the best."

It was difficult to part with my family. But this time, it was easier and happier, with one exception. My father invited our immediate neighbors over for a wine toast to my safe travels. They then invited their neighbors, and as word spread, half the town's population showed up with empty pitchers. "Tradition," my father explained. "You can't turn them away."

Until my train arrived, they decanted two large barrels of wine into thirsty pitchers, and the Kolo circle dance wrapped around the waiting train. The celebrants invited the train engineers. This resulted in an additional six-hour delay. Memories of my beloved uncle Jonathan flash by. The sounds of my hometown filled my ears, and nothing came out of my mouth for a moment. Those were the happiest times of my life. Lord, why don't you let us stay in these happy times of our lives? Humans are not so bright. They like misery as much as happiness.

EIGHTEEN

My return to the capital sucked me into a pile of military duties. It eagerly awaited my return to make up for every minute of my convalescence. I quickly learned that the merciless job of each commander was to suffer from an endless load of senseless correspondence. In its original form, military stupidity filtered through bureaucracy from the high command.

I had planned to visit Miss Selma Medova in Bellcity this weekend, and I rushed to complete the reports on ill-fated proposals for a fictional confrontation of our army with the Austro-Hungarian forces across the river's borders. After the Balkan wars, our generals, well into their second childhood years, dreamt and prepared for another war of Biaresens' liberation in every neighboring country, including America, wherever that country might have been.

Two days later, an unexpected order came from headquarters. I was to report on Saturday at the Ministry of Foreign Affairs to Secretary Bogdan Danski for my upcoming assignment.

This confusing order puzzled and disappointed me, and I questioned the reason for this change. No one from my post could offer a clue, and my commanding officer advised me to keep the questions to myself.

I sent a telegram to Selma and asked if she could come to the capital on Sunday. Her reply stated she would be on the train arriving at 10 a.m. She had arranged to stay overnight with her aunt Mara in the capital, and she would return to Bellcity on Monday morning. Her image lurked in my mind, and some mysterious words echoed in my hollow cranium. "She is not easy to forget."

My elevated spirit thought of romantic gestures, warm greetings, daytime amusement, and my undefined plans for Sunday evening. I gathered the courage to ask an older captain about his courting experience, and I hit the jackpot. He opened his heart and poured out the charming details of his memorable experience with the woman he fell in love with and married.

151

"Every woman loves romantic gestures expressed with splendor. The first act that opened Zaza's heart started with a bouquet of red roses I brought to her house when I asked her parents for permission to court her. Our walk in the park, chaperoned by her two aunts, consisted of bubbly conversation. Our hearts were filled with anxiety to touch each other's hands. Unfortunately, the wide invisible barrier between us was enforced by the hawkish aunts who stepped between us every time we moved closer than four feet. Two weeks later, on my tenth date, weekends excluded, I brought with me a romantic musical trio and sang with the band, "My sweet dove, would you take my love?" Although her father wasn't happy about the ruckus this event caused, he invited my parents to come when I was ready to ask for her hand.

"Our secret correspondence, enabled by my witty sister, who arranged it during Sunday church services, consisted of yearning with an impatience that threatened to explode. When her father declared that a one-year waiting period was a traditional custom, both Zaza and I rebelled. It didn't help. We waited and learned to love each other with a lesser burning desire and greater respect for our tradition. It was one of the longest years of my young life, but it was repaid by the most beautiful smiles and air-kisses Zaza sent my way."

"Thank you, Captain Zoric. Yours is a true love story. I shall remember the red roses."

"We are still in love with each other, Colonel, sir. Seven daughters, three sons, and twelve grandchildren fill our lives with stronger love and greater happiness."

"Captain, you remind me of my father. He's also a traditional man."

He smiled, saluted, and walked away, then stopped, turned around, and said, "Colonel, sir, may I offer a suggestion for you and your lady friend?"

"By all means, Captain. Please do."

"On Sunday evening at the Summer Palace in Deerhill, there'll be the officers' ball. I assume you've received an invitation. I can arrange for the fiacre to take you and bring you back."

"Captain, thank you for thinking of all the details. My lady friend will be staying with her aunt, who lives near the Summer Palace. I will consider your suggestion. However, would you please keep the fiacre on standby for Sunday, starting at the train station at 10 a.m.?"

On Saturday morning at 9 a.m. the Secretary of Foreign Affairs, Bogdan

Danski, received me in his office and invited me to attend the cabinet meeting. In the conference room, a group of his advisers, seven high-ranking officers, and five civilian appointees occupied a long rectangular table. He seated me on his left and raised his arm. The murmur stopped.

"Gentlemen, our minister of defense, the Honorable George Tanasic, informed me of the latest military maneuvers by the Austro-Hungarian Empire on our western borders. Our brothers in the occupied Sanobia are subjected to calculated terror and population uprooting. The young Sanobians were beaten, imprisoned, and often executed by the remaining Muslims of the Ottoman Empire in the Balkans. The latest accusations by the Habsburgs, insist that our royal government is encouraging and supporting the liberation movement by the young Sanobian revolutionaries. Pressure from the Austro-Hungarian Empire is mounting with their army maneuvers on our western borders. Minister Tanasic is expecting increased provocations by the Habsburgs in the next few months. We must learn their plans and inform our allies of their latest plots.

"Gentlemen, Defense Minister Tanasic has requested an audience with His Majesty King Tarpe, and I was summoned to attend. The meeting is set for noon. I have only thirty minutes before I leave for the palace. Are there any urgent matters or concerns we need to cover at this time, or could we postpone them to our next meeting on Monday morning?"

A young man stood up and spoke with fervor.

"Your Honor, Mr. Secretary, may I bring up again the most urgent issue facing our nation?" "The radical party is openly promoting a liberation war against the Habsburg Empire. Their leader, Joseph Stepan, is calling on the Royal government to deploy our armies to Sanobia. The upheaval within our military and government is causing serious problems for a diplomatic solution. The secret society, known as the Liberators, is heavily involved in training Sanobians. Terrorist activities are being organized across the border. It has established a network of revolutionary cells throughout Sanobia, and it operates primarily under the leadership of radical Biares army officers and some government officials. It has a growing influence over army and government officials, and it's becoming a real threat to our kingdom's security."

"We are aware of the Liberators' negative campaign and the harm it brings to the table of diplomacy," Secretary Danski responded. "Our prime minister, Maydan Bogdanov, has informed His Majesty King Tarpe and the

Parliament, of the open ultimatum from the Austro-Hungarian Empire to the Kingdom of Biares to hand over all Sanobian revolutionaries operating inside of Biares and to arrest Joseph Stepan.

Gentlemen, we have serious concerns within our own borders, and we're determined to address this issue immediately. We must eradicate all radical political currents that feed anti-government sentiment. This is our number one priority.

For this purpose, I am appointing Lieutenant Colonel Babic to take command of the special operations undercover unit."

Caught by surprise, and uncertain of my own considerations, I stared open-mouthed at Mr. Danski.

Spontaneous applause erupted, and everyone stood up in stupefied admiration. Although I kept nodding my gratitude, my soul wandered away and I was left in a state of complete astonishment.

"I'll see you on Monday morning, Lieutenant Colonel Babic," Honorable Secretary Danski said and walked out.

NINETEEN

Finally, I was free. My thoughts turned to Sunday and the visit with Selma. So many things needed to be done. My custom-made uniform was ready for fitting this afternoon. I drifted through my mind in search of a gift. I didn't know what to get. What do men buy for young ladies? And what should I get for her aunt? I was a simpleton with only military manners. I could no longer hide behind the uniform. I thought of the red roses. Where can I find a fresh bouquet of flowers in November? I had one of those helpless feelings when a fellow commoner dreams of being a nobleman while his imaginary advisors scream in his ear, "Be a man, don't be an ass, for your time will quickly pass."

I missed my imaginary advisors.

On the other hand,
One of them could say, to my dismay,
"It might be hereditary meekness,
That adds to your weakness.
When confronted with your women,
To submit and forfeit,
Your right to be first,
May turn into your worst nightmare."

When I thought about it, I realized they might be right. My mother always won her arguments. My grandmother controlled Grandpa's wild behavior, and my uncles never married because they feared women. My alley cat Marinko, agreed. Any time a woman tried to pat him, his claws were ready to strike. If he succeeded, a posse of men and dogs would hunt him. But he was clever and disappeared for days. Men would get drunk and forget about the cat. The dogs, well, were too lazy, and they didn't like to chase cats.

Not far from the ministry building, a sign pointed to the bazaar, the most popular shopping center in all of Biares. It offered many choices. If they found a man, his wobbling head would be wearing a puzzle on his face. To spend or not to spend, that is the question! The stoic expression of a women reflected in a window simply asked, how much?

A French boutique displayed the latest in ladies' fashion. Italian leather craftsmen exhibited handmade goods for ladies and men. The two jewelry stores, owned by Greeks and Turks, faced each other across the busy avenue. The shop windows had a beautiful arrangement of expensive jewelry. Gold, pearls, and diamonds glistened in the morning sunlight. A few passersby stopped for a minute or two. They shook their heads in a moment of indecision, keeping their hands on their wallets. 'Maybe next time? Now the children need shoes for winter.' They murmured and walked away.

At the end of the bazaar, a small shop sold books, magazines, and a stack of framed paintings depicting bouquets of flowers. I stopped and flipped through them until I found one that caught my eye. Red roses! How appropriate.

An older man walked out of his booth. With a pair of glasses over his long nose, a paint palette in his left hand, and a paintbrush in his right he hovered over my crouched body and said, "Ah, that! Do you like it? I did it five years ago for my Kathy. She loved red roses. We had them in our garden, and every spring they bloom for her. She had vases with fresh flowers all over the house. I painted all of them, but when she fell ill, I stopped painting her favorite flowers. This is the last one. If you like it, you may have it for free. The time has come for me to stop painting red roses. They remind me too much of her."

"I'm sorry, sir, but I cannot take your painting as a gift. I'm willing to pay whatever price you ask. Although I was hoping to find real flowers at this time of year for my lady friend, I think the painting will be a suitable gift for her aunt."

"Real flowers? Well, it might be your lucky day. I was planning to paint a fresh bouquet of camellias I cut this morning. I would be happy to include the flowers in the price of the painting."

He rushed back into his kiosk and brought out a glass vase full of dazzling pink camellias. "They're from my Kathy's Garden of Eden. The flowers are our gift to your lady friend. I would be grateful if you paid me fifty dinars for the painting."

I didn't respond as I thought about my limited exposure to artwork.

It was possible that the value of this painting would be much more in any gallery.

"My name is Lieutenant Colonel Dino Babic. Would you mind holding the two items until this afternoon when my adjutant will bring the payment and pick up the flowers and the painting?"

The man stood quietly. He smiled with some inner satisfaction, and said softly, "Thank you, sir. I'll be here waiting. My name is Dr. Polic, and the kiosk is known as Doc's Corner."

I parted thinking about how faith could find its course in the most unexpected circumstances.

"Lieutenant Balada, I've bought two items from an antique arts and books store in the bazaar. One is an oil painting of red roses, and the other is a bouquet of camellias in a glass vase. Could you give me an idea about the price of an oil painting in a regular art gallery?"

"Well, sir, it depends on many factors, such as the origin, the name of the artist, the appraisal, and its catalog valuation."

"What if the artist is unknown, the painting is not hanging in a reputable gallery, and it comes from a second-hand shop?"

"I'm not an expert, sir, but I've browsed through the open arts fair in Mezun past summer, and I've seen amateur paintings sold between a hundred and three hundred dinars."

"Great, please put five hundred dinars in a sealed envelope addressed to Dr. Polic, at Doc's Corner, and deliver it after lunch. He will have the two items ready for you. When you return, pack the painting in gift-wrapping paper and refresh the water in the vase. Use the shay carriage, and have it ready for me this afternoon at about 4 p.m."

"Yes, sir, Colonel, it will be done. May I spend a few more minutes in the bookstore?"

"Of course, Lieutenant, I forgot that you're an avid reader. I'm sure you'll enjoy the visit to Doc's Corner. Take your time and be back before 3 p.m."

I don't know what prompted me to schedule the visit to Selma's aunt on the day before Selma's arrival. I convinced myself that I should pay respect to this old lady with the hope of learning more about her niece. An intriguing question popped into my head. Why? But the urge was much stronger than any reasonable analogy. One explanation that loomed over the shadows of the past was a more intense image of Selma.

At 3:30 p.m. a hand-delivered order from the Ministry of Foreign Affairs specified that I must leave on Sunday morning at 8 a.m. with the cavalry regiment for the northwest garrison in the border town of Tall Pines. It instructed me to report to Colonel Stanko Suton for details of my new assignments. My disappointment, coupled with my displeasure over the unexpected military orders, shattered my illusions about Selma's meeting tomorrow. All my plans and hopes vanished as if there never was a tomorrow for us.

I still had the scheduled visit with Aunt Mara for this evening. I also had the letter of explanation for Selma. Common sense prevailed, and requesting Aunt Mara's approval, I sent an advance announcement of my planned visit. My adjutant returned with a note. "You're most welcome, Colonel Babic."

At 5:00 p.m., with my gifts safely stored in the back chest of the Shay carriage, I drove to the residence of Mrs. Mara Katanski.

Built at the turn of the century on the northern slope of Deerhill, the two-story brick house stood like a guardian on the narrow cobblestone road. It overlooked villas placed at random along the winding path down to the majestic Danube. I drove the carriage to the back and tethered the horse to a large tree. The sun dipped behind the mountain peaks, and the twilight shadows rolled over the remaining daylight.

I took the flowers and the painting and headed toward the entrance. Music came from an open window. In the lamplight, a woman stood by a child at the piano and directed her playing.

I pulled the string on the doorbell. The music stopped. A child's voice echoed with excitement. A woman in the window peered into the shadows. She raised her hand above her eyebrows and called out, "Is that you, Colonel Babic?"

"Yes, ma'am, it is I."

"Mariana, open the door. Our guest has arrived."

A charming little girl, not more than five years old, appeared from behind. Mrs. Mara Katanski approached. "This is my grandniece Mariana. She was named after me."

The little girl curtsied and whispered, "We're pleased to meet you, Colonel Babic."

Her manners suggested a proper upbringing.

"Thank you for receiving me at this hour, Mrs. Katanski." I bowed, but the two gifts in my arms prevented me from kissing her hand.

"Come in, Colonel," Mrs. Katanski said.

Led by little Mariana, I entered a spacious reception room decorated with classic furnishings. An oval dining table with chairs for eight was set in a separate space between two walls with bay windows. A stone fireplace had various sculptured busts of famous people on its mantel. A bookshelf, from floor to ceiling, was filled with books. On each side of the open stairway to the second floor, separate doors led to other parts of the house. A small round table with four cushioned chairs sat in front of the fireplace. Mariana took me by the hand and walked me there.

"Please, sit here, Colonel." She pointed to the first chair.

I placed the two packages on top of the small table and unwrapped the vase with the flowers. I took the wrapped painting and turned to Mrs. Katanski. "This is for you, ma'am, a small memento from me. The flowers and the letter are for Miss Medova. I'm so sorry that I must leave before her arrival. I also apologize for not bringing a gift for your grandniece."

"Oh, but you have, Colonel Babic. Your presence is a splendid gift to her. She talked about you before you announced your visit."

Puzzled, I wanted to ask, how so?

"Mama is coming tomorrow. We will share your flowers," Mariana said.

I looked at a mirror above the fireplace, and I saw reflection of my astounded face.

Mrs. Katanski pulled me out of befuddlement. She rang the hand bell and the housekeeper appeared from one of the doors.

"You may serve tea now."

"Right away, ma'am."

The charming little girl, who resembled Selma in many ways, sat across from me as if she were an artist, scanning her model with an inquisitive look. The admiration was mutual, but I couldn't find the words to link up with her thoughts.

The housekeeper brought in the teapot and teacups on a silver tray and placed them on the round table. Mrs. Katanski poured tea into my cup and asked, "One or two?"

The idiot in me didn't know what "one or two" meant, but the wise one said, "one." He didn't know either. I satisfied my curiosity when Mrs.

Katanski opened the small jar full of sugar cubes and dropped one into my tea. I managed to say thank you. That phrase started our conversation.

"Colonel, sir, I presume you gathered that Selma has talked about you with me and Mariana. She shares many of her experiences with us. During her last assignment, she wrote letters about you, your family, and your magical vineyard. My grandniece is enamored with stories about you. She has prepared many questions, but her bedtime is here, and she will bid you goodnight."

"Dear sir, you must promise to return and spend more time with us." Little Mariana curtsied and extended her hand.

TWENTY

During the early hours of the morning, I ordered the departure of two cavalry regiments from the Southside garrison. After a thirty-minute walk through the capital's sleepy outskirts, we arrived at Central Station. We lined up along the auxiliary rail track and waited for the military train to pull in. The main passenger station operated on four rail tracks for incoming and outgoing trains. On its right-hand side, each track had one narrow platform.

I ordered my men to dismount and water the horses. In the shade of a tree, I sat and pondered. Why was I not informed ahead of time about the details of my assignment? I considered the growing hostility between our small kingdom and the Habsburg Empire, but I couldn't figure out my role in it. I had a hunch that my late brother's fate played an influential part in my engagement.

First Sergeant Dobri reported. "Colonel, sir, our train is delayed due to the lack of horse cars in the main depot."

"How long?"

"Maybe an hour, or more. The two passenger cars are on their way and should be here soon."

I didn't ask how soon. In military terms, it will probably take longer than getting horse cars.

"Sir, our garrison food wagon is serving breakfast. Would you like a plate of porridge and a cup of coffee?"

"Just get me a cup of coffee, please."

The passenger trains pulled in and out of the four main tracks.

From the sea of crowded platforms, travelers boarded the cars, rushed to their compartments, and stuck their heads and arms through the windows. The screams and confusion of people on the four narrow platforms, over-whelmed by locomotive whistles and iron wheels screeching, caused panic. Farewell wishing shouts turned into, "Let's get out of here."

As if watching from the front row, the train engineers enjoyed this stage of chaos. They blew the train whistle, released more steam at the daring pass-ersby, and laughed out loud.

An older gentleman stepped up into the locomotive on the first track, yelled at the engineer, and clobbered him over the head with his cane. The crowd cheered. A man stepped down and walked away. The loud noise stopped, and people resumed their normal arrival and departure routines.

"Who was that man?" One of the passengers called out from a car window on the first track.

A response came from the second track. "He is definitely the head master of the Transportation Department."

"I think," an older woman surmised, "he is a gentleman working as inspector, mind you, on Sunday at this station."

"No! Did you see his cane? He is the chief of the capital's train station."

Another authority declared, "You are wrong. He is the secretary of the Royal Transportation and Navigation Department."

I believe one of my people from Koles released the final conclusion. "He is Duke Nevski, from Tsarist Russia. He is the guest of our Royal Majesty the Queen, checking out our transportation network, and he is very eager to ride our world-famous Royal Daily."

An old locomotive arrived dragging the two military personnel cars. It poured a huge black cloud of smoke. It quickly filled the crowded station with ghastly fumes. Like rats, people scattered in all directions. Our horses panicked and bolted from the rope-bound corral. My men chased after them. The soot-covered devilish train engineer, inside this hell on wheels, smiled and waved. I covered my face with a napkin and waved back. The horses had more common sense. The engine stopped, and the smoke cleared away.

By 9 a.m., we boarded two cars, officers in the first and cavalrymen in the second. The comfort of my cabin provided a quiet ambiance behind a closed window. More coffee and crunchy biscuits tamed my hunger, and my yawning indicated the need for a nap.

"Lieutenant Colonel! Wake up, sir."

"Yes, Sergeant Dobri, I'm awake."

"My apologies for disturbing your sleep, sir. Horses are loaded and we are ready to depart."

"What time is it?"

"Ten o'clock, sir."

"All right, sergeant. Give the signal. No, wait. Are we using the same old chimney belcher that delivered the two cars?"

"No, sir. A new locomotive is at the back of our train. The smoke is clear."

"Thank God."

Another train arrived on the first track. Passengers poured out and rushed to the gate. Family members and friends stood on the outside edge of the platform. People shed tears of happiness, as they ran into each other's embraces. Our train moved at a very slow pace. A little girl yelled, "Mommy, Mommy!"

I recognized the voice and jumped to open the window. They hugged and kissed in a longing reunion. My train moved faster and the distance between us increased. I opened the window, but it was too late to call. A fading image of Selma appeared beyond many scenes as if the rolling clips of goodbyes were the final scene in my daydream. Goodbye Selma.

Two hours later our train stopped at an isolated station. The small stucco-clad shelter had no attendant. An old dog slept in the shade of the building, undisturbed, in his own dog's dream. An officer stood by the door, his horse tethered to a signal post.

Lieutenant Balada knocked on the door, and entered my compartment. "Colonel, sir, there is a telegram for you from the Ministry of War. The officer from the third army garrison insists on delivering it to you personally."

I stretched and yawned. "What's happening?"

He shrugged. We stepped out of the car and greeted the officer.

"Lieutenant Colonel Babic, we have a telegram for you transmitted to our Dava Garrison. I am Captain Radoslav Ilic, and I'm ordered to deliver the letter from General Vasic and the telegram from the Ministry of War."

"At ease, Captain."

The letter from General Vasic expressed his apology for not delivering the telegram to me personally as instructed by General Komadina, the Minister of War. Severe back pain was preventing him from moving, and he was very sorry for missing the opportunity to meet me, the Biares' national hero.

I opened the telegram. The message read, 'Lieutenant Colonel Babic, your order is to return to the capital and report to me immediately. This is of the utmost urgency. To alleviate delays, we have cleared all train traffic on your way back. Upon your arrival this afternoon, an automobile will be waiting for you.' The Minister of War, General Komadina."

I couldn't pull myself together or understand the meaning of this sudden change. I thought of my family, but they all looked healthy and happy when I left.

"Lieutenant Balada, inform the train engineer that we are returning to the capital. Tell him not to worry. The track will be clear all the way."

"I have already done it, sir," Captain Ilic said. "My order is to accompany you, but if you don't mind, sir, I would like to ride in the locomotive with the engineer. He is my cousin, and the two of us have many things to talk about."

"Well, then, enjoy your ride, and don't miss the capital. We'll see you there."

He saluted with a smile.

The ride back allowed me to ponder this sudden change. In the end, I had no clue.

In the window of my compartment, a reflection of Copernicus appeared directly opposite me.

"That, what's on your mind, will eventually decline. Your fate will challenge you again. But don't call us if you get in trouble. Follow your convictions and use the wisdom we planted in you. You are a Biaresen, and you should know that 'What's on your mind is also on your spine.' Use your ticker to get there quicker."

Don't ask me what all this means. From the book of morals, handed down to me by my imaginary advisors, the answers were in a faraway land, where a crowd of enthusiastic citizens of Koles gathered and debated until the jugs of plum-rum in their hands were empty.

I learned from my monk brothers in Lanhidar to cover the tracks in my dreams, so no evil would follow me. It worked. I slept until we arrived at the capital's train station.

A rap at the door woke me up.

"Colonel, sir, we have arrived. Your chauffeur is waiting outside," Lieutenant Balada said.

The two of us walked out and stepped down onto the platform. A bright, sunny afternoon greeted us with the sparse warmth of midwinter. From inside the engine cab, Captain Ilic stood at attention and saluted. Behind him, the train engineer and his helper joined in, one with a coal shovel over his shoulder, and the other with his left hand on the whistle lever.

"How did…" I asked.

"We stopped at the next station with an auxiliary track, and moved the engine forward." Lieutenant Balada explained.

Outside the main entrance, a chauffeur stood next to a shiny, hardtop, four-door automobile parked in the designated waiting spot for our royals and government officials. A silver-colored rope, tied to four white posts, separated this unique display of modern technology from the gawking crowd.

In Biares, such sensational exhibits were rare. The royal four-door cabriolet, acquired in 1910 for the annual Christmas Parade and summer liberation day, saw the light twice a year inside the winter palace grounds. The royals sat in the automobile inside the pavilion when the snow fell.

The engine ran in neutral, and a brass band played in front of the vehicle. Invited dignitaries and government officials, cramped in the small pavilion behind our cabriolet, inhaled the cloud of exhaust fumes. They gasped for air and rushed out coughing and heaving until the clean air entered their lungs. Those who didn't pass-out ran to the refreshment stand and washed their throats with the proven Balkan medicine, the plum-rum.

My adjutant, Lieutenant Balada, and I rode in the back seat of this luxury bouncer, but did not inhale any fumes. Our cobblestone streets offered many chuck holes. The engine sputtered and released less fumes. Copernicus found it most entertaining as he bounced on his tightrope.

Minister of War, General Komadina, received me in honor of my heroic deeds with due respect. The strong grip of his handshake assured me of his four-star general superiority. Deep brown eyes pierced through me in search of evidence that I was who I had been told I was.

I stood at attention and waited. He walked around me a few times testing my resolve. Up close, his breath tickled my hair. His eyes mellowed. The tension of his facial muscles receded.

"At ease, Colonel."

I took a quiet, deep breath and relaxed.

"When considering the choice for this mission, several factors have influenced our decision to call on you for an assignment worthy of your reputation. You are the grandson of our great hero of 1878 liberation wars, Spiridon Silan Babic, seven times wounded warrior, the avenger of our fallen.

You are the brother of the most celebrated scout in the history of our kingdom, late colonel Petro Babic, and you are the hero of the wars with Thracia. The most relevant factor in our scrutiny for the best candidate is your close relationship with our prince George." General Komadina stopped, inhaled, and continued. "You will swear on this Bible, that you will keep the secret, and never reveal under any circumstances your holy assignment in this mission."

I put my hand on the holy book and swore to keep the secret.

"Now sit down and listen carefully. The Red Wing Revolutionary Party of Bessarabia has kidnapped Prince George. He is being held for ransom. They are demanding the release of their leader, Robis Bakalov, plus a hundred thousand rubles in gold in exchange for Prince George. Duke Jovan of Lodovia, the host of Prince George can assure the monetary part of their demand. However, he will not release their leader, his mortal enemy Robis Bakalov, under any conditions."

He stopped. He gazed through the window as if clinging onto the bliss of faith, then swiftly turned to me, "Lieutenant Colonel, you are our only hope. You speak Russian. You have proven your abilities to make crucial decisions for a favorable outcome, and you are still an unknown military hero. We are sending you to Lodovia under an assumed name to find the way to infiltrate the Red Wing party and liberate our prince George. This is your mission. Life threatening challenges will follow you every step of the way. Major Sandik will provide specific details, travel documents and arrangements, one-day undercover operations training, and the reason for your visit to Lodovia. You must sever your relationships with friends and any personal relationship with a woman. Do you have a girlfriend, Colonel?"

"No, sir, I don't. I am a widower. The janissaries brutally murdered my wife. I am still morning for her."

"Please accept my deepest sympathies for your loss. Forgive me for inquiring about your personal life, but we must be absolutely certain there will be no one to jeopardize our mission. Is there anything between you and Nurse Selma Medova?"

The question surprised me. He didn't wait for my answer.

"Lieutenant Colonel Babic, this chapter of your life is over. You will exclude Nurse Medova from your present and future association. Your mentor, Hieromonk Theodor Ivanov, now Major General Theodor, highly praised your innate military skills, your ability to make quick decisions, and your undaunted courage to face danger. In our meeting with His Majesty The King, he suggested that you resume the role of a monk and travel under your given chrismation name, Brother Samuilo. No one will question your devotion, your association with Mount Athos, or your role as a monk from Panteleimon. In fact, if anyone from the Bolshevik expatriates should recognize you, it would only affirm your association with the leaders of the Bolshevik party, Ulyanov (ie. Vladimir Ilich Lenin) and Leon Trotski."

TWENTY ONE

It took a week to get me through a rigorous, painstaking transformation from an obedient regular soldier to a crafty, covert secret service snooper. That's what they trained me for. An innocent Eastern Orthodox monk, introducing myself in all future encounters as a student of the doctrine of Imiaslavie (lit. "glorification of the name"), a very popular ideology among Russian monks on Mount Athos in the first two decades of the 20th century. It resulted in a major controversy, but when efforts to convince the "name-glorifying worshippers" to renounce their teaching failed, in the summer of 1913 the Russian Navy forcibly removed over 800 monks from the Mount Athos Russian Monastery Panteleimon.

The followers of Imiaslavie teachings dispersed and remained active in Bessarabia and the Caucasus. Major Sandik insisted it was a credible reason for my journey and a clever cover-up for my secret assignment. "Even if you are questioned by the authorities while passing through borders, no one will doubt your religious beliefs."

To ensure my fluency in the Russian theological language, a Russian-born priest spent hours with me correcting pronunciations, grammar, saints' names, common psalms, and the proper way of administering the liturgical practice of Zapivka (sacramental wine) of the Body and Blood of Christ. All the clergy consumed the Zapivka, still undergoing fermentation.

I liked that part of my rapid course very much. When Father Dema, at the end of each class, generously toasted with holy wine, I topped it off by singing his most beloved hymn, "Let My Prayer Arise."

I departed from my beloved country on the train that would take me through Romania, Lodovia, Bessarabia, and perhaps into Mother Russia if my fate allowed.

There were enormous obstacles. "Learn not to ask questions", Father Dema preached. Major Sandik forewarned, "Trust your eyes, but rely on your common-sense decisions." My seven advisors interjected, "You are playing with fire, and we are coming along to protect you." They were back in my head.

My contacts and additional details waited for me in Lodovia. The remnants of the now outlawed, infamous monks of the Imiaslavie movement would be the most reliable link to the Red Wing Revolutionary Party. Unthinkable! Those outcast nincompoops? "Don't make quick judgments," Copernicus reminded me. "They might be in cahoots with the Bolsheviks."

Oh goodness! That's what I needed again. To play chess with the Bolsheviks.

The flatlands of Pannonia rolled by the window like a silent movie. The train chugged along and got swallowed by the early December winter night. The lights inside my compartment flickered, stayed steady for a few minutes, then completely faded. A light in the passageway illuminated an older couple, dressed in their native costumes, sitting across from me. Next to them, a young man in a three-piece lounge suit, a starched collar high on his neck, and a felt hat with a dent down the top studied a small booklet.

On my bench by the entrance door, an overweight priest of an unknown denomination wiped the sweat off his face and neck and mumbled words in an unfamiliar language. A stream of perspiration rolled down his fat cheeks from under his large round hat. The space between us shrunk, and I wondered if the sixth passenger would be a child or a dwarf.

The hypnotic rhythm of iron wheels over the railroad tracks created chug-along sounds, and I fought to stay awake. The curious faces of passengers looking in through the glass door changed into my seven mischievous advisors. As my uncle Jonathan's 'scientific dissertation' states, they were mental creations that may have originated back in my childhood. Well, I wouldn't go that far.

While I was still awake, it might be a good time to tell you about my lifetime companions. The Founder, the almighty ruler of this unruly bunch, Ole-under Minimus, had a final say in all inconclusive decisions about my guidance. "We'll see," was one of his unique words of wisdom. So they renamed him, "Willsee" Minimus. Chief Advisor Andronicus, the second in command, primarily nodded in approval of all decisions. His suggestions rarely passed through the rigorous censorship of Copernicus, my personal advisor. I don't know how he was appointed to this role, but Copernicus was irreplaceable. Next to him, Bento Spinoza, an extraordinary, foolish, and cantankerous character, instigated a moral philosophy centered on the control of passion, leading to virtue and happiness. I liked him, especially when he returned from his favorite hiatus, the plum-rum distilling festival.

The remaining three, Aristotle, Nostradamus, and Confucius, were my consciousness advisors. I had no patience to listen to their unending oratories and unfounded exaggerations. Fortunately, they were only in my head, and when I dedicated my time to God, they'd leave me.

The loud opening of our compartment door woke me. The border-crossing agent stepped into our compartment, struck the light fixture with his hand, and announced in three languages, "Welcome to Romania. Please present your travel documents."

The light flickered again and faded into darkness. The agent swore, raised his fist, and hit it hard. Bright light spilled out and hummed a steady sound.

Aha, a good smack made the train lights glow. After all, we don't live in the dark ages anymore.

The agent checked my papers and said, "Would you bless my new Bible, Father?"

I pulled out the small bottle of oil, spilled a drop on my finger, and anointed the first page with a cross.

He smiled, kissed my hand, and said, "Thank you, Father. May God keep you safe on your journey."

Our train stopped in a small town. It was a cold, wintry, and cloudy day. The warm air in our compartment froze on the window and formed shapely ice crystals covering the view of the countryside. When the train moved, a young woman with a baby in her left arm, and a travel bag on her right, entered our compartment. She scooted down into the seat between the fat priest and me. She put the bag on the floor, and pulled out her left breast, then guided the hungry mouth to her red nipple. Her baby pushed and pulled as milk poured out. A short while later, the infant fell asleep. I followed.

At noon the following day, we arrived at Ungheni, the entry port of Lodovia. I opened my eyes and faced the young man sitting across from me. Others had already left, and the corridor was empty.

The young man addressed me. "It is our time to disembark, Brother Samuilo."

"Who are you? How do you know my name?"

"My name is Progon Ivanovich Levski. I am your liaison with Duke Jovan of Lodovia. Here are my credentials and a note from the Biares Minister of War, General Komadina. From here on, we will travel separately. We cannot be seen together. You will get off here and change trains for Balti. Your destination is St. Stefan Monastery, about fifteen kilometers northwest of town. Abbot Radesku is sending a monk to meet you at the station and take you to the monastery.

We believe the Red Wing has infiltrated the abbey with the help of the displaced Imiaslavie monks. This may pose a considerable challenge for you. The story about the brutal acts of the Tsarist Navy is greatly exaggerated by the Red Wing rebels. You will be confronted and questioned about the incident and your purpose for coming here. You must maintain that your only reason is to join Hieromonk Hilarion in the Caucasus and follow his teachings. Any doubts about your visit would be dissolved if someone at the monastery recognized you as the monk from Mount Athos. One person that you can trust is Father Ranko. He knows who you are, and he will provide you with other details during your confession in his cell. Your goal will be to find the Red Wing infiltrator and establish a link with their leaders. Be aware that my platoon of sixty combat-ready troops will be available from the nearby army garrison at any time your signal is passed on through Father Ranko.

"I wish you Godspeed and mercy on your soul if your mission fails. I will pray for you, Brother Samuilo, and I will pray for the soul of the Royal Highness, Prince George."

He walked out and exited through the back door of the railway carriage. As the last passenger, I stepped down from the front exit. The station had only two tracks with one platform in between. Our train puffed steam from its tired engine and gave one more reminder with its whistle for departing passengers. On my way out, a group of peasants with bundles of purchases passed by me and rushed through the entry gate, huffing and puffing in rhythm with the train engine.

I spotted the ticket counter and purchased the ticket for Balti. The clerk told me my train was running late. He advised that I leave the station and get a hardy lunch at the famous Ungheni restaurant which specializes in goose liver delicacies and fried calf-brain gourmet salads. I listened, then nodded, and walked away. Out of my shoulder bag, I pulled out the smoked piece of meaty bacon and a slice of the remaining corn bread. I sat by the water fountain and munched on my ration while a hungry squirrel watched for dropped crumbs. I shared a few and I could swear I heard him say "thanks" before he ran up the tree and disappeared. My train arrived just one hour behind schedule.

"We will be in Balti on time," an older conductor assured me. "You are our only passenger, Father."

In Balti, our train arrived on the first track. The six empty platforms indicated that people only traveled during daylight hours. The stationmaster stood next to the locomotive and talked to the train conductor. I passed by and exited into the waiting area, where I searched for the monastery monk. No one was waiting for me. The clock on the wall showed a quarter to nine. A woman was washing the concrete stairways before the main exit.

"My good woman, could you tell me what road to take to St. Stefan Monastery?"

She sized me up, then pointed to the left, "There are only two roads in front of the railroad station. The one on the left will take you to Holy Hill where the monastery is located. But, Father, it is too far for you to travel at night. It is also dangerous, and you may get lost. Why don't you stay overnight and take a safe walk tomorrow morning? Our priest lives around the corner. I'm sure he would be happy to accommodate you tonight."

"I will be eternally grateful. May God repay your kindness."

I followed her to a nearby cluster of brick homes, hardly visible under the cloudy skies. She knocked on the front door of the first house. A woman holding a kerosene lamp opened the door. Behind her, a man with a pair of wire-rimmed glasses gazed at the two of us.

"Mother Kara, it is I, Mirna. Good evening. Forgive me for disturbing you, but this monk just arrived and wanted to walk to St. Stefan Monastery. I brought him here, and I wonder if you could take him in for tonight."

"God bless you, Mirna. Of course, we will. Every servant of God is welcome in the house of the Lord. We will humbly receive our brother in Christ. Come in, come in." The woman stepped aside.

"I am working tonight, Mother Kara, and I must go back. I thank Thee and Father Marin."

Mirna turned to me. "You will be safe here, Father."

Mother Kara closed the door and led me to a small bedroom. "This is where you will sleep tonight. Please take your robe off and refresh yourself. The wash basin and water pitcher are inside your room. I'll take your robe and have it ready for tomorrow. When you are done, please join us in the dining room."

Oh, how welcoming these people were. I squeezed my handbag against my growling stomach and nodded shyly.

I found the hosts praying at the dinner table set for three. I stopped at the open entrance, kneeled, and prayed. My prayers echoed the familiar lines from long ago. Images of monks from Mount Athos, icons in the monasteries, the music of big bells, and the whirl of pilgrims tirelessly searching for the word of God, passed through my memory lane.

I often ask myself if I should pray for forgiveness. I never did. Copernicus urged my characters to confess. The righteous one did when he was a monk, but the bad one shied. As the roles between the two changed so many times, I was unable to tell the right from the wrong. My grandpa once told me that all people are born with two personalities. Much obliged to you, Grandpa.

At dinner, I told them about my destination and my desire to learn more about Imiaslavie preaching from the Hieromonk Hilarion. They were gracious and didn't ask many questions. Father Miran praised Abbot Radescu and wished me a safe journey.

I excused myself and retired to my bed in the back of the house, where I asked God's forgiveness for lying to my hosts.

In my dream someone was calling me to wake up. I opened my eyes in total darkness and closed them again. I lay awake. Through my closed eyelids, a smidgen of dawn teetered. A while later, a rose-pink light entered my room. I got up and walked to the washbasin. The pitcher was full, and my robe lay clean on the chair. Mother Kara probably made these preparations when I was asleep.

Dressed and refreshed, I walked outside. Heavenly stars illuminated the road to the monastery. I kissed the cross on the door and left.

The crisp winter air filled my lungs, and steam poured out of my mouth.

My body resumed its normal strength with a brisk walk. A short time later, people emerged out of the fog. Farmers passed by on their way to town. Oxcarts loaded with sacks of vegetables, milk cans, and other marketable products traveled at a slow pace. Women carried baskets on their heads. Some men, harnessed to homemade carts, pulled them in a swaying motion like snakes, head down, dust clouds up.

"Bless our day, Father." Different voices repeated the call.

"May the Lord be with you," I responded.

When the fog lifted, burned by bright sun rays, the empty road in front weaved through the hilly countryside and disappeared.

An hour later, I arrived at an unattended well on the side of the road. A sign for St. Stefan monastery pointed to the start of an uphill narrow path to the right. I stopped and drank some cold water, refilled my canteen, and continued my journey.

Around the bend, the rooftops of the monastery compound appeared. A bell rang in the tower. I picked up my pace and arrived in front of the tall wooden gate. A side door had a small lookout square. I pulled the doorbell chain, and a young monk's head appeared through the opening.

"Who goes there?" He asked.

"God's servant, Brother Samuilo from Mount Athos. The Right Reverend Abbot Radescu is expecting me."

The young monk opened the door and walked out. "Welcome, brother in Christ, Samuilo. We have been expecting you." He hugged me and kissed my cross.

"No one greeted me at the station last night. God provided comfort at the house of Father Miran and sister Kara."

"Follow me, Brother Samuilo. You'll be sleeping with us in the main house."

"Would it be possible to get a cup of tea and a biscuit before we go?"

"By all means. I will also get you a clean robe and some clothes. You have been on the road too long."

The warm water from the showerhead refreshed my body. I quickly changed and walked out into the hallway where my new acquaintance waited.

"We will have tea in the small dining room."

The abbot's office was situated in the lower flat of the building. We entered the hallway, and my young monk informed the receptionist of my arrival.

Then he led me into the monastic office of Abbot Radescu. A small, skinny man, with thick lenses in his wire-rimmed glasses tried to locate me as I approached to kiss his hand. His shaking arm moved in front of my face and my attempt vanished into thin air.

"Welcome, Brother… in Christ… Samuilo…" He stopped. His squinting eyes searched.

A priest dressed in a black cassock approached Abbot Radescu and whispered in his ear. The old abbot nodded and slid into his tall chair. The priest motioned for us to leave.

"Brother Samuilo, I am Father Ranko. Follow me."

I should only trust the priest, Progon advised. I opened my mouth but stopped when I saw his finger on his lips. At the bottom of the courtyard, on the other side of the main building, stood a small chapel. When we came to the entrance, Father Ranko turned to the young monk, "You can leave now. I am taking Brother Samuilo in for confession. I will call you when we are done."

He gestured for me to walk in. The chapel lay silent. Candles illuminated icons on the walls and the iconostasis. With every breeze, their ghosts danced with the flames. At the bottom of the chapel, behind the large iconostasis, a door led into a cell.

Father Ranko closed the door and pulled the heavy curtain behind it. A tiny oil lamp provided enough light for us to see each other. We kneeled on the floor and faced the icon of the Holy Mother of God. We prayed in silence and through humming. Deep in my reverie, the ghosts of Galia and Petro flew over the monastery rooftops. I peered into the cupola ceiling, but the tiny cell was cloaked with the sins of souls in penitence.

Father Ranko turned to me. His whisper could hardly be heard, but his steady voice was comprehensive. "Brother in Christ, Samuilo, your visit here is timely, and my prayers for your safe arrival have been answered. We have an enormous task ahead of us and very little support from St. Stefan's brotherhood of monks. Ever since we opened the gates to our Imiaslavie brothers of Panteleimon, St. Stefan Monastery has turned into a nest of revolutionary theologians. They are heavily influenced by the infiltrated Bolsheviks and Red Wing Revolutionary elements. Our abbot is old, almost blind, and on the way to his final rest. The situation is dire, and it has become dangerous for the remaining core of true Orthodox monks within the walls of this old monastery. Some of our young students have experienced terror and walked out of the seminary. Our dedicated monks are so scared that they stay in their cells and only go out at night to scrounge some leftover meals in the kitchen…"

I interrupted his long, gloomy speech. "Why isn't Abbot Radescu doing something about it? Why is the church tolerating this alarming situation? From Commander Progon, I understood the secret police is aware of it and ready to step in any time you give a signal."

"Abbot Radescu will never disallow the sacred privilege our monastery provides to anyone who seeks asylum. He does not make prejudicial distinctions in the treatment of different categories of people. In his eyes, we are all children of God." He sighed and crossed himself, lifting his head. "Let us talk about your mission. You will be questioned, observed, and followed within the monastery estate. Stay close to the Imiaslavie monks, and inquire only about Schema Monk Illarion and his whereabouts in the Caucasus Mountains. One of the monks or Bolsheviks from Mount Athos may recognize you. If he approaches you, that will be our link to the Red Wing kidnappers."

"How would I know he would be the link?"

"Among the infiltrated antisocial elements, the secret police of Bessarabia have identified three Bolsheviks and five Red Wing rebels. However, we don't know how many of the fifty-two Imiaslavie followers are associated with the kidnappers of Prince George. The Red Wing rebels are spreading their revolutionary movement across Lodovia, Bessarabia, Bucovina, and the western outskirts of the Russian Empire at a rapid pace. They could be moving their kidnapped hostages for ransom anywhere within this large territory. Ten of Commander Progon's best undercover agents have joined our brotherhood incognito. They are dressed in worn-out monks' attire, officially coming from Mount Athos. They will only be known to me, and their main responsibility is to watch over you. They are trained in Imiaslavie gibberish, and their Russian is fluent. We will take your confessions every morning here, and you will report to me all the details of your daily encounters. May God be with you, Brother Samuilo."

I kissed his cross and walked out of the claustrophobic space onto a clear, sunny day. I was relieved that I would not be alone. I could breathe easier now. The courtyard buzzed with monks and visitors. The locals traded their goods for the monastery's honey, candle wax, religious ornaments, and icons. A barrel of blessed wine with a tap and one wooden cup served a line of visitors in the middle of the courtyard.

My young escort approached me. "Brother Samuilo, a group of monks from Mount Athos would like to meet you."

"Oh! How do they know about me?"

"I told them while I was waiting for you. They are eager to hear the news about Panteleimon and their brothers who stayed behind. Please follow me. They are waiting for us in the garden."

Outside the monastery walls, a large plantation contained a cultivated spread of vineyards, vegetable gardens, fruit trees, and two wind-powered wells. A wide path led to a straw canopy in the middle of the flower garden. Ten monks sat in a circle and prayed. We stopped before it, kneeled down, and joined in. The prayer lasted a while before one of the monks stood up, crossed himself, and turned to me.

"Brother in Christ, welcome to our circle of prayer. The Name of God is God Himself, and no other name is Holy. I am Brother Yakov, and these are my Imiaslavie brothers from the Great Lavra. We heard that you were coming from Mount Athos on your way to join our beloved teacher, Schema-Monk Illarion, in the Caucasus Mountains. We have many questions for you. Would you share your memories with us?"

"I won't be of much help. It's been a year since I left Holy Monastery Panteleimon and moved to Lanhidar."

TWENTY TWO

During the first three days of my stay at St. Stefan, both young and old monks asked me questions about how forced changes affected the people of the Great Lavra, but I had no answers.

"Brothers, as I mentioned before, I left Panteleimon long after the problems arose. I believe many of the Imiaslavie brothers have more recent memories to share with you."

"Brother in Christ, how and when did you become a follower of our movement?" One of the monks from the circle of ten asked.

"Some of the purged Imiaslavie brothers escaped and found refuge in Lanhidar and Zograff. Father Ratnikoff was my teacher and mentor. He convinced me to become a follower of Imiaslavie, and he promised to take me if I wish to join the brotherhood of Imiaslavie in the Caucasus. Sadly, Father Ratnikoff died of meningitis just before our departure."

Their curiosity about me seemed to diminish. I walked and prayed in the open, alone. When my turn for confession arrived, I stepped away from my daily routine.

On the fifth day, an unexpected event occurred when I entered a secluded park on the outskirts of the monastery. A small group of monks surrounded the two chess players sitting on the ground. The game's intensity lingered over the chessboard.

I stopped by and leaned over. Without looking at me, the spectators spread out and let me join the circle. One player had five white remaining figurines; a king, rook, bishop, knight, and pawn, and the other had the same in black. The monk with the white had a move.

"Attack!" Copernicus yelled in my ear.

"Shut up!" I yelled back.

Everyone turned to face me.

"Who are you talking to, Brother?"

"Hey, Vasiliy! Look who is here," one of the players stood up and shook

179

my hand.

"Holy Mother of God. It's young Samuilo. The monk who fell from the sky into the Great Lavra compost pit." The second player jumped up and hugged me. These two monks were unfamiliar to me. Six spectators watched intently our reunion. Their eyes were filled with a mixture of curiosity and suspicion.

"Rejoice, you idiot! This is the moment you have been waiting for. Hug them back and play along." Copernicus shouted.

The act of remembrance was clumsy. I scrambled for the right words. "Brother Vasily, Brother Grigory? May God forgive me for not recognizing you. When did you arrive?"

Their reply was more convincing. "We arrived from Orid monastery a few days ago. We are staying until Friday, then we will go on to the Caucasus Mountains. We hope to join our teacher, Hieromonk Ilarion."

"It is God's will to bring us here," I said. "This is also my destiny. I was praying to find one of my Imiaslavie brothers on my journey to Holy Father Ilarion. My prayers have been answered. Thank you, Lord."

"God is Great." The monks pronounced.

"Stay with us, Brother Samuilo, until we finish the game. Then we can talk about our travel plans."

"We are done," Vasily exclaimed. "Checkmate."

Everyone burst out laughing.

"You are a stinker, Brother Vasily," his opponent said.

The three of us walked away from the rest. We talked cheerfully about made-up pass times, names, and locations until we were out of earshot.

"It was very clever of you to name me Grigory, Brother Samuilo. Luckily we didn't introduce ourselves to other monks. My name is Filip." He whispered.

Vasily scanned the area around us, then said, holding his hand to his mouth. "We have tracked down and discovered the new hideout location from one of the rebels. Father Ranko will give you details and further instructions."

"How did you find out?"

"We have our means of persuasion."

"What means? You are in the holy place."

"We are at war with terrorists. We don't ask many questions, but we get the answers."

Anxious to hear more about the new location, I rushed to the chapel. Father Ranko lay on the floor praying. His skinny body formed the cross. I kneeled and recited my favorite prayer; I know my path to You. I know my sins, I will carry the torch through Hell, and I will be your slave. My sweet Lord, take me for what I am. I am nothing, but my beliefs are immortal, and when my earthly days are over, I will take them with me into the Kingdom of your Father. Amen.

"Brother Samuilo, we have good news for you. The Bessarabian police agents have located the fortified hideout in the hills near Soro. They have surrounded the area, but the rebels are threatening to kill all the hostages unless their conditions are met.

The Duke of Lodovia and Count Artukov of Bessarabia have accepted some of the terms. Ransom compensation and prisoner exchange would be negotiable, but the release of Robis Bakalov is outside of any consideration. In fact, it is uncertain if he is still alive. As you can see we are dealing with unpredictable circumstances and the outcome could be disastrous. We are sending you to negotiate the release of one or all hostages. The caves in the hills are impenetrable, and the only solution is long-term starvation. But that would also be a double-edged sword. You must pray for guidance from our Lord Jesus Christ. Use your senses, your skills, and your instincts to make the right decisions. They have requested a neutral party, an Imiaslavie monk, to represent Lodovia's government. That aligns with your mission. May God bless you and protect you. Commander Progon's agents will accompany you to Soro, where negotiations may take place. I will pray for you, Brother Samuilo."

It was a lot to take in, but the relief that waiting was over lifted my spirits. I now considered the action. The soldier in me awakened. I licked the flame in my mind and spat out the fire. It landed in the pot of ideas and burned the hope. "Cool it, soldier," Copernicus yelled. "Use your brains."

"If I have any left?"

"That's why I'm here."

On Friday night, before midnight, during the mass, the three of us sneaked out of the monastery. Our walk through the wooded, hilly area took an hour to get to the main road. About three hundred meters away, a man was holding the reins of four horses while the full moon shone on him.

Vasily made an owl call, and the man replied.

"Let's proceed."

We walked downhill, crushing dry branches. Partridges and rabbits scattered, and some quails whistled, running away from us. The horses whinnied softly as we approached.

"Captain Vasily, the horses are fed and rested. I have some food and water for us in one of my bags. At your command we are ready to go." The man in peasant attire spoke.

"Very good, Sergeant Arnad. How much time to Soro?"

"If the moon stays with us, about three to four hours. We should be there at dawn."

Vasily looked at me. "Can you ride a horse, young brother Samuilo?"

"I believe I can." My swift mount removed any doubts. I figured they did not know my true identity.

"Well, then, let us not waste any time."

They mounted their horses, and the guide took the lead.

The strenuous ride through the night over the hilly land of Northern Bessarabia took longer than expected. We stopped three times to rest our horses and have some cold food and coffee. At dawn, we stopped in a village about twenty kilometers from the town of Soro. We dismounted in the public square. Water from the nearby creek was diverted to fill the wooden tub for the animals. Our horses lined up and drank the fresh water. We sat on the ground and rested.

Captain Vasily said, "Lieutenant Filip, ride into town and inform Commander Progon of our arrival. To avoid suspicion, In a few minutes, we will move out of the village in a few minutes and wait in the old mill outside of Soro."

The village slept while we walked through. No dogs or roosters made any noises. The sunlight from the east announced the arrival of a new day. We mounted and rode at a slow pace. A half hour later, we crossed the river Niestra and arrived at the mill. The abandoned stone building was empty. We dismounted and tethered our horses. Captain Vasily took off his robe and undergarments, and jumped into the river. He released happy shrieks.

We followed. The water was freezing. We shivered. A few moments later, the shock diminished, but one part of my body retreated.

"What happened to your other brain?" Copernicus asked.

"Go to hell!"

"I am already there."

Sergeant Arnad poured a fresh cup of coffee. The hot liquid soothed my remaining body shakes. My empty stomach growled. The scorched bacon released salty molten lard into a frying pan. The sergeant dipped pieces of bread in it, topped them with slices of goat cheese, fried bacon, and sweet paprika, then served it to us. Warm grease ran down our chins. Each lip-smacking mouthful of food was sucked through faster than we could chew.

I thought about my grandpa who loved bacon. On every occasion, when a family, a neighbor, or a friend slaughtered a hog for winter food supplies, he would be there, with a jug of brandy and a drooling mouth by the fire-pit. As a child, I could never figure out why he did not look like all the other slobs in my hometown. This generation of fat, lazy, and slovenly brotherhood of men seemed to have jumped from puberty into middle age without looking in a mirror. My Grandpa was different. Although fried bacon was his favorite meal, and he could eat a ton, he spent a lot of energy driving his old bicycle around the county as a commissioner for war restitution. There were many war widows in our county, and the county was pretty large. As a child he used me to tell Grandma Nella that he had gone to play chess with the boys. Now I know how exhausting chess games with those widows were.

An hour later, Commander Progon rode in with Grigory and two other agents.

"We have arranged the meeting for tomorrow," Commander Progon said. "Three of their negotiators will wait for you at noon in the middle of the Niestra stone bridge. The bridge is about one hundred meters long and about ten meters wide. They will frisk you for weapons, and all they will find are your prayer rope and wooden crosses. In the event of a serious threat to your lives, each cross has a hidden ten-centimeter blade that can be ejected by pressing the horizontal cross bar. Our two agents are well trained in hand-to-hand combat. They will show you how this stiletto works.

"The rebels are well aware of our presence, and our knowledge of their hideout. But caves are many and complex. It would take an army to chase them out."

When he stopped for a moment, I asked, "Do we know, in addition to Prince George, who are the other three hostages?"

"Well, not exactly. One is said to be a politician from the Bukovina principality, and the other two are merchants from Rumelia. We have no background information about their capture. Prince George is the rebels' biggest prize and the greatest challenge ahead of us."

"What is the current status of the negotiation? Is there a change in their demand? What am I bringing to the table? Finally, why would they want to talk to me?"

"The rebels were advised yesterday that the payoff for the four hostages is increased to one hundred and fifty thousand rubles in gold. There will be no prisoner exchange, and the release of Robis Bakalov."

"What happens if they refuse our terms? What would be the next step?"

"We will know more after you meet with them. You will present our latest counter-offer, and if they agree to consider it, there could be a glimmer of hope for a peaceful way out. We don't believe they would be authorized to refuse any of our proposals on the spot. This could be a long negotiation. Every word, tone of voice, facial expression, and new consideration will be evaluated after each meeting."

The two agents spent most of the afternoon teaching me basic negotiating skills. To maintain proper posture, my voice must not show emotion. Before responding inhale slowly.

Look them straight in the eye and speak only when your turn comes. Be neutral. Do not show any concern for the hostages. Play the role of a messenger. Dictate our terms and wait for their reply. On one or two occasions, say a prayer and confirm your religious identity. The two of us will join you. Use the old Slavic language. At the end, ask them to bring out the hostages. It is your duty to give them a Confession of Faith. Insist on this point and be firm."

"Brothers, I thank you," I said. Commander Progon did not tell me your names, and I don't know if you are policemen or monks. You seem to know a lot about religion."

"We are both, Brother Samuilo. You may call us Gus and Ion. The less we know about each other, the less risk we pose. I am Gus." He removed his hood to reveal a square faced man, with a broken nose, and bushy black eyebrows.

His twin, I presumed, showed almost identical features in a lighter shade. He said, "I am Ion."

Looking back, after so many years, the two could have been real twin brothers from my hometown. They had those unique features of my beloved citizens of Koles—red noses, illustrious drunken expressions, and never-ending smiles.

At 11:30 on the following day, the three of us waited on our side of the bridge. At the midpoint, two rebels stood on each side, one with a white flag in his arm.

"When he starts waving the flag, we walk." Gus said.

As he spoke, the flag rose up.

"Now."

A few minutes later, we faced our three counterparts, the rebel negotiators. The tall one in the middle stared at me with his dark eyes. The two others, young and stiff as if chiseled out of stone, released clouds of hot air with their short breaths.

I stared back at the tall rebel. His lips twitched. He turned his head to Gus. I relaxed and inhaled. I pulled my cross and said, "Brothers, let us pray for the peaceful resolution of our negotiation."

"We are not your brothers, and you can pray as much as you want, but that will not help you unless you meet our demands," the tall rebel exclaimed in a sharp voice.

I ignored his comments and dropped to my knees. Gus and Ion followed. We prayed and asked Our Lord for His guidance and mercy. A flame of hatred shot out of their eyes. Where did this hostility come from? Were they not raised as Christians? How potent could Marxist ideology be in the hands of young men?

"Well, what have you brought to the negotiating table this time? Our conditions are firm, but we have agreed to hear your proposal." The tall rebel said.

"Brother in Christ, your request for unofficial, neutral negotiators chosen from the order of Imiaslavie monks, has been granted. The three of us were selected to help negotiate the most favorable solution between the two sides. The kingdom of Biares, and the dukedom of Lodovia have agreed to the ransom payment of one hundred and fifty thousand rubles in gold. There will be no exchange of prisoners, and no other conditions from the Red Wing Party will be considered. We ask you to convey this proposal to your leaders. Before we proceed with further negotiations, we demand that you bring out the hostages so that we may confirm they are alive and well. May God help you find the path to brotherly love."

The rebel's face flushed red. He stared us down and screamed. "You are not in command here!" He clenched his fists. His voice cracked.

"You best go and report our message to your superiors. We will wait for you here." I replied.

A whole minute of a faceoff between us ticked away before he said, "We will be back at 9 a.m. tomorrow."

TWENTY THREE

At our headquarters in town, the police commissioner, Commander Progon, and Count Gasha of Lodovia discussed the submitted offer. They agreed that the rebels had no other choice but to accept it.

I thought differently, but Copernicus advised me to keep it to myself. The night was long. Bad dreams of long, dark tunnels occupied my sleep. I woke up several times before falling into the abyss.

Once, I saw the face of Prince George passing by me in a two-way tunnel. What does it all mean, I asked Copernicus. "Patience, my boy, it will be over soon."

A fresh pot of coffee was a welcome treat. It woke my sleepy brain, and re-energized my readiness for action. Gus and Ion gobbled down grilled sausage, ham, and sliced boiled eggs, stuffed a couple of extra sandwiches in their pockets, and nodded when they were ready.

Threatening clouds hung over the bridge when we arrived at nine o'clock. The sudden rush of cold wind from the east blew over the river and caused the surface to ripple. The white flag went up and swayed. As we started for the meeting point, a premonition of imminent disaster flashed through my mind, then faded.

The other party came out walking. They dragged one of the hostages by the rope around his neck. His hands were tied behind his back. A shudder of fear passed through me as I searched his face. Thank God it was not Prince George.

"What is the point of this? Will this hostage be their counteroffer?" Gus whispered.

At the meeting point the tall rebel addressed us.

"This capitalist pig is condemned to death. He devised ugly schemes, delivered empty promises, robbing innocent people of Rumelia. If your bosses should refuse our demand, this criminal will be executed at noon, and every day after it another hostage will face the same fate. We will not entertain your future proposals without the release of Robis Bakalov. You will have until noon to decide."

"They would not dare take this suicidal step," Count Gasha screamed in the police station.

"We must stay our course and not waver from their threats," Commander Progon calmly advised. "Brother Samuilo, advise the rebels that we will not accept their counteroffer."

"Even if they execute the hostages?" I was obviously disturbed by this decision.

"We will have to test their resolve. If they are committed to their act, we will change plan of action. Our units are ready to attack. We pray and hope for a harmless rescue of hostages.

"Go back, Brother Samuilo, and tell the rebels we will not release Robis Bakalov."

The bridge had a different setting now. At the beginning of the bridge on the rebels' side, the blindfolded hostage was in front of the one-meter high concrete barrier. His hands were tied. A man, about five meters away, held a pointed rifle at him. The three negotiators waited for us at the meeting point.

Shaken by the vision of the foregoing conclusion, I presented our decision with a pleading voice, "Brothers, although, we were instructed to convey the refusal of your counteroffer, there are other God given means to find an amicable solution and prevent the human sacrifice. Let us pray." I dropped to my knees and began, "Our Father, who art in Heaven, hallowed be thy name…"

The rifle shot echoed across the bridge. The body of the hostage collapsed and folded. His corps made one last jerk, and calm took place. The three of us stared befuddled. In this situation, nothing would make any sense. Wars are senseless. Why should this be any different?

On the following day, we returned with the revised offer and the request to postpone further executions until the reply came from the Duke of Lodovia.

"You have one day," the tall hateful rebel turned to me. "Your God is not helping you much. Does he?"

His sarcastic remarks were hurtful, but my faith was stronger, and my mind was sharper. We left the tragic scene behind, and returned. Fear and unpredictability grew ahead of us. From our headquarters in Soro, urgent messages were dispatched to the Duke of Lodovia.

The reply said: No change. I asked commander Progon, "Would old Duke Jovan let Robis out, if pressed by the Tsar and King Tarpe. Was this not too much of a risk for Prince George?"

"You must understand there is always a certain risk of standing between two enemies. You should continue to negotiate with the air of superiority. We hope that rebels will not risk the fate of their beloved leader."

"But what about those innocent hostages. Will they have to be sacrificed in your chess game?"

"There will be no Kings and Princes if we allow the riffraff of our society to take control of our government. Casualties are the consequences of war. This is an extremely difficult mission for us."

"My God, sir. You are risking the life of my Prince. I will not allow it, even if I have to take his place." I stormed out furious. The snow has started falling. My face was red hot, and some of the flakes melted as they touched my skin. Tears in my eyes, mixed with wet snowflakes, rolled down my cheeks. I was in a panic. My mind raced. Senseless thoughts popped in and out. I will not let them sacrifice Prince George. He is my Prince. He is my brother.

The three of us considered the options.

"What would happen after we convey the new message?" I asked.

Gus pressed his lips with his fist and mumbled, "They will kill another hostage. We will stand by and watch. The shot will echo across the valley, and the town will know the second execution took place."

"Do we have a chance to break through and rescue the hostages?"

"All odds are against us." Ion said." We don't know how many armed guards are inside the caves. The way in and the way out could be leading through a labyrinth of passages and hidden chambers. Commander Progon told us that according to world-renowned speleologist, professor Derenski, the Soro caves are full of stalactites and stalagmites. The main cave is accessible only through Prut river branches and through a manmade tunnel dating back ten thousand years before Christ. Only a few speleologists have dared to venture into the caves and made their way back. The rebels must have found someone who could take them through the maze, and out, some other way. Do you think we would be able to find a way in?"

"No, I do not. But I will insist on seeing the remaining hostages before we make the prisoner exchange."

"What prisoner exchange? Duke Jovan is not releasing Robis Bakalov," Gus questioned my plan.

"Brothers, I fear that Prince George is left at the mercy of Duke Jovan who believes that the rebels will balk, run with the money, and forget their leader Robis Bakalov. But the old duke is wrong. These people are idealists, and in the end they will win, while the dying class of bourgeoisie will be replaced by the Marxist revolutionary ideology. Robis Bakalov is the most wanted terrorist. But, there are hundreds like him, waiting for their moment in history to lead the masses into a bloody world revolution. We must not give them the opportunity to sacrifice captives in the name of the socialist revolution."

"Do you have an idea how to get into their hideout?"

"I have a plan."

In that moment I was ready to commit myself and march into hell for this noble cause to save my prince. I conceived a daring plan that would yield immediate success. I didn't share my idea with Gus and Ion in fear of endangering my position in the negotiation process. I would not allow any errors that could result in my removal. Throughout the stormy night I pounced on the perilous plan, searching for the trouble-free exit from captivity. My dreams, mixed with the thundering clouds, vanished into morning.

On the following day we arrived at the meeting spot at 9 a.m. The bridge on their side had no guards. We waited in the shade of the center arch. The town's tower clock rang ten times. No rebels. Gus and Ion sat on the barrier's edge and lit their cigarettes. As the river's waves rolled down its course, I watched them in awe.

At 10:30 a.m. the rebels came into view at the end of the bridge. They led another hostage on a leash tied around his neck. He was blindfolded with his hands tied behind his back. His whimpering echoed across the water. The two guards positioned him against the bridge fence. One stood with a rifle ready to shoot.

I strained my eyes.

"It is another merchant, Brother Samuilo," said Ion.

"Thank God," I whispered.

The three negotiating rebels walked toward us.

"They are not the same," Gus commented. "They are short and stocky, with beards and moustaches. They seem older."

"They could be decision makers," I said. "Let us see what they want."

The three rebels marched in step as if in a parade. They stopped in front of us, lifted their right hand, and yelled, "Long live our leader, Robis Bakalov."

All wore the same gray slacks, black jackets, and Russian sailor caps. They waited. A minute or so passed in a mutual study of each other's features.

I broke the spell. "Welcome Brothers in Christ to our meeting. We are hoping to find a resolution and save the lives of innocent people in your captivity. We are also hoping to save others that would die in the ensuing confrontation between our overwhelming forces and your small group of defenders."

As I anticipated the cutoff, one of the rebels stepped forward and spoke. "We have come to the final phase of our negotiation. This is the last time we are meeting, whether you agree to our conditions or not. We are ready to sacrifice our lives if you refuse to release our leader, Robis Bakalov. On my signal, the second hostage will be executed, and the other two will be shot this morning."

While he deliberated to give the signal, I grabbed his hand and said, "Please, Brother, don't. We have come with the greatest desire to meet your demands. I can vouch for the Duke of Lodovia to release Robis Bakalov, but only under one condition. You must let us see and talk to the hostages. This must be done before we make any further arrangements for the exchange of captives. Can you, Sir, make a decision now?"

The spokesman and his negotiators stepped about ten meters away from us. They huddled and whispered. Brisk moves and occasional loud expressions gave the impression of lively arguments. A minute later, they returned.

"You say you can guarantee the exchange. If so, where would the exchange take place?"

"Right here, on this bridge. You have your side and the caves with a secured exit. We have no knowledge nor skills to pursue you through the Soro Cave. The process will depend on our findings about the condition of captives in your possession. Can you let us see them?"

"Yes, I am authorized to make a decision if you meet our demands. First of all, we will have to see Robis Bakalov on your side of the bridge. He will have to stand on an elevated podium so that we can see him from a safe distance with binoculars. We will do the same on our side. Should you make the wrong move, we will execute the captives. The exchange can be scheduled for tomorrow. You may go back and tell your masters our conditions."

I stood there and shook my head. "No. We are not going back before we see the captives. Those are our conditions. Neither side has an advantage. You don't want to risk the life of your leader, nor do we the lives of our people in your custody. It is now, or we walk, and let the army take over."

It was the scariest moment of my life. I gambled and bet on the presumption that once the three of us got inside the hideout, our military skills would overpower whatever obstacles, men, and unknown pathways we may encounter.

The force of my words worked. The rebels deliberated again. Their leader came back and said, "We will let you to come and see the captives. Your two companions will wait for your return here. We will have to frisk you. It will be easier if you remove your robe."

"I am God's servant. I only carry my cross and the prayer rope." As I spoke I took out both items and gave them to him. He looked over at the cross, and ran the prayer rope through his fingers.

I took off my robe and let one of the rebels pass his hands over my garments. He nodded to his leader who handed back my cross and rosary. "Put the robe on and come with us."

"Brother Samuilo, take our crosses and give them to the hostages. They will find peace and receive the power of prayer from the Holy Spirit." Ion extended his hand with two crosses.

I turned to the rebel leader. My heart pounded violently. He nodded and said, "We will have to blindfold you when we get to our side."

Not far from the stone bridge, the entrance into the Soro Caves began with steps spiraling into darkness below. The rebels lit torches. They put the blindfold over my eyes and led me down. As we descended, I counted fifty-four steps before we entered a small passage. Boot steps sounded from the right over the pebble walkway. The voice of another man saluted the rebels. It was the second guard point.

"At ease, Comrade. All under control?" The rebel leader asked.

"Yes, Comrade Volski."

The murmur of running water came from my left side. We took a low ceiling tunnel to the right and I counted thirty steps before we came to a stop. The third guard greeted us here. We continued through a wider tunnel leading to the left. Water was now dripping from above. Forty-eight steps later, we entered a larger underground cavity, where sounds resonated across an open space. They took off my blindfold. Torches illuminated the large cave. I estimated about sixty or seventy meters for its diameter, and maybe twenty to thirty meters for its height. This cave had ten or twelve tunnels on the other side. I tried to remember all the details of this labyrinth. My eyes adjusted quickly to the darkness.

"We will wait here while one of my men brings the hostages," the rebel leader said.

"But it is too dark in here. "Could we take them out in the daylight?"

"No. We will light more torches."

I heard the sound of a waterfall on the other side of the cave. There was a very dim light in one of the tunnels. Perhaps the hostages were kept there. I strained my ears for human voices, but the waterfall muted other sounds. From one of the tunnels light shined and disappeared. A few moments later, it reappeared above the heads of five people. An armed guard pulled the three hostages stringed behind him with a rope. The second guard urged them on with his gun barrel. The three wretched men swayed, and stumbled, as dragged by the rope out of the tunnel.

My heart ached. Copernicus warned me to stay calm. When they approached, the hostages collapsed to the ground. I twisted the vertical bar of the cross in my pocket and removed the stiletto. The commanding voice of comrade Volski stopped the guard. He pulled the handgun out of his pocket and pointed it at him.

"If you make another forceful threat, I will shoot you. You are endangering the life of our comrade Bakalov. Mistreating and torturing our political hostages is not our practice. You are dismissed. Report to Deputy Party Commissar Sverdloff immediately."

The man saluted and marched out in a hurry.

Comrade Volski addressed me, "You see, Brother Samuilo, if I may call you so, we are not an unruly army of revolutionaries. We follow the strict codes of the party, and we weed out bad seeds among our members. You may now take your time and visit our prisoners. Our guard and one of my negotiators will stay with you while the two of us will go and report the status of our negotiation to our headquarters. You have one hour to examine their mental and physical condition. When we return, we will expect your promised obligation to bring Robis Bakalov to the exchange point on the stone bridge. Remember, should anything go wrong, we would shoot the hostages. Makayev, light up two more torches."

My head was buzzing with plans. I resumed the role of Biares soldier. My muscles tightened to the point of breaking. I caressed the stiletto and waited.

A few meters away, Volski and his companions exchanged a few more words. I saw the handgun changing hands. I took the torch from the guard to shine on the faces of the hostages. In front of Prince George I coughed and whispered quickly, "This is Brother Samuilo. Nod if you heard me."

His eyes opened wide. I placed the cross against his mouth and said, "let us pray, Brother."

When love is in your heart, no matter how heavy a burden of life befalls, it will be as light as an angel's feather. When enter the kingdom of heaven you will take a confident step. His blessings will give you the strength to walk in his path, united as brothers. Glory be to God, the creator of all happiness, the liberator of sin, the King of Kings, and the merciful Almighty Father.

While I prayed, I kept my eye on the young guard. He was maybe fifteen or sixteen years old. He held loosely the sling of his rifle. A shadow of uncertainty flashed across his innocent face. "His fear is your friend. Concentrate on the negotiator." Copernicus advised.

Comrade Volski and his companion walked out through the same tunnel we came from.

I played the role of examiner and asked each hostage questions regarding their health, the treatment by the rebels, and the food they received. The slow recovery from their lengthy period of incarceration and abuse inspired me to regain the courage I needed to execute my plan.

"Do you have any drinking water in your canteen, Brother?" I asked the rebel negotiator.

"No! I do not. Why?"

"I need it to give a Holy Communion to my brothers in Christ. Instead of wine, I will ask the Lord to bless the water and use it as a consecrated drink. Can you get some for us?"

I think this question presented an unexpected problem for him. He scrambled for an answer and then asked the young guard, "Comrade, do you have the canteen with you?"

"No, Comrade, I do not. But I can go and get one from our post on the other side."

"Go ahead. Fill it up with water and bring it."

All the chances I had in my life did not line up as easily as this plan took place.

I approached the rebel expressing my satisfaction with the condition of the hostages. At about three to four steps from him, he pulled out the gun and said, "Don't come any closer."

"Why, Brother, I am not armed?" I opened my arms to remove doubts in his mind. In my right hand I had the cross.

It was a moment of relaxation in his eyes that I took advantage, freed the stiletto out and stabbed his right hand. He screamed and dropped his gun. I grabbed him and closed his mouth. "Put your left hand on the wound to stop the bleeding. It's not so terrible. We'll wrap it and tend to it later. Your man will come running. Keep quiet."

I picked up his handgun and stood behind him. The boy came back as expected. His right hand held the torch, his left the canteen, and his rifle swung on his back with each step. "What's happening, comrade? Who screamed?"

I stepped out of the shadows and pointed the gun at him. "If you follow my orders, everything will be all right. Put the canteen down and drop your rifle on the ground. Keep the torch in your hand."

I turned to one of the Rumelians and told him to take the rifle. He jumped as if awarded, and took the gun. He pulled the bolt, and turned to me. "This gun is empty. No bullets."

I asked the boy, "Do you know the way out?"

He was still shivering.

"Relax, Boy. We will not hurt you. You can go free after you lead us out. I promise you that, as God is my witness."

The boy looked at the rebel negotiator, then nodded.

"Don't worry about him. We will mend his arm and leave him behind.

When the rebels find him we will be long gone."

I finally addressed Prince George. "Your Highness, are you all right? Do you need any help? Here, please drink some water."

He was still confused and shaken, but he took the canteen and drank.

We moved fast. The man from Bukovina cleaned the wound on the negotiator's right hand with water, and wrapped it with a piece of cloth. He tied his arms behind his back, his legs with shoestrings, then stuffed his mouth, and leaned him against the wall.

I approached the boy and said. "Listen carefully. At each of the three guard points, you will tell the attending guard that you are taking us to the bridge for a prisoner exchange. Say it cheerfully, 'Our leader, Robis Bakalov, will be freed today.' We will walk in front of you with your rifle pointed at us. Tell them the chief negotiators are coming behind us. Be very careful. Say it clearly and as instructed."

I gave the two stilettos to the Rumelian and Bukovina hostages. "We will have to disarm the guards and neutralize them. I don't want to risk anything. If you use stilettos, aim for the throat."

"But it takes time to disarm and tie the bastards. Let's just shoot them." The Rumelian said.

"No. Not under my command. I will give them the same choice as I did for the boy. They can come with us, or stay behind tied down."

He grumbled but accepted my decision and we moved out. The boy led us through a series of tunnels and passages, and before we came to the guarded checkpoint, he alerted us that we were about fifty meters from it. We lined up in front of the boy and he acted better than I thought. He yelled at us and swore using bad words he mispronounced, probably not educated to know their meaning. No matter. The screaming sound brought the guard from his post

"What is going on?" He asked the boy.

"I have the order to take these criminals to the bridge for an exchange of prisoners. Our leader, Robis Bakalov, will be set free today. Long Live the Party!"

"Why are you alone? Where are the others?"

"The negotiators are coming along shortly. They went back to report the agreement about the exchange to the headquarters. You can come with me, or you can wait for them. I don't need more help."

I was impressed with this boy. He reminded me of my younger days, when I had a lot of courage and very few brains.

The guard shrugged and stepped into a line behind us. He lowered his gun barrel to the ground and tried to light up a cigarette. His rifle was without a sling. He struggled to keep it under his arm. The boy said, "Let me hold your gun." The guard handed over his rifle and lit his cigarette.

"What?" He asked, holding a lit match. The flame illuminated the surprise in his eyes. His rifle was now in my hands, pointed at him.

"You can come with us and help us go through the remaining check points. We will set you and the boy free when we get to our side of the bridge. Or you can choose to stay, tied down, and wait for your comrades to find you and put the blame on you for our escape. You decide."

My convincing words didn't require much consideration. He stepped in line and we moved on.

The second checkpoint had no guard. We passed through quickly and encountered the last checkpoint with a guard soundly asleep on a small stool. We circled around and climbed the spiraling steps, listening to his loud snoring until we reached the top. From our tunnel, the sunlit riverbank exhibited a portion of the stone bridge. "We are almost home." I whispered in Prince George's ear.

Unsure of himself, he smiled, and nodded. My poor brother George! How I missed him. In some of our Balkan traditional customs, Prince George has taken the place of my late brother Petro.

His sunny personality that was very engaging had many traits resembling the people of our peninsula. His natural curiosity, an oddity of the royal family, made him very popular among his people. He climbed the tallest mountain peak in the Balkans. He competed in the Tour de Balkan motorcycle race and came in third. His popularity grew when he won the race in a sack. He never competed again. Why? His prize was a kiss from an obese woman weighing one hundred and twenty kilograms. He told me he had nightmares for months. He was about sixteen, like the boy. I wondered about this young rebel. Many questions went through my mind about his origin, his reasons for association with the Red Wing Party, and his future.

"What is your name?" I asked the boy.

"George."

I giggled.

"My name is Simon," the other guard said.

"Very well, George and Simon. We will use the same ploy as we did before. You are taking us to the prisoners exchange meeting. As soon as I get behind, I will disarm him. He can come with us, or we can leave him behind. Are you ready?"

"Yes, sir, we are." Young George said.

We crossed the last barrier and started the walk over the bridge uninterrupted. With every step closer to our side, I breathed a sigh of relief. The familiar feeling of tension before a battle ran through my nerves. We increased the pace, checking over our shoulders. The bridge's length appeared a thousand meters away. Prince George could barely walk. I lifted his right arm and helped him stand. Simon took the other arm and we carried him. Halfway through, Gus and Ion ran toward us from the other side, screaming and waving. "Down! Down!" I heard. The bullets flew over our heads, and we dropped to the ground. It was too late. One of the bullets hit George. He was lying on his back. His eyes were frozen blue. His last breath was already gone. Poor little boy, may the Lord bless your soul.

END OF VOLUME II

Gene Luke Vlahovic is of Serbian origin. Born and raised in former Yugoslavia, he acquired the love of literature from reading the European Classics at his early age. Gene Luke is the author of books published in the Serbo-Croatian language by the traditional publishers, Prosveta Publishing House, in 2002 and 2004.

The Award Winning novel, The Artisan, is author's first novel written in the English language. The second book is the trilogy titled Pilgrim of Fate, Volume 1 published in 2019. Volume II and Volume III are scheduled for release in 2022/2023. The latest publication in the Serbo-Croatian language is Memoirs of the Last Generation of 1959 Gymnasium's Graduates, released in July, 2021.

Gene Luke is the founder of the Brevard Authors Society, and an organizer/promoter of many writers' events, book festivals, and literary contests. He continues to support his fellow authors with free educational seminars in formatting, book cover designs, publishing, marketing and promoting.

Gene Luke lives in Rockledge, Florida and enjoys writing new stories in three languages. He is published internationally in the republics of former Yugoslavia and in the USA.

ALSO BY GENE LUKE VLAHOVIC

THE ARTISAN

Timo, a young Serbian POW in WWII Germany shares the gift of his artisanship and earns sincere gratitude from the farmers of Lomnitz, and love from the village teacher, Frau Gottfried, who is a member of the Hanover Oprea House in peace time. This forbidden love flourishes in a war time isolated village. It denounces ....

PILGRIM OF FATE

In a small kingdom of Biares, at the turn of the 20th century, mute boy Dino grows up in the town of Koles as a free spirited adventurer until the age of fifteen when he opens his mouth and sings the most beautiful melody that makes him famous overnight.
He is forced to leave his hometown and ....

YEARNING

The collection of short stories about the immigrants from the Balkans who settled in the industrial midwestern cities of America and dreamed of returning someday to their homelands. Their names and origins are engraved on the monuments in the cemetaries of Midwest ....

THE CHAMPIONS OF MIDWEST

In 1950 the first Serbian soccer club of America was formed by the immigrants, and the soccer team became the formidable force in the Wisconsin State league. The chronicle follows for five decades the glory of championships and memorable victories against United States professional soccer teams.

GENE LUKE AUDIOBOOKS

Narrated by Brian Wiggins.
Released 2019 by ACX
Available on Audible

Narrated by Brian Wiggins,
Released 2020 by ACX
Available on Audible